Praise for *Saigon Tea*:

Marathon drinking … standover thuggery, urgent sex, random violence … pet budgies that are deep fried … an excellent description of the intimacies of sausage manufacture … this novel has a strangely innocent ring to it.

Debra Adelaide, *Sydney Morning Herald*

Rare, laugh-out loud read … a riotous novel … so pertinent and provocative.

Juliet Rieden, *What's On Weekly*

Full of life, humour, passion and violence — I loved it!

Wendy O'Hanlon, *Sunshine Coast Sunday*

Funny, moving and often tender … hard to beat … very funny and very true.

Christopher Bantick, *West Australian*

Reilly writes with an insider's knowledge and the result is provocatively funny

Jan Hallam, *Sunday Times*

A great read with some very funny moments — thoroughly recommended for the beach or poolside.

Ken Spillman, *West Australian*

Sex, music, bad food, bar girls and lifestyle magazines and how you shouldn't get in over your head …

MX – Melbourne

Romp and rump in equal measure … in a time of either stone-cold academic theory or else cliché-driven bestsellers written by the dead, *Saigon Tea* is positively more-ish.

Barry Dickens, *Big Issue Australia*

Graham Reilly emigrated from Glasgow to Australia as an 13-year-old in 1969. His family arrived to live with their Uncle Charlie in the Altona district of Melbourne with £200 and a biscuit tin full of family photos. His cousins described them as 'a sorry sight' at the airport having left Scotland in mid-winter and arrived, 32 hours later, on a scorching summer's day.

Reilly went on to graduate at Melbourne University and work as a newspaper journalist eventually joining *The Age*, Melbourne's largest broadsheet daily, to which he contributed sporadic fiction pieces which fostered an urge to write novels. He married a diplomat and became father to two children. In 1999 his wife Amanda was posted to Saigon and his chance to dedicate more time to his writing came about. During his two years there he worked for the English-language daily *The Vietnam News* and wrote this novel and one other, *Sweet Time*.

He is currently writing the sequel to *Saigon Tea*, entitled *Five Oranges*.

That's the ba up oan the slates noo.
Old Glasgow saying

Boom boom boom boom.
John Lee Hooker

SAIGONTEA

GRAHAM REILLY

www.11-9.co.uk

First published in Australia and New Zealand in 2002 by
Hodder Headline Australia PTY Ltd

This edition published in 2004 by 11:9,
an imprint of Neil Wilson Publishing Ltd
303 The Pentagon Centre
36 Washington Street
GLASGOW
G3 8AZ

Tel: 0141-221-1117
Fax: 0141-221-5363
E-mail: info@nwp.co.uk
http://www.nwp.co.uk

A catalogue record for this book is available from the British
Library.

11:9 is funded by the
Scottish Arts Council National Lottery Fund

ISBN 1-903238-78-1

Typeset in Utopia
Designed by Dan Prescott after Bookhouse, Sydney
Printed in Poland

For Amanda Paxton

Many thanks to Helen Rechter, John Spooner, Barry Dickins, Arnold Zable, John Donnelly, Caitlin Reilly and Grace Reilly.

Acknowledgements

"Boom Boom"
composed by John Lee Hooker.
Published by Tristan Music Ltd/Mautoglade Ltd.

"Dancing In The Street"
W.Stevenson/M.Gaye/I.Hunter
Copyright © 1964 Stone Agate Music Corp/Jobete Music Co. Inc
Used by permission of EMI Songs Australia Pty. Limited
All rights reserved.

"Theme From Shaft"
Words and Music by Isaac Hayes
Copyright © 1971 IRVING MUSIC, INC.
Copyright Renewed. All Rights Reserved. Used by Permission

Quotations from *Apocalypse Now* courtesy of American Zoetrope.
All Rights Reserved.

The following terms are Trademarks ® and as such are recognised by the publisher: Laphroaig, Corona Extra, BMW, McEwan's Export, Tiger, Stella Artois, Heineken, Beck's, Holstein, HP sauce, Irn Bru, Drambuie, Coca-Cola, Who Wants to be a Millionaire?, Citroen and Zippo.

'Would ye look at those two.'

Jessie Canyon leans out the window overlooking the back, her elbows resting on the worn sandstone ledge. What a sight. She always tells people that this is a view to die for, that having to look at it every day made you want to just throw yourself right out the window to land with a scream and a thud on the dirt and muck four floors below. You'd have to make sure to jump close in though, otherwise you'd land on some poor woman's washing line and that would be her day at the steamie wasted. It's a fair walk to go all the way back to the washhouse with your pram laden up with dirty clothes and sheets and a wean perched on the top like the king of the castle. Just look at it. It's a wasteland, so it is. Something has to be done about those middens, what with the rubbish overflowing and being blown all about the place by the wind. Still, there's not much point in the council spending any money on these old tenements because they'll be under the wrecker's hammer soon enough and folk will be flittin' to the new housing schemes anyway.

'What is it?' Alexander 'Sandy' Canyon emerges from the darkness of the scullery, stripped to the waist and drying himself with a towel.

'The boys, look at them runnin' aboot there chasin' that ba'. They'll be playin' for the Celtic soon,' Jessie says, shaking her head in disbelief at how wee Danny's matchstick legs can hold

1

him upright, never mind propel him around that makeshift pitch like a puppy chasing its own and everybody else's tail.

Sandy pokes his head out the window and sees his two sons playing football with a gang of their pals. They are using one wall of the old washhouse as one goal and two washing line poles as the other. Even from this distance he can see that his boys' faces are glowing beetroot from the game and the busy afternoon sun. He chuckles to himself. It won't last. The Glasgow summer, eh. Here today, gone tomorrow.

'And the Celtic would be lucky to have them, so they would,' he says, wincing as he watches Frankie stumble and fall on the hard clay. He nods in approval as the boy pulls himself up, rubs at his scraped and bleeding knee and jumps back into the game.

'I'd better get them up in a minute. They've got the scouts the night,' Jessie sighs. 'Just look at it oot there. It looks like a bomb had struck it.'

'Well, a bomb did strike it, mind, during the war. My granny got killed. Just about everybody in the whole close did. It was terrible.'

'Aw aye, so it did,' she says, retreating back into the living room, one of the only two rooms in the house. 'I was evacuated away tae Fife then.' She holds her husband tight around the waist and squeezes herself into him. She can smell the soap on his skin, feel his strong miner's arms. 'I can't wait to get out of this place. I'm sick to death of it, so I am.'

'Aye, me an aw. We'll have our own bathroom eh? And an inside toilet. Imagine that. I've never had an inside toilet. I won't know what to do wi' masel'.'

'I'm sure you'll figure it out, Sandy,' she smiles, running her hand through the damp hair on his chest. 'But, I'm tellin' ye, we'll never be able to get those weans oot the bath. They're talking aboot having a bath every night. They've already worked out what boats they're gaunny take in wi' them to play battleships an' that.'

'Ma . . . may. Ma . . . a . . . ma . . . ay!'

Sandy laughs and strokes his wife's cheek. 'Talk ae the devil.'

Jessie frees herself from her husband's embrace and sticks her head out the window again. Frankie and Danny look up at her, like two wee boys gazing at the sky on a clear night, searching for shooting stars.

2

'Will ye throw us doon a piece, Ma,' Frankie yells, his hands cupped around his mouth. 'Two pieces an' jam.'

'Aye, two pieces an' jam,' Danny repeats, squinting up at his mother and holding two fingers in the air.

'Aye, all right,' she shouts back, her voice floating down to them like a parachute swaying in a current of warm air. 'But just a few more minutes, eh. You two have got the scouts the night and your faither will be away to his work in a minute.' She watches them scurry back to the game, having a race to see who gets there first.

'I'll be glad when you're off this nightshift, Sandy. I'm fed up wi' it, so I am,' Jessie says, slicing the half loaf of bread on the table.

Sandy goes back to the window, rubbing at his wet hair. 'Me an' aw.' He watches his elder son score a goal and run about like he'd just won the World Cup for Scotland. 'Frankie's got some left foot on him, so he has. Ye know, I asked him the other day whether he wanted to be a fitba' player when he grows up.'

'Aw aye. What did he say?'

'He said naw, he wanted to work in the library, so he could read all the books.'

'That'd be right,' Jessie laughs, spreading raspberry jam on the sliced white bread. 'He's ay got his heid in a book, that yin. Did ye ask Danny as well?'

'Aye, I did. And do ye know what the wee bugger said?'

'No, what.'

'A bookie. He said he wants to be a bookie. Can ye believe that? No a fireman, no a doctor, no an engineer. He said he wants tae go tae the Ayr races and the dogs at Carntyne. A bloody bookie, eh? Ye widnae credit it.'

'My god! I don't know what I'm gaunny dae wi' that boy,' she says, shaking her head in disbelief. 'Ye know Mrs Duncan fae up the next close. She said Danny and her boy were playin' bools for money. Imagine that, bettin' on the marbles. She said Danny took threepence off him and he ran away home greetin'. I don't know where he gets it from, a' this gamblin', honest I don't.'

'I bloody well know. He told me he's been runnin' messages for that swine, Sammy Skelly, buying him bacon rolls and cups of tea an' that.'

'Jesus, Mary and Joseph. The boy's only nine and he's runnin' messages for a bookmaker? I hope you told Danny to stay away from him.'

'Bloody right I did. I told him I'd skelp his arse if I caught him anywhere near that bastard.'

Sandy picks up his jacket and his bag with his piece and his tea caddy in it. 'I'd better be away to my work. It's gettin' late. I'll take the boys doon the road.'

'Here, gie them this,' Jessie says and hands him two jam sandwiches wrapped in brown paper. She rises on her toes and kisses him on the cheek. 'I'll see you the morra then.'

Sandy Canyon strolls down the street, his heavy steel-toed work boots singing on the cobblestones like the clickety hoofs of the rag and bone man's old Clydesdale, his bag slung over his shoulder, his jacket folded over his arm. He whistles away to himself and watches his boys running and skipping ahead of him, dodging each other's feeble blows. 'I'm Cassius Clay,' Frankie whoops, excited.

'Naw, I am. I'm Cassius Clay, you're Sonny Liston,' Danny yells back, his fists dancing a spirited jig through the air. Sandy beams to himself. They're a couple of wee toerags, so they are.

'Right, you two,' he says when they reach the busy corner of Shettleston Road. 'I'm away to catch my bus. Francis, you look after your brother. Daniel, I want you to hold Francis' hand when you're crossing the road and do as he tells you like a good boy scout, eh.'

Danny gives a saintlike nod. 'Aye, da.'

Sandy ruffles Danny's hair and feigns a right hook to Frankie's head. Frankie ducks and weaves his way around an imaginary ring. The two boys follow their father's every step as he walks leisurely towards the bus stop, suddenly breaking into a clip as he turns and sees his bus coming up the road. They wave as he takes his seat at the back of the bus, not stopping until it trundles into the distance.

'Right, we'd better hurry up or we'll be late,' Frankie says, holding out his hand for his brother.

'Och away,' Danny grins, poking his tongue out and making himself go cross-eyed. 'I can cross the road masel'.' Before Frankie can grab him, Danny spins on his heels and scampers away down the road, looking back now and again to smile and

leap into the air, frantically whirling his arms, like a dement-
ed windmill.

'I don't what I'm going to do wi' that boy,' Frankie Canyon,
four feet eleven and aged ten and three-quarters, says to himself.

'Honest I don't.'

Danny Canyon feels the sweat run slowly down the inside of his shirt. The fan whirring drunkenly above his head does nothing to contain the tributaries of moisture that creep snail-like along his skin. It just shifts the heat around from one corner of the room to another, each stumbling revolution a breath of stale, spent air.

Some people prefer Saigon in the dry season, but not him. There is no let-up from the heat, no relief. At least with the wet, the daily downpour cools the air, cleanses it, washes the piss and excrement off the streets, drives the hawkers out of your way for a few minutes, a blessing if you've lived here as long as he has. And the sound of the rain, the way the clouds gather together like fellow travellers at a religious convention bellowing their praise for the Lord. Hallelujah!

Fortunately, you can buy a raincoat here for ten thousand dong, not even a dollar. Full length, in a variety of offensive colours. With the first spit, the raincoat vendors appear as if from holes in the ground. They are vapours that coalesce into human form with a rack of plastic macs ready to rescue those caught on the hop. Then, when the rain subsides, they evaporate, return to their subterranean world, get collected by their brothers-in-law, maybe. Who the fuck knows. They disappear.

Danny stares at the ceiling, forces himself to. He thought terror was supposed to concentrate the mind, but he can't seem to focus on anything important. It's strange the things a man thinks of when someone is holding a large stainless steel knife to his throat, the blade serrated in parts, the hardwood handle stained dark from years of sweat and fear. And blood? He's not thinking of anything particularly existential, no reflections on the meaning of life, or whether God exists or whether it's just a bad joke that's gone on too long. Is forty too young to die? Come in number eleven, your time's up. Here's your chit for the afterlife. Behave yourself this time. No, nothing like that.

He's thinking about the 1966 Jaguar Mark 2 he used to have when he was working as a bookie's runner in Glasgow, paid for mostly by the money he should have been returning to the bookie. White duco, red leather interior, walnut dash overdosed with dials, knobs and switches. A bucketload of style, confidence and class in a 3.8 litre engine. He's thinking about how he'd had to sell it quickly to raise some travelling money when the bookie in question decided to lay claim to Danny's car and his genitalia. Thank God for Australia and its open arms policy towards migrants, even dodgy ones like him. No questions asked. Here's your ticket and your hat with corks on it. Come on in, son. What was Celtic's forward line when they won the European Cup in '67? What would it be like to have it off with that Helen Mirren? Come on in, Inspector Tennison. Can I call you Jane? Just make yourself at home. Take your clothes off, I'll be with you in a minute.

And salad rolls. He hates them but he can't seem to get the taste out of his mouth. When he first arrived in Australia it seemed people ate salad rolls any time of the day or night. It almost put him off settling there. Australia is a country with too many vegetables on its hands. He sighs and wishes the lovely Assumpta hadn't gotten electrocuted in *Ballykissangel*.

His head is thumping, as regular as a heartbeat. Why can't he focus on anything? Thank Christ he managed to get that phone call in yesterday to Francis before these people turned up on his doorstep. His brother said he'd come as quick as he could. Danny asked him if he might be able to get here sooner than that. Where is he? He swore he would come. Francis was so surprised to hear from him. It has been a while, after all. But he didn't seem too surprised that Danny was up to his eyes in trouble. Aye, and who can blame him? It's not as if he hasn't been there before. 'Hold on, son,' Francis had said. 'Just hold on.'

Perhaps he should just give these bastards the money they want, the weekly share of the business that he and Mai have worked so hard to build up. But then they'd probably just want more. Not probably, definitely. That's the problem with Saigon, everyone wants a bit of what you've got—the police, the gangs, the bloody military. But if he gave in, sure he'd be poorer, but he'd be alive. There's something to be said for that. There'd be no blade pressing at his throat, no threats against his family, no waking up dead at the bottom of the Saigon River.

Danny's mind wanders and he reminds himself his motorbike needs fixing. Outside in Dong Khoi Street he can hear the night proceeding as usual, unaware of his predicament. The clickety clack of the foodstall vendors announcing their arrival with hot sticky rice, noodle soup and morsels of chicken and pork. The street hawkers trying to unload everything from shrinking T-shirts and fake American war-era Zippo lighters to coconuts and recently manufactured Cham Dynasty artefacts. Thousand-year-old dirt sprinkled on week-old concrete makes for a tidy profit.

He breathes in the ever present rumble and hum of the motorcycle madness, the basic score of life in Saigon. Seven million people, two million motorbikes. Jesus. He can hear the cyclo drivers parked by the corner of Mac Thi Buoi Street cajoling the tourists into a trip around the town.

'You! Where you go? I take you round, one hour. Two dollar. Number one.'

His mind revolves with the fan above his head and he pictures the shoeshine boys with their eager smiles and little wooden boxes containing their apothecary's kit of brushes and polish, their eagle eyes able to spot leather footwear at a hundred yards. He sees the beggars with their missing limbs, victims of landmines or desperate parents in need of another income to supplement their hopeless, bare-as-bones existence; the others with their napalmed skin, like fruit that has dried too long in the sun, looking for a few dong to get them through the day. 'Sir, monsieur, can you help me?' What's a thousand dong anyway? Sweet bugger all.

He smiles to himself as he thinks of the tourists emerging innocently from the Continental or the Grand or the Majestic, draped in cameras, moneybelts, maps, and shirts that should be illegal, looking forward to their day of wide-eyed exploration before they inevitably offer up their shoulder bags to the motorbike thieves who happily relieve these sacrificial lambs of their money, passports and postcards with one yank or surgically precise snip. Aid from the West.

He can see the girls falling out of the Monkey Bar at the slightest whiff of foreign flesh, flesh that is usually drunk, desperate or dollar-rich. The doors snap open for the prey must not escape, and the alluringly-clad women spring from behind the black-tinted glass, a colourful parade of store-bought sensuality, turned on and off at will like taps over the bath. Pay me and I will love you. Pay me more and I will love you more. They beckon and yell, titter and taunt, all painted-on skirts, cascading hair and slender arms waving in the warm, soulful evening air.

'Dahling! Dahling! Come over here. Number one bar. Number one ladies! We like you very good.'

For a moment he dwells upon the ripe pleasures they have to offer but is quickly brought back to earth as he feels the tip of the knife pierce his skin just below his jaw line, one lonely trickle of blood meandering down to his shirt collar. He wonders if it will stain.

'Penis enlargement?'
Frankie Canyon is so stunned by the very idea of it that his glass of Laphroaig hangs suspended and expectant in midair, waiting for some sort of instruction about whether to proceed to his now half-open gob or to sit it out on the coffee table while its master waits for further elaboration from the author of this unfathomable statement.

'I kid you not,' Jimmy Stewart says, a man known in the scheme as someone who would never lie about matters of such importance. If Jimmy told you the Pope was secretly married to Gina Lollobrigida you'd be inclined to believe him. 'I saw it in yon GQ magazine. Up the back. Nae kiddin', there was an advertisement offering hair replacements and various other forms of cosmetic enhancements.'

Frankie interrupts, raising his hand slightly, tilting his head to one side. 'Was that hair weave or hair plugs?'

'Micro plugs. Individual strand replacement,' Jimmy says, running his fingers sadly through his thinning hair.

'Individual strand, eh,' Frankie says, thinking of the time he rewired the house. 'Fiddly.'

'Anyhow, so I'm flicking through this GQ and they've got the men's health bit up the back and, as I said, there was an ad for hair replacement, fat removal, pectoral implants, testicle replacement, penis implants and . . .'

'Fucksake,' Frankie says, unable to contain himself, cradling his head in his hands. 'The things people will do to themselves. It's criminal, so it is. What is the world coming to? I can't get my head around penis implants at all.'

Frankie shifts uncomfortably in his seat, takes another gulp of his drink. It's not that he's not progressive. Shite, he had long hair when he was a teenager. Wore flares even. Read a book on Tantric sex, which his missus, the highly-erotic Eileen, calls frantic sex ('Just stick it in and go like crazy, darlin'). But penis implants?

'What is a penis implant anyhow?'

Jimmy is au fait with the procedure, having read the article. 'Well, as far as I can tell, they snip a tendon at the base of your wullie which releases a good couple of inches of it from inside the body, right. Then they stick a big dod of fat from the top of your thighs in it tae make it bigger and fatter. Here, I've got some pictures.'

Jimmy rummages through his plastic bag, his cigarette dangling from his mouth, the smoke making him squint as it rises steadily into his eyes, and comes up with the magazine, holding it aloft triumphantly like he's just won the European Cup. He flicks through the pages, past articles about blokes who like to wear dresses on the weekend, an eight-page spread on designer socks, and a piece about the rise and fall of Demi Moore—'Are her breasts too big for her boots?'—until he locates the special cosmetic surgery sealed section.

'Here you are, Frankie. That's the operation. See how . . . '

'Jesus Christ,' Frankie says, wincing. 'That's disgusting. I've never . . . My God. Look at that. It's splayed out there like a sausage on a piece.'

Frankie is completely gobsmacked. More than twenty-five years down the shipyard and the factory with those hard bastards, and twenty years living in one of the toughest housing schemes known to mankind (Vikings, Visigoths and Vandals would have found it tough going here) and he's never seen anything like this before.

He knows someone who'd had a tooth implant after his missus had belted him with a frying pan, but implants in the pelvic region were completely new territory, a bit like the west end of Glasgow where all the men are tall with big legs, and are called Callum and are doctors or civil engineers and wear kilts on Burns night and don't know what hire purchase is.

The two of them sit on the settee, speechless in their disbelief. Their brows furrowed like a fork across a plate of mash, they turn the magazine this way and that in an attempt to come to grips with what is portrayed before them, like teenage boys with their first copy of *Playboy*.

'You know what they say,' Jimmy says. 'Long and thin goes right in and makes the babies, short and thick does the trick and satisfies the ladies.'

'Is that right? I didn't know that. Makes sense I suppose,' Frankie nods. He thinks to himself that it doesn't seem that long ago since Christiaan Barnard performed the first heart transplant operation, and he dwells momentarily on the progress of mankind. 'I'm telling you Jimmy, I've never seen that kind of surgery on *Chicago* fuckin' *Hope*, have you?'

They both break up laughing, smoke, whisky and spit decorating the living room wallpaper, which suddenly takes on a new embossed texture. Frankie lies back, half on, half off the couch, and with one hand wipes the tears from his eyes. Jimmy is on the carpet and struggling to regain what passes for his composure, but keeps choking on his laughter as he tries to speak. He just can't imagine it, that kind of operation. It'd be like wearing a black string vest, or buying a tube of facial scrub for men from the Body Shop. But with one substantial exhalation of fetid cigarette and alcohol breath he manages to get a few words out.

'Frankie. In all seriousness, but. Would you have it done, like? Cosmetic surgery. Penis enlargment, an' that.'

Frankie surveys his groin and gives it a peremptory rub, takes a nip of his whisky and leans forward towards Jimmy who is now staring with singular intent at his own crotch.

'Well, if I did, Jimmy, I'd have the whole playpen done, wullie, the lot. A complete new rig. In fact, I'd get the Jimi Hendrix model. I hear he had the biggest kit in pop music.'

'Is that right?' Jimmy says, his interest perking up. 'But it'd be black, Frankie, yer wullie.'

'Listen son, if it's fourteen inches long I don't care what fuckin' colour it is.'

'And it could probably play the guitar as well, eh.'

'Aye, behind its head.'

Jimmy pauses, mulling the broader implications of cosmetic surgery. Does it make you any less of a man? Any more of a man? Would you tell your pals down the pub that you were thinking of having a tummy tuck? Can you pay for it in weekly instalments?

'Do you think you'd get a discount if you got the lot done at once? Like twenty-five per cent off, that sort of thing,' he says with the faux earnestness only the dead drunk can muster.

'Aye, I'm sure you would. You'd probably get a box of steak knives thrown in as well. I'm telling you, Jimmy, I'm buggered if I know what the world's coming to. Fancy a pint?'

What Frankie fancies is the idea of a walk, even if it is just to the pub. He loves to immerse himself in the chill of a late winter's evening with only the occasional yelps from weans playing football in the street or the low crackle of bus wheels as they push their way wearily through the winter slush.

The frost-laden air is a slap in the face, like aftershave without the pong. It wakes him up, revitalises him, makes him feel alive, gives him a sense of anticipation, even if he doesn't quite know about what. It is more a vague reassurance that something good might happen.

Just being out of the house, the journey itself, is enough to make him feel he has choices in his life, that he has a destiny and he controls it. That not everything is pre-ordained by class, circumstance and religious affiliation, or whether you eat fresh vegetables or serve them up straight out of the can.

Mostly he likes to walk by himself. It felt strange at first, just walking, as Chuck Berry put it, with no particular place to go, no destination in mind, no greyhound on a leash to legitimise your stroll, to give it a reason, a context. Walking for walking's sake was not a common pastime where he lived. There, if you weren't walking somewhere definite, the bookie's, the pub, the shops, you could easily be seen as a bit mental, which was not an unreasonable assumption. A walk around the scheme was not exactly a leisurely stroll around the Duke of Argyll's estate. There is nothing much in the way of nature, hardly a tree, barely a blade of grass. Asphalt, cement, dog shite. Endless rows of pebble-dash houses just waiting to be demolished like a man on death row preparing to die. That's your heather-covered highland glen of Glasgow's east end.

But mind, once you get walking, get a decent rhythm going, it doesn't really matter what is around you. Get the head down, review, readjust, rearrange in your head—bills paid or overdue, promises fulfilled and unfulfilled, opportunities presented and denied, squandered. Sort things out, settle the nerves, iron out the stresses of the day's work, come face to face with yourself, with your responsibilities to your family, to a brother in trouble, a brother who needs his help.

A man needs a plan to keep going. That is Frankie's credo. Otherwise, what is there to look forward to at the end of the day? Beer? A documentary on the telly? A new book? More beer? The football replay? Maybe. Not bad, but nowhere near enough.

No, Frankie needs to walk. What do the Italians call it? A *passeggiata*. Get dressed up in your finest clobber and stroll, glide, saunter down the boulevard, nodding here, waving there, feeling the gentle late afternoon sun caress your face. Stop to chat about children, wine, food, lovers.

Not that a clamber around the scheme is vaguely reminiscent of an early evening wander around the Piazza San Marco, except perhaps when you hurry by St Clare's chapel, head down, hoping Father McGonigal doesn't notice you and ask awkward questions about why you hadn't been to mass for the previous thirteen years. 'Oh aye, well I slept in Father,' works for a couple of weeks, a month maybe, but once you got past a decade it did tend to lose that aura of credibility, although Frankie is always ready to point out that the Catholic Church has a few problems with credibility itself.

'So run that one by me again. There's a Father, Son and Holy Ghost, and the Son got crucified but, and then he came alive again and some angels took him back to heaven. And his mother was a virgin right? Not from this part of the world, obviously.'

Francis Aloysius Canyon stuffs his hands deeper into the pockets of his overcoat as he and Jimmy walk, shoulders hunched, up the road to the pub where the village used to be before it was overrun with corporation housing and fried food. He glances up at the Number 11 bus as it makes its way down the road to Barlanark, then on to Shettleston, and Dennistoun. His side of town. Before they flitted to the scheme, he and his younger brother Danny, and their two sisters, Fiona and Anne, lived in Shettleston, on the fourth floor of a tenement right across from the police station. 'Very handy,' Frankie's mother often announced proudly as if it were a feature of the house, like central heating or built-in wardrobes.

It was a good house, though, good for a young boy whose world was defined by being loved by his parents. And visits by the toffee apple man. He didn't mind that the toilet was on the landing and shared by three families, that it had no running hot water, or that it had only one bedroom, with an inset for a double bed. His sisters were wee then, so they slept in the big cot and he got the fold-down bed with Danny.

He loved that time just before he drifted off to sleep. He'd had a wash in the sink and his mother had warmed his pyjamas by the fire. He'd pull the sheets right up high and rub them against his lips. Was there anything ever so luxurious? She'd bring him a piece with butter and sugar on it and the slow syrupy crunch would set him off to sleep.

When he woke in the night, he'd slip out of bed and go stand by the big bay window and just stare out of it. He'd linger over the lights of the police station. He could make out men in uniform, talking on the telephone. He'd watch couples coming out of the fish and chip shop, fish suppers under their arms, in a hurry to get home for their dinner. He'd catch the odd footstep in the close, a muffled cough in the street, the bus trundling down Shettleston Road, whining and grunting as if it had smoker's cough as the driver changed the gears, up and down and across. He'd creep back into bed but was always too excited to get back to sleep.

Sometimes, early in the morning, he'd hear his father coming home from the nightshift. The sound of his boots on the stairs. That smell he had. Metal and oil and sweat. The smell of work. The feel of his beard on his cheek, ticklish, painful and delicious. Hearing his father wash himself in the scullery sink. Smelling liver and onions in the frying pan. A sheepish hello as he got up before he was supposed to, still rubbing the sleep from his eyes. 'Go back to bed Francis,' his mother would say. 'It's only five o'clock in the morning.'

'Och, he's all right Jessie, he just wants to see his old man.' His father would lift him up high to the ceiling, his pyjama top riding up around his shoulders. 'That's ma boy,' he'd say. 'That's ma boy.'

Frankie and Jimmy walk on, not saying much, just listening to the sound of their shoes on the concrete and watching their breath condense in front of them like a magical mist leading them to the pub. Follow me and you shall have as many pints as your heart desires.

The Number 11 is almost empty. There are a few people on the top deck, illuminated like cardboard cutouts in a puppet show. No one moves, they just sit there, slumped against the window, waiting to get where they are going, so they can just get home, get warm, and get on with their lives.

For the last twenty-odd years Frankie had caught that bus to his work. Up at six, cup of tea, cereal, pack the piece, out the door, down the stairs, through the close and into the dark, blue street to join the others as they dragged themselves into another working day.

Frankie worked hard, there was no doubt about that. Eileen, while quick to acknowledge his faults and eccentricities—only talked when he had something to say, hated television except nature documentaries, read too many books, walked too many miles, thought he was really a black soul brother in a Glaswegian's pasty white skin—she was the first to admit that he was a good worker.

But he worked hard because he couldn't see any other way to get through it. Being a welder was not exactly his dream job. But the time went fast when you got wired in. It wasn't what he'd thought he'd turn out to be. He'd hoped to stay on at school, he was clever enough for it, and his teachers were disappointed when he left at sixteen. But he had no choice after his old man had taken a heart attack down the pit. He was only thirty-six. Fucking thirty-six. He'd had pneumonia and had gone back to work before he should have. But they were skint. What choice did he have? That's what everybody said at the funeral anyway.

He still remembers the day the police came to the door, the shine of their shoes, the swish and sway of their black plastic raincoats. He'd just got home from school and was in the kitchen making himself something to eat while his mother was peeling some carrots. She'd nicked herself with the knife and was sucking at her finger and the younger ones were crowding around her to get a good look at the blood. There was a knock at the door and he said he'd get it. Hughie Brown was supposed to be coming up to get him and they were going to kick the ball around the back. But when he opened the door, chewing away on his piece, he saw it was the polis, two of them.

'Is yer mammy in, son,' the taller one said, gazing down at the sixteen-year-old boy, friendly, reassuring, the way the dentist does before he slips the gas mask over your face to send you to oblivion.

He left the polis waiting on the landing and went to get his mother. He stayed in the kitchen with the weans. Then they all heard her scream and somehow he knew right away what the matter was. The four of them just stood there, saying nothing, waiting for someone to tell them what to do.

Danny was talking about getting a job with the bookie's and he started working at the shipyards two weeks after his father died. His uncle Paddy put in a word for him. Paddy drove a crane and Frankie was taken on as an apprentice welder. He didn't hate the work, but he didn't like it either. He just felt he was missing out on something. His childhood maybe. A future.

Some nights after work he'd sit in a booth in Coia's Café in Dennistoun, just sit there with a cup of tea, and slip a few pennies in the jukebox. He'd agonise over the songs like a prospective bride over a wedding ring in a jeweller's shop. So much to choose from: Led Zeppelin, Deep Purple, Free, Neil Young. The old favourites from the sixties: the Beatles, Manfred Mann, The Rolling Stones, Cream, Jimi Hendrix. But he always ended up with black music. That's where his money would go. Soul, blues, pop, as long as it was black it was just fine with him. John Lee Hooker, Wilson Pickett, James Brown, The Temptations, Nina Simone, Etta James. Real music. Doesn't seem that long ago. And what have we got now? The Backstreet Boys. Fucksake.

Frankie shakes the chill off himself as he and Jimmy edge their way into the pub. He does a quick recce, not that it could be anything other than quick, given the size of the place. More like a living room than a pub, just a small rectangular bar with a few stools lined up in front of it and a couple of tables and chairs either side of the fireplace. A photograph on the wall of Charlie Tully in his Celtic strip. Reminds him of the old joke. The Pope and Charlie Tully are walking down the street in Rome. Somebody asks, 'Who's that wi' Tully?'

Some folk describe it as cosy, but Frankie thinks it's too unpredictable to be that. He's been there on too many nights when some poor bastard left without his teeth or with a broken bottle embedded in his cheek. But it has atmosphere, right enough, and he prefers it to the big shop up the hill, even though some nights they put on a smorgasbord. Frankie isn't averse to being presented with a wide variety of food to choose from, but there is something he can't quite come at with a smorgasbord. It doesn't matter what you eat, it all tastes the same, like it has been sprayed with the essence of bad breath.

Frankie settles himself in at one of the corner tables, taking off his coat and hanging it on the back of the chair. 'What'll it be, Jimmy?' he says, already reaching into his pocket for some pound notes.

'Pint o' heavy, thanks pal.'

He edges his way to the bar, acknowledging familiar faces with a nod or a hello. There's a few in for a Wednesday, when usually everybody is skint, it not being pay day until the following day. There's a few desperadoes in the other corner, enveloped in a force-field of cigarette smoke, bad language and who-the-fuck-are-you-lookin'-at demeanours. He knows a couple of them, they went to school at St Leonard's together. But they got themselves in with the gangs, the Pak and the Toi, wee boys with big chips on their shoulders, always talking about who they were going to do next. This cunt and that cunt and some other cunt are in for it. Meet us by the swing park at nine.

Frankie gets them in and squeezes back to the table where Jimmy is browsing through his magazine, shielding its contents from nearby drinkers lest they think it less than appropriate reading material for this part of the world. He lingers momentarily on an article about designer living and the minimalist approach to interior decoration. Rooms with hardly any furniture in them. Sounds like his place, he thinks to himself.

'Frankie, this magazine's got a lifestyle section an a'. There are a couple of pages about garden furniture here. Very nice.'

'Aye, well. You haven't got a lifestyle. Lifestyle's only for people who've got a life. Besides, what are you wanting with garden furniture? You haven't even got a bloody garden,' Frankie says, taking a mouthful of his pint and grinning to himself.

'I have so got a lifestyle. I drink a lot and eat shitty food. I live in a dump. All I need is a mobile phone and an electric rice cooker and everything will be hunky dory, pal. It says so right here in this magazine,' Jimmy exclaims, his finger stabbing away at the relevant article. 'Besides, it says here this handcrafted, cast iron outdoor setting fae Italy would sit just as easily inside your home as it would on the terrazzo.'

Frankie smiles. 'Terrazzo. Doesn't he play on the left wing for AC Milan?'

'Jesus fuck, Frankie, a terrazzo isnae a fitba' player it's a . . .'

Frankie interrupts, raising his hands as if professing innocence to a referee. 'Aye, I know what a terrazzo is. I'm just kidding you on.'

'So what is it then, smart arse?'

'Well, you take one terrazzo, top it with grated parmesan cheese and bake it in the oven for approximately forty minutes or until brown. Serve with buffalo mozzarella, tomato and basil salad. Accompany that with a nice bottle of chilled Chianti. Eileen and I always have that on a Sunday night in front of the telly. Very nice it is too.'

Jimmy gives up, shakes his head, takes a cigarette from his pack and taps it against the table. 'What is Chianti, anyhow?'

'It's the preferred drink of men who have penis implants.'

They both let out a sudden explosion of laughter, rocking back and forth in their chairs. The other drinkers turn to look at them, wondering what's so funny and why they don't know about it. And wondering whether they are laughing at them?

Two fresh pints arrive, delivered carefully by Big Andy the bartender, who presents them as if they were offerings to the gods, a religious experience. He all but gives them the Papal blessing before he sets them down gently on the table. 'There y'are lads, get yer gobs around those.'

Frankie takes custody of his, cradles it. 'Thanks, pal. Magic.'

Andy puts his hands on his hips, leans back slightly. 'So, what's new wi' youse two? I saw you there gabbin' away like two auld fish wives.'

Jimmy lifts up his pint, sips at it, his mouth a ring of white foam. 'Aw nothin' much. Just talking aboot life, an' that.'

'Aw aye. You've got one, have you? Can I borrow it? I'll bring it back in the mornin'.' The bartender shuffles away, laughing to himself, telling some irate punters to hold their horses, he'd be there in a minute.

Frankie leans forward in his chair, rubs his finger across his nose. 'Listen Jimmy, I need to talk to you. Danny rang.'

'Danny, your brother? What, fae Australia?'

'No, from Saigon.'

'Sai where?'

'Saigon, Vietnam. Where the war was.'

'Aw aye, Ho Chi Minh and a' that. Jesus Christ. What the fuck's he doin' there? I thought he lived in Australia.'

'No, he moved a while back. Runs a bar with his wife.'

'What did he want?'

'He wanted some help, Jimmy. And he needs it now, right away. He's got himself into a bit of bother. You know Danny. But I'm right worried about him this time.'

'When did he ring?' Jimmy says, rubbing the stubble on his chin.

'Last night. There was this magic programme on about whale sharks, you know, and I was just about to sit down and watch it when the telephone rang and it was him.'

'Jesus. Tell me everythin', son. I'm all ears.'

One and a half million wildebeest are making their annual pilgrimage across the Serengeti in search of green pasture and water. It's the end of the dry season and the plain is now a dustbowl, the grass just dry lifeless sticks. Many of the wildebeest are weak from hunger and thirst. Out here on the scorching plain death lies behind every tree, in every thicket, by every depleted waterhole.

Hardship and predators plague a journey that lasts thousands of miles until they reach the flourishing grasslands. For Tabatha, the hungry lioness, and her three cubs, the wildebeest are a godsend. It has been a lean summer and her ribs can be seen painfully outlined against her skin as she crouches low behind a fallen tree, waiting for the best moment to strike. She picks out her target, a sickly young wildebeest by the edge of the herd.

Frankie turns his head and yells into the kitchen. 'Here, Eileen, there's a good programme on Discovery Channel about the annual migration of the wildebeest.'

Eileen emerges wiping her hands on a tea towel. She's been washing up after Frankie had cooked the dinner. Lasagna, salad, home-made icecream.

'What, are those poor wildebeest getting it again? You'd think after all this time they'd learn not to stray from the pack.'

Eileen takes a seat and they both watch silently as the inevitable happens. The chase is brief and brutal. Tabatha's powerful claws grip the animal's flesh like a vice and bring it violently to the ground in a storm of dust and despair. She clamps her huge jaws around the neck of her fallen prey, which struggles vainly to raise itself from its predicament. Its legs kick, then twitch and give a final shudder. It's all over Rover. The denouement is predictable, but sad and moving nonetheless. Tabatha and the weans get stuck in.

'They kill by asphyxiation, your lions,' Frankie says, breaking the funereal silence.

'Is that right? So they just squeeze the life out of it? I could do with a bit of a squeeze myself, Francis.'

Eileen sheds her apron like a snake sheds its skin and snuggles up to Frankie on the settee. She tenderly strokes his cheek with her index finger, a faint aroma of dishwashing liquid in the air. They agree, as if by telepathy, that Routine Number Four is the preferred special of the day. Frankie plays hard to get. Eileen's favourite.

'Do you want to make mad passionate love, Francis?' she whispers, breathing heavily like a big cat after the hunt.

Frankie kids on he didn't hear her and flicks the channel. There's a programme about the reproductive habits of whale sharks due to start in ten minutes.

She shifts closer and links her arm through his. 'Did you hear me? I said do you want to make mad passionate love?'

With his free arm Frankie turns up the volume with the remote control. 'What?'

'I want you to make love to me Frank.'

'Och, I don't know. The whale shark documentary is on in ten minutes. You know it's one of my favourites,' he says, quickly glancing at her before turning his gaze back to the television.

She rakes her fingers through his thick dark hair. 'You can do an awful lot in ten minutes, love.'

He fiddles with his slippers. He notices the cloth is wearing a bit where the big toe sticks up. Like a wee erection, he thinks to himself.

They are quiet for a moment as she rubs what is yet to be a bulge in his trousers. The trousers are part of a suit, but he hasn't worn the jacket in ages.

'I'll suck it,' she says, in her best Joan Collins *Dynasty*-voice.

He picks up the TV guide. It's a good night in front of the telly. Three documentaries in a row. A trifecta. He takes a desultory nibble at the remains of his biscuit and sips at his tea, but it's tepid.

She brushes some biscuit crumbs from his thighs. 'I'll do that thing you like with the clotted cream.'

He stares at the fire, or what passes for a fire. These two-bar radiators with the plastic coal for effect are nothing like the real thing. What possessed him to box in the fireplace and put in this piece of shite he'd never know. But she'd wanted to modernise the place, she said. Make it more classy. Classy my arse. The electricity bill has gone through the roof. And that wee stupid bloody fan inside that was supposed to emulate the real flames of a roaring coal fire, you'd have to be an eastern mystic and visionary to see any similarity. You could sit there till kingdom fucking come and all it would ever look like would be a light bulb inside a red shell of plastic coal. Wullie the coal man said they'd rue the day they did away with the coal and he was right enough.

'C'mon Frank. Tell you what, I'll put on those leather thigh boots, the ones you got at the pub for a tenner.'

'Oh aye.' Frankie snatches a quick glance at the clock. Five minutes and the whale sharks are on.

Eileen slowly undoes the buttons of her dress and throws it provocatively onto the chair behind her. She slides her leg over his, her left thigh snuggled up against his crotch. She starts singing softly . . . 'Who's that black private dick that's a sex machine to all the chicks?'

It's his fourth favourite song. Foul play. 'Shaft!' he replies, a glimmer of a smile at the corner of his mouth.

'Damn right!' she whispers, sliding her tongue into his ear.

Frankie puts the remote control on the coffee table and caresses the inside of her thigh. 'Who is the man that would risk his neck for his brother man?' he coos.

'Shaft!'

'Can ya dig it?' Frankie moans, as he cups his hands around her slowly undulating behind.

Eileen rips at the buttons of his shirt and makes a mental note to sew them back on again. 'Who's the cat that won't cop out when there's danger all about?'

'Shaft!' he shouts, as he bites her left nipple.

'Right on! RIGHT ON!' she screams, transported to the long back seat of her very own big black Cadillac. 'What about the whale sharks, love?' she inquires breathlessly as she unzips his trousers and prepares to take him into her mouth.

'Och, I'll tape it.'

It's late. Frankie and Eileen are horizontal on the couch, a tangle of wayward limbs and appendages. The documentary on whale sharks is over. 'Gentle Giants of the Sea'. They'd managed to catch the last ten minutes. It turns out they don't actually mate that often, which Eileen found disturbing. The telephone rings.

'That'll be the phone,' Frankie says, tilting his head to the corner of the room where the standard lamp is. 'I'll get it,' he says.

'No, I'll get it.'

'OK.'

'You're supposed to insist a wee bit more, Frank,' Eileen moans, extricating herself from their post-coital embrace. She picks up the phone.

'Who is it?' Frankie inquires, reclining comfortably on the settee.

'It's Fiona.'

'Fiona who?'

'Fiona, your sister.'

'Aw aye. What does she want?'

'Something about her teeth.'

'She hasn't got any fuckin' teeth,' he laughs.

'She says she had too much to drink last night and managed to throw up her dinner and her teeth right out the window and into Mrs McKechnie's garden.'

'And what does she want me to do about it?'

'She want's you to go and fetch them.'

'What about Eddie? You know, her husband.'

'Eddie says there is nothing in the marriage vows about denture retrieval.'

Frankie reflects on this. There was nothing in the marriage vows about him beating the shite out of her every Saturday night either, but that hadn't stopped him. Useless prick. Frankie was fond of his sister, but this was taking the notion of family responsibility a bit far. Blood wasn't necessarily thicker than vomit.

He raises himself up into a sitting position and shakes his head. 'OK. I'd better put some clothes on, I suppose.'

He begins gathering up his clothing, which has somehow managed to disperse itself around the room. He retrieves a sock from the top of the standard lamp, his underwear from the fireplace. He is having trouble buttoning up his shirt when the phone rings again. 'I'll get it. It'll be Fiona. She'll have lost one of the weans or something,' he says.

There is no response. Eileen is already in the bath singing 'These Boots are Made for Walking'

'Francis. It's me, Danny,' says the voice on the other end of the line.

Frankie immediately recognises his brother's voice, the deep gravelly timbre it always had, even from when he was a teenager.

'Danny. Where the hell are you?'

'Sauchiehall Street.'

'What the . . . '

'Naw, I'm just kidding. I'm still in Saigon. I'm in Saigon and I'm fucked.'

'Jesus Danny, what's going on?'

Danny feels the ropes bite tighter into his wrists. Every time he moves they dig deeper into his flesh. His back aches and his eye feels swollen. Look at those men, laughing at him as they light up yet another cigarette. Maybe they are going to do more than smoke it? His shirt is soaked with sweat. If he ever gets out of this he will definitely fix that fan. How did he get himself into this mess? It seems like only yesterday that he arrived in Melbourne, a pasty-faced and freckled boy from Glasgow, fleeing his past in search of a future. That first day at the slaughterhouse, he can still feel his eyes water at the smell of it, still feel his throat constrict at the taste of it. Welcome to Australia, a new job, a new life.

Danny tries not to breathe, or at least to breathe as little as possible. But no matter how small he makes his inhalations and exhalations, his chest barely moving like some Eastern mystic in self-induced suspended animation, the fact remains that the place smells terrible, as if all the world's most eye-watering, stomach-gagging, head-spinning, bone-crushing odours have been combined into one giant stink by some fiendish alchemist and released at William Mortimer & Sons, abbattoirs and selfproclaimed manufacturers of the world's finest smallgoods.

Danny waits patiently as one by one the men, and a handful of women, register with a bloke holed up in what looks like an overgrown sentry box positioned just inside the gate. When it's his turn, he hands over the application form he's already filled in and waits for a response from the box man, who studies Danny's details.

'Daniel Canyon. Born in Glasgow, eh?'

'Aye, that's right.'

'Me missus is from Glasgow,' the box man says glancing up for the first time, and looking vaguely interested in the twentysomething, sandy-haired and sharply-dressed young man before him.

Danny and the bloke in the box, whose name turns out to be Dennis, spend the next few minutes discussing how he had met Shirley when she started working in the boning room fifteen years ago, and how they had a couple of kids, and how she took him on a holiday to Glasgow last year to show him where she grew up, and how he had met all her cousins and uncles and aunties, but the weather was shithouse and the beer was as weak as piss.

'Dunno how you drink that shit,' Dennis says, putting Danny's application form in a drawer while picking up a big black telephone.

'Bill, I've got a bloke for you here for smallgoods. Be a good TA for Young Bob I reckon.'

Danny hadn't expected to be taken on so quickly. In this instance, being a Glaswegian appears to have been an actual advantage, the first he had encountered since he came screaming into the world at the Glasgow Royal Infirmary more than two decades before.

Young Bob seems pleased to see him, explaining that he has been without a trades assistant for several weeks and he is sick to death of carrying his own tools, raising his own ladders and generally having no one to do all the shitty little jobs he doesn't want to do himself. And, he points out, he doesn't have anyone to talk to in his workroom-cum-humpy-cum-sleeping quarters behind the sausage-making machines where the Greek women reign supreme in their long white coats, white rubber boots and sausage mince-encrusted plastic gloves.

As a son of Glasgow, Danny had eaten more than his fair share of pork and beef links, and many a square slice, but he'd never actually witnessed the manufacturing process on an industrial scale, so he was looking forward to becoming acquainted with its secrets. He knew from his days with the bookies that there was nothing more advantageous than a bit of inside knowledge.

Young Bob was the fitter and turner in the smallgoods section and as such it was his responsibility to maintain all machinery associated with the sausage-making process in tiptop working order at all times of the day and night given that the world of smallgoods production never stopped. As Bob was often heard to say, a sausage never sleeps.

After Danny is fitted out with a new pair of blue overalls and work boots, he immediately embarks on a tour of the sausagemaking equipment and associated paraphernalia in order that he might fully understand their workings and lubrication requirements, for which he will be primarily responsible on a twice-daily basis.

Young Bob leads Danny around the smallgoods floor like a king showing off his castle, a young child his toy box. He strolls with his head slightly bowed, his hands behind his back, his balance maintained by the weight of the fourteen-inch shifting spanner leaning Tower of Pisa-like from his back pocket. Occasionally, he rotates his shoulders slightly to acknowledge various members of the staff, his sausage serfs, as he likes to think of them in his more medieval moments.

Young Bob had earned the right to adopt a kindly paternalistic attitude to his charges as he had been a fixture at William Mortimer & Sons for so long. When he arrived at the works as a sixteen year old in the late fifties, he'd immediately been given the moniker 'Young Bob' by his more elderly workmates on the maintenance team, although the modern human resource manager's concept of a team as such did not exist in Australian slaughterhouses then. They were a collection of blokes with spanners, screwdrivers, wrenches and welding equipment who shared an interest in mechanical devices and discount meats.

'So they still call you Young Bob then, even though you're not really that, ah, young,' Danny says, trying to be as diplomatic as possible.

'Yeah, the name's kinda stuck. Anyway, I'm buggered if I know where the last twenty years has gone. It just seems like yesterday that I started work here with me dad. He was a sparkie. Top bloke. Got electrocuted in the skinning room in '62.'

'I'm sorry to hear that.'

'Yeah, well, it was a long time ago now. Can't see a sheepskin without thinking of him though.'

Young Bob takes Danny by the elbow and ushers him towards a sleeping giant, a bulbous beast of a machine, and introduces its features like a man proudly showing off his brand new car. He circumnavigates it as he speaks, nodding and pointing, his steps, slow, measured and full of purpose, his grasp of detail, his recall of even the most obscure particulars, at once impressive and awe inspiring.

Danny notices right away that the beast is set precisely in the middle of the room. By virtue of its size and significance, all other machines are kept at a distance, placed deferentially along the perimeter walls, but angled slightly towards it as if in tribute. Do not crowd this beast, give him room to breathe, Danny thinks to himself.

Young Bob runs his open palm across the curved dome, his fingers spread spider-like and trailing off as he moves around it. He takes a grease nipple between his thumb and forefinger, tweaks it, and is satisfied that the machine is sufficiently lubricated and ready for action. 'It is ten feet and three inches in diameter, nearly five and a half feet tall, with a lower protruding rim thirty-two inches wide. The outer casing is cast iron and, as you can see, the inner lining of the rim is stainless steel. It weighs three and one-half tons and was manufactured by MacIntosh and Sons in Manchester, England, and transported here in parts and reassembled by my former boss and mentor, Albert Duffy, master fitter and turner, formerly of Her Majesty's Navy. I'm happy to say that as a young apprentice I was privileged to be part of the assembly team.'

But what catches Danny's eye, transfixes him with their sheer flesh-pulverising power, are four shiny blades, each consisting of half a dozen crescent-shaped slabs of razor-sharp steel, placed at two equidistant points above the rim, into which they would be lowered, Danny assumes, when it is time for them to do battle with the recalcitrant matter that would soon become sausage meat of the highest grade.

'This, my boy,' Young Bob says, caressing the outer casing with what some might regard as an unhealthy eroticism, 'is the mainstay of our little operation here. The mother of all mincing machines. The Big Chopper. Not bad is she?'

'Very impressive, aye,' Danny says, unable to resist running his finger along the edge of one of the blades.

Young Bob shakes his head with obvious disappointment while firmly removing the offending hand from the vicinity of the pristine blade, like a parent removing his child's greedy fingers from the biscuit tin.

'Listen Daniel, if you want any sort of future in the smallgoods game there are rules to be observed at all times and rule number one is never, ever, put your hand, or any other part of your anatomy, in The Big Chopper. I'm saying this for your own good. I don't want any nasty accidents.'

'Have you had any nasty accidents then?' Danny inquires, suitably chastened, but slightly irritated.

'We've had a few, yeh.'

Danny waits for the elaboration he certainly feels is called for in this instance like a nut awaiting the turn of the spanner. 'Any that you can remember, then?'

Young Bob stands quietly for a moment, but then ignores the question and stoops to check the alignment of the blades, for blades that are not aligned correctly are accidents waiting to happen. He squints, his head meandering from side to side, then gives two of the fixing bolts a quarter turn with his shifter.

'Those bolts have to be tight as a fish's arse, mate. Any looser and they'll fly off at fifteen thousand revs a minute. Any tighter and you'll strip the thread. Then you've got real trouble. As in everything in this life, Daniel, it's a matter of getting the right balance.'

Danny nods in agreement. He's right, balance is the key. Yin and Yang, bacon and eggs, Morecambe and Wise, Butch Cassidy and the Sundance Kid.

Young Bob emerges from the depths of the protruding rim of The Big Chopper and points to a large scar, several inches deep, in the concrete wall behind them. 'That's what happens when a blade comes loose.'

'At fifteen thousand revs a minute?'

'At fifteen thousand revs a minute, Daniel. Not a pretty sight, is it? Fortunately for all of us, its path was slowed down by a stack of boxes packed with premium quality pork luncheon, otherwise that rampaging blade would have flown all over the room, felling anything that might have got in its way.

A blade on the loose shows no mercy, son. It knows friend nor foe. It's not a pretty sight I can tell you.'

'So, what happened? Was anybody hurt?'

'Again, unfortunately yes. And the pork luncheon was ruined. A total waste. We had to do three days of double shifts to catch up and that's not counting the curing time. I'd say all in all we lost about a week. Extremely disappointing.'

'What about the person injured by the blade. Was it bad?' Danny inquires, hoping for some of the blood soaked detail.

Young Bob stops in his tracks and looks Danny straight in the eye, his gaze lingering for a few, perfectly still seconds. 'The less said about that the better. Follow me.'

Danny trails behind Young Bob as he continues his guided tour of the smallgoods department of William Mortimer & Sons in a blur of basic information, historical context, sociological analysis and exaggerated hand movements. Facts and figures, outputs and inputs, curing times and temperatures, textural specifications, ingredients, ratios, boiling and mincing capacities of each machine, staff requirements, hygiene standards, preferred outer skin thickness relative to particular products, maintenance and lubrication requirements, packaging and, finally, a breakdown of market penetration and future sales strategies.

'Any questions?' Young Bob inquires, turning ballroom dancer-like in a half circle from the pork luncheon boiler, his hands spread beneficently before him, satisfied that all necessary information has been imparted thoroughly and to the best of his ability in a manner that is informative and entertaining.

'Aye, any danger of a cup of tea?'

The works canteen overflows with men and women in various combinations of working apparel, mixed and matched according to the particular responsibilities of the wearer. The intensity and location of blood stains provides Danny with an instant job description, like a soldier's uniform in a sea of sailors or a nun's billowing habit in a bus full of atheists.

The women from the hyper-clean vacuum packing section, where slabs of rib eye, porterhouse, tenderloin and other choice cuts are hygienically sealed and dispatched to Japan and Korea and various markets hungry for quality flesh, chat-

ter animatedly in Spanish, their calf-length, button-up dresses as white as new snow on the roof. Their thick woollen socks
peek out of their rubber boots, warding off the shuddering
chill of the cool room. They hold hands and link arms and
whisper endearments that sound like distant salsa music on a
warm summer's night.

The slaughtermen keep their own company in the corner of
the vast room by the open windows, the intense summer light
ricocheting off their murderous knives and shooting across
the room like bullets off a rock. Their full-length rubber
aprons, now hosed down and hanging idle by the door to the
killing floor, have managed to protect them only partly from
the thick dark blood that erupts violently, like beer from a
shaken can, from the slashed and torn throats of butchered
animals. They are still drenched, their sleeveless overalls just
patches of white against a crimson wash.

They attack their sandwiches and meat pies and chips in a
storm of salt, pepper and tomato sauce. They slurp and laugh
and chew with their mouths agape and look quietly, discon-
certingly dangerous.

The workers from the sheep skin de-fleecing and curing
room, their days spent in a murky half-light amid the olfactory tang and eye-watering sting of acid and brine, sit pallid and
grey. The clutch and utility of their cutlery is impeded by the
absence of thumbs, fingers, middle, fore and index, wrenched
off and mashed by the many-toothed and merciless fleece
removing machine which, like a bull terrier with its jaws fixed
in a vicelike grip, refuses to the finish to relinquish its unfortunate victims.

They munch disconsolately on their leftovers warmed-up
from the night before, mumbling among themselves, pushing
their food around their plates in a fruitless search for a corner
to hide it in, so that they might, at last, light up their cigarettes
that hang, shaking like tall grass in a light savannah breeze
between their dry, chapped lips. They rasp and cough and
rumble as they tell filthy, subterranean jokes.

Danny holds his steaming cup between both hands as he
speculates about the small herd of tussle-haired and bearded
men in their mucky brown overalls, scratching and sniffing as
they carry their trays to an empty table by the door. Agile and
animated, the lads from the skin shed, where the fleece-free
hides rest up before the next stage in their transformation to

a panoply of leather goods, bubble and squeak with energy. Throughout the day they leap from one hanging rail to another, moving old skins, hanging new ones, the swarming flies but a minor inconvenience in their quest for a perfectly ordered shed. They devour their food, a smorgasbord of everything that is on offer, before heading out in a riot of camaraderie to play as many ball games as they can squeeze into fifteen glorious, skin-free minutes. They whoop and yelp and call everybody mate.

So this is morning smoko, Danny thinks to himself. Here he is, in Melbourne, in Australia for God's sake, having a cup of tea at his new place of employ, surrounded by the detritus and smell of death, the bloody overalls, the shrapnel of flesh and bone and gut that clings to the back of a leg, the nape of a neck, the palm of a hand. Dried blood on boots, minced meat behind the fingernails. The promised land, eh? The fuckin' lucky country.

He should eat something but he's not hungry. There's an emptiness in his stomach, a small knot of incipient panic not helped by the cloying smell that hangs heavy in the air, so thick you could cut it with a blunt knife. Young Bob says he'll get used to it, that in all this death there is a kind of life, that it's part of the natural cycle of things. From the grass in the paddock to the stomach of the beast, to the sausage in the butcher's shop window to the mouth of the man in the street. Bob, what a character. There he is now, waving, beckoning Danny over to sit with him and his mates. Danny gives them the thumbs up.

He watches as they take their tins from the small oven that's bolted to the battered brick wall, their oil-stained hands wrapped in gloves or tea towels, or bits of rag so as not to burn themselves; although by the look of it, their skin is so thick from years of hard graft, it probably wouldn't make much of an impression anyway. Just a slight hiss, a momentary whiff of burning flesh that registered neither pain nor alarm on their working man's paws.

Earlier, he had looked on in amazement as Young Bob dexterously undid a couple of small and difficult-to-get-to nuts with his bulbous, preternaturally swollen fingers, like an elephant dancing through a field of daisies without damage to leaf or bloom.

In their navy blue overalls, Young Bob and his mates immediately stand out from the rest of the workers. Blue means
maintenance staff, maintenance staff means a step up the
rung from the killers and boners and gut workers, and a step
up the rung means more pay, better hours, less blood and
shit, and a feeling that you can go about the place with a bit of
status, a bit of respect. I'm a fitter, I'm a welder, I'm a mechan-
ic, I'm a sparkie for fuck sake and I've done my apprentice-
ship. Yeah, I've done my time, and I can pull apart a pump, or
a four-foot electric saw or a vacuum packer and put them
back together again and there won't be a bolt or a washer or a
screw out of place.

Danny gazes at the men as they carefully lift the lids of their
round aluminium tins of stew and spuds, sausages and beans,
chops and veggies, inspecting and sniffing and stirring, before
reaching into their variously coloured canvas knapsacks or
weathered airline bags. They withdraw bricks of buttered
white bread, placing them next to bucket-like mugs of steaming tea in what Young Bob would call a neat and orderly fashion. Their talk is a caw and twang of an older, whiter Australia,
when coffee was instant, when veggies were boiled, when
women stayed home and bred kids and roses, when questions
of cultural identity were not yet questions.

Young Bob is on his feet, gesticulating and shouting above
the throng. 'Hey, Danny, me boy, get your skinny Scottish arse
over here. That's an order.'

Danny, in an ersatz semaphore manages to communicate
that he's just going to get himself another cup of tea. Standing
in the line, with people poring over and poking at the depress-
ingly modest fare, Danny observes the men in blue tucking
happily into their food, now tumbled onto plates, dipping
their bread into the juices, talking football, kids and caravans
and holidays by the sea, talking about the Chilean girls in
Export Meats that they'd be happy to provide with a bit of
colour in their cheeks, should they be so inclined. They slip on
spectacles and squint at the form guide, lead pencils licked
and tenderly circling those horses thought to be in with a
chance.

That's probably what his old man did during his morning
break, Danny thinks to himself. Sat there with his pals, talked
shit, talked kids, talked lassies. He never did visit his father at

his work, although he'd always wanted to, just to see what he did all day long and what made him so buggered of a night time. Maybe it wasn't the done thing, but his da never took him. Maybe he didn't want to give his son any ideas about following in his footsteps. His father had always wanted something better for him than a miner's life.

Danny, on the other hand, couldn't wait to get out of school, get away from that dirty sandstone monument to Victorian sobriety and discipline with its wrought iron paling fence and its separate playgrounds for boys and girls and an outdoor bog that was like a dark and smelly purgatory. A place where some bastard would come up behind him and laughingly push him into the reeking urinal so he'd piss all over himself to emerge stinking and desperately trying to wipe himself down as the prick in question and his skinny pals with their fags and spit, laughed and gobbed and pointed and jostled each other in the ribs.

'Look boys, wee Danny's peed himself again. You should go and see a doaktir aboot that son.'

But they never picked on Francis. Francis had a quiet self-possession about him, an inner toughness that warned people off, like a lighthouse beacon near a perilous reef. Sure, the hard boys taunted him, and shouted insults across the yard or from the safety of the back of the bus, but they never followed them up, never scratched the surface for fear of what they might find under there. Anyhow, Francis just ignored them, gave them a look, turned away as if they didn't exist. He'd only ever seen his brother lose his temper once, when that useless piece of shite Malky Armstrong took wee Fiona's skipping rope outside the school and wouldn't give it back. Fiona was just a wean, she couldn't have been more than six, and she was bawling away, red-eyed and inconsolable. It took two teachers to drag Francis off, but only after he'd broken Malky's nose and kicked in two of his front teeth.

Danny knew he was reckless, quick to act, slower to think. If he'd given it a bit more thought he would never have nicked that money from Sammy Skelly, bookmaker and bastard of the first degree. What possessed him he'd never know. He was making good money, enough for the family to get by, with a bit left over for him for the occasional new suit and the payments on the car. And Francis was working as well, so things could have been worse. So what does he do? He fucking fucks it up. If he'd still been alive, the old man would have killed him. He always hated anything that wasn't all above board.

What's it been now? Seven years? Seven years since he got the phone call at work from Frankie to tell him his father was dead. It was hard to hear for the din of the fourth race at Ayr blaring away on the radio. Highland Fling ran second by a short half head and he lost fifteen pounds. Should've backed it for a place. Frankie was in the polis station across the road from their house. They'd let him use the phone because of the circumstances. Gave him tea and a biscuit and called him son. Our ma couldn't do it, she couldn't move, couldn't talk, couldn't believe it.

Five hundred quid. If it wasn't for five hundred quid and Sammy Skelly's hard men he'd still be there in Glasgow with the rest of the family. Driving the Jag, going to see the Celtic, dancing, dog track, the works. Maybe even giving young Fiona half a crown for the sausage she always left for him on the side of her plate for precisely that purpose. She knew two wasn't enough for Danny. Danny was always a three or four sausage-with- mash-and-peas-for-dinner man.

And here he is now, surrounded by the fuckers in all shapes and sizes—thick, thin, short, fat, round, square and stumpy. Sausage city. What did Young Bob say this morning by way of an introduction to The Big Chopper? Son, a sausage is more than a short cylindrical tube of minced pork or beef or other meats encased in a skin, natural gut or synthetic, typically sold raw to be fried or grilled before eating. A sausage, me boy, is a cultural statement. A connection with the past that told a thousand stories about a nation's economic and social history. A wurst is a window to the world, he proclaimed with a certain amount of evangelistic fervour, his thumbs tucked into the side pockets of his overalls as he rocked back and forth on the heels of his steel-capped work boots.

'It's from the Latin, you know. *Salsus*. That's how far your sausages go back mate. A bloody long way, that's for sure. The Romans were well aware that an army marches on its stomach, and that army, some would say the greatest army in the history of mankind, marched on sausages. Tons and tons of 'em.'

'Aye, well I didn't know that,' Danny replies. 'I know my father liked his curried. I don't know much about the Romans, but.'

'Well, just think about it for a minute,' Bob says lowering his head as if observing a minute's silence for a departed loved one. 'The Romans conquered all of Europe from Scandinavia to France and Germany. Spain as well. North Africa. England.'

Danny interjects, raising his arm slightly. 'Never conquered Scotland, but. We kept beating the shite out of them. They had to build a wall to keep us in. Bunch of lassies.'

'Well, that may be true. But my point is Daniel that, through their various conquests, they were exposed to sausages from all over the world. Do you know how many varieties of sausages they would have come across in their travels?'

'Well, pork and beef links for starters. Haggis maybe, when they were in Scotland, before they got their arses kicked.'

'Good point Daniel. Haggis is, after all, just one great big sausage. Did you eat haggis yourself back in the old country?'

'Aye, just the once. My da brought it back from a trip to Inverness wi' the ex-servicemen's club. I threw it up all over my wee sister. And the dog. The dog seemed to enjoy it, but. Licked it all up.'

'That's unfortunate,' Young Bob says, looking momentarily disturbed, no doubt trying to conjure up this colourful scene in the life of the average Glaswegian family.

'So,' says Young Bob, smugly. 'How many types of snags do you think the Romans ate?'

'I couldn't honestly tell you, Bob. How many?'

'Nah, go on. Have a guess.'

'Ten?'

Young Bob grins the grin of a man in the know and shakes his head. 'Not even close. Not even close, mate. I'll tell you what, I'll give you another guess.'

'Naw, really, I've got no idea.'

'Nah, on you go.'

'Twenty.'

Young Bob exhales deeply in an expression of profound disappointment. 'At least a hundred. Some authorities say a hundred and thirty-five. The mind bloody boggles, doesn't it.' Young Bob, like a man overtaken by the holy spirit, inclines his head heavenwards and reels off a rosary of varieties.

'Blutwurst, bockwurst, bologna, bratwurst, braunschweiger, cervelat, chorizo, frankfurter, goetta, holsteiner, knackwurst, landjaeger, linguica, lyons, mettwurst, milano, mortadella, just to name a few,' he says relishing the sound and taste of the words. 'And you can't forget pastrami, polish, vienna, weisswurst and wiener. And I'm not even out of Europe yet. I could go on. They did some lovely sausages in Constantinople.'

'Naw, I think you've made your point. What exactly is braunschweiger, anyhow?'

Young Bob smiles like an aficionado glad to have found a receptive ear, as he takes Danny by the arm and ushers him into his workroom. 'Braunschweiger, me boy, has a very interesting history . . . '

Danny collects his cup of tea and squeezes between the tables to where Young Bob and his cronies are seated like the working man's version of high table at college. They sit there, studiously licking pencils, scratching thinly thatched pates, deftly selecting sandwiches from the pile, or spearing the preferred vegetable from their steaming tins, without taking their eyes off the form guide or the sports pages of the newspapers in front of them.

'Daniel, me boy,' Young Bob says, pointing to the vacant chair next to him. 'Fellas, this is Daniel Canyon, me new TA. He's just off the boat from bonnie Scotland. Isn't that right?'

'Aye, that's right enough.'

Danny finds himself at the centre of a flurry of handshakes and 'good on yas' and 'pleased to meet yous' as Young Bob presents his mates and fellow workers, 'the who's who in the zoo', as he puts it.

'Frank, Terry, and that's Wally. The little fella there, that's Davie. Bill, Joe, and the bloke with the big grin, that's Happy Jack. Always smiling, he is. Isn't that right, Jack?'

Jack grins and nods happily, a boiled potato impaled on the end of his fork. Young Bob leans in to Danny and whispers in his ear. 'Jack's me best mate. Started the same day as me, all those years ago. Jack's a great bloke, he's like me brother. If I'm not here, he'll look after you, no worries. And if your car breaks down, he's your man. Can put in a new gearbox in the dark. Bloody amazing.'

'So what brings you out here, Daniel?' the diminutive Davie asks.

'Och well, seemed like a good idea at the time, you know,' Danny shrugs.

'So, what do you reckon of the place so far?'

'Smells a wee bit.'

'Aw, yeh, but you'll get used to it, don't you worry about that. The smell of blood and guts becomes normal after a while. It's the smell of Happy Jack here that takes a bit of getting used to,' Davie replies, casting a mischievous glance in his mate's direction.

Happy Jack looks up from his paper and smiles, cheerfully mouthing the words 'bugger off'.

The questions come from all directions, with Young Bob acting as self-appointed moderator.

'Are you married Daniel? Do you prefer Daniel or Danny?'

'I'm not fussed. No, I'm not married.'

'There's some lovely sheilas around here, mate. Just about your age too.'

'Too young and beautiful for old farts like us though.'

Everybody laughs, chests rattling, dentures shifting, bits of sandwiches and lamb chops spat out like pellets from an air gun.

'Yeh, you should try and get onto one of those girls in Vacuum Wrapping. Suck you dry, I reckon.'

'Steady on.'

'Or one of those Vietnamese sheilas in Packing and Dispatch. Beautiful little bodies on them. Always smiling, they are. I tell ya, if I was forty years younger I'd . . . '

Young Bob calls a halt to the proceedings as the siren sounds for the end of morning smoko.

So that's it, Danny reflects. The first bit of the first day in a new job in a new country. It could well be a new world, though, for all it has in common with Glasgow. Get outside this meatworks and it's clean and orderly with little patches of lawn on the footpaths and trees plonked right in the middle like a single candle on a cake. No trees on the pavement in Glasgow, pal. Just rubbish and dog shite.

Here the cars drift lazily by on the wide tree-lined streets, the sounds of their engines hanging in the hot afternoon air. So different from back home. He can still hear those little four cylinder Prefects and Anglias and Cortinas coughing and spluttering up Shettleston Road in the thick January snow. No snow or slush or sleet here though. The heat, it fair jumps out at you from every corner. Beats down on your head by nine o'clock in the morning. And the way it shimmers off the asphalt like a mirage in the desert, it could be another planet altogether. Makes you sweat just looking at it. The bloody sun can turn your skin red raw in a few minutes and a few days later you can peel it off like rotten old wallpaper that's been up in the living room for too many years. It makes you squint and sweat and turns your tongue to sandpaper. No wonder these Australians drink like fuckin' fish. Glasses, pots, cans, slabs, kegs. They don't care what it comes in as long as it's cold and wet. Cold and wet. Just like Glasgow.

And the houses, the size of them. Brick veneer and weatherboard with three or four bedrooms and front gardens and backyards you can play football or cricket in, with peaches and apricots and lemons dripping off the trees just asking to be picked and bitten into with the juice running down your neck. Christ, the six of us slept in one room when the old man was alive. Bodies and beds everywhere and no bathroom, just a washcloth and a sink. And fruit only came in cans. But Jesus, me and Frankie loved those mandarin pieces with big dollops of ice cream. Or canned pineapple or Ardmona pears. And it's here in Australia where the fruit in the cans comes from. The origin of the fruit. Who would have thought, eh?

Everyone here looks tall and healthy, except for the Italians and the Maltese. They look short and healthy, full of pasta and wine and green peppers that they grow themselves in their backyards with their grapevines hanging over their carports. Carports for fucksake! A safe place to put your motor off the street, right there by your own house, to stop some bastard from scratching the paint work or stealing your hubcaps. Back home, the Jag was always missing a hubcap or two. Or a windscreen wiper. Why would anyone take one windscreen wiper?

And every Sunday morning there's blokes out there with their lawnmowers cutting the grass to within an inch of its life. The bloody noise of it when all you want to do is have a bit of a lie in. The constant drone. It's as if a million bees have decided to fly over your house and just hang there outside your window until you wake up, bleary-eyed and cursing.

You can't go past those barbecues either. Magic. The smell of sizzling chops and sausages and onions. Gets up your nose and into your gut and gets you dribbling away like an idiot. What a country. Behind their fences in their quiet leafy streets, everybody's got a dollar, and a car, and plenty to eat. And a tan.

The birds in the trees sing away like they were in the Eurovision Song Contest, or something. Better than some of the contestants he's seen over the years, that's for sure. Birds everywhere, and not just sparrows or crows or pigeons. Birds with brightly coloured feathers, blues and greens and yellows and reds. Cockatoos and rosellas that descend on your back-yard in one huge great cackle and scream, before flying off like banshees, leaving you to the sound of the mowers and the muffled bark of a distant dog or the rusty creak of a flywire door rattled by the hot northerly wind.

But they are strange sounds, sounds muffled by a blanket of silence. The sounds of suburbia. No sounds of humanity, just machines and animals and the rustle of trees. There's no bug-ger on the streets, no life, no women yakking away and having a fag sitting on their chairs on the pavement in the summer. No men kicking a ball around or just talking shite. No hordes of kids running madly about, playing kick the can or hide and seek or chasey. Here, everything goes on behind closed doors or behind fences. Lots of fine cars in the driveway, but no peo-ple. A funny way for folks to live, eh?

Still, at least it's warm and you can earn a decent wage. There are opportunities here, that's for sure. Not like back home where you can have a bucketful of aspirations and get a thimble's-worth of chances, where the opportunities are only for a select few, and certainly not for those from the wrong class, the wrong side of town, with the wrong accent, the wrong bloody life.

The job, well it mightn't be so bad after he gets over the smell. Start at seven-thirty, a twenty minute break at a quarter past nine, lunch and a lie down at ten past twelve, afternoon smoko at three and out the front gate, hands washed, face scrubbed and bag packed with a little something for dinner at twenty-five past four. Pretty good really. Better than working all hours of the day and night for that bastard Skelly. Smelly Skelly.

Danny takes a last gulp of his tea and places the cup on a table as they head out the canteen door and into the bright sunlight to get back to work.

'So what do you think of the job then, Danny?' Happy Jack inquires as they head down the wooden staircase.

'It's a wee bit early to say yet.'

'You'll be right, mate. Young Bob will look after ya. No worries. He's a top bloke.'

'Likes his sausages, eh?' Danny says.

'Yeh, and his dogs.'

'Dogs?'

'Yeh, he breeds 'em.'

'Aw aye. What sort?'

'Dachshunds.'

'Who would have thought?' Jimmy says, shaking his head in amazement at how a flighty boy from Glasgow could spend years in a Melbourne slaughterhouse before ending up running a bar in downtown Saigon.

'Same old Danny, but,' Frankie moans, waving to Big Andy to bring over another couple of pints. 'Still betting on anything that moves. He can't help himself.'

And now he needs my help, Frankie reflects. And it's not as if it's the first time either. Once, he'd had to have a chat with that bastard John Cameron after he kicked in Danny's door at three o'clock one morning and dragged him out of his bed and beat the shite out of him. Even before he ran off to Australia he couldn't pay off his debts. Danny did manage to batter Cameron over the head with a cast iron jemmy one night as he fell out the pub and it was Frankie who had held the prick's head in the canal until he passed out, but not before Frankie had tried to reason with him and sort out a repayment schedule. Unfortunately, the big man refused to be a party to it and ended up with nothing but a sore head and a stomach full of filthy water.

When Cameron turned up dead one morning on the waste ground near the train station, his face caved in on one side as if someone had just stepped on it, the police pulled Frankie and Danny in for a word. They had to let them go for lack of evidence and the well known fact that Cameron had more enemies than Adolf Hitler. But the story of how Frankie Canyon had sorted out Big John Cameron became part of the local folklore anyway.

Maybe this time Danny's bitten off more than he can chew. The local police want as much out of him as they can get, and for what? Missing a few payments to keep them off his back, to oil the works for the smooth running of his bar, free of complications and of fabricated allegations of drug trafficking and prostitution. Keeping them well fed and happy in their spacious homes. And those bastards—what did Danny call them?—the local mafia. Who do they think they are, tying him up and threatening him with a slow and painful trip to the bottom of Saigon River if he didn't pay off his gambling debts with interest on top that could only be described as extortionate? That's taking liberties. That's pushing the fuckin' envelope, so it is. Things get serious when you start talking heavy like that because once you go there, there's no way back. You've played your last card. Start off with a wee weapon and suddenly it's not big enough or nasty enough. Remember those idiots at school? Used to stab the Protestant boys from up the road with compasses. Stuck the pointy end right in their kidneys. The poor buggers couldn't piss right for weeks. Well, it didn't take them long to trade in the compasses for chains or flick knives, did it? No, the tongue is the most effective weapon. For a while, anyhow.

Frankie sighs loudly, as if exhaling his uncertainty and acknowledging the fact that he has no choice. 'I'm going to have to go to Saigon, and quick. The thing is, Jimmy, I'd like you to come with me.'

Jimmy is flabbergasted, like a man who's just been told he only has a few more days to live in the middle of a brewery strike. 'Me? I know I've been tae the Greek Islands but that doesn't exactly qualify me for a dangerous mission to the jungles of Southeast Asia. Vietnam is in Southeast Asia isn't it?'

'Aye, it is. But it's not a mission and it's not going to be dangerous. We're just going to have a word with these people who are giving Danny a hard time. Reason with them. Negotiate. See if we can help out. What have you got to lose? Look on it as a holiday. I hear they've got some nice beaches there. And palm trees with coconuts in them. The beer's supposed to be good too. And Danny said on the phone that the women are right crackers.'

'What, better than in Australia? Better than those tall, leggy blond Scandinavian birds that sunbathe naked all over the bloody Mediterranean so that a man's up tae his eyes in tits and pubic hair?'

'So I've been told.'

'Och, well that settles it then. I'm sure all those gorgeous Vietnamese women are just waiting for an ugly forty-one-yearold bus driver fae Glasgow tae light up their lives. As fuckin' if, pal.'

Frankie smiles. 'Foreign women just love that Scottish accent, Jimmy. They think it's sexy.'

'Aye, well, I'll put a cardboard box over my head and just talk, eh. That should do the trick.'

Frankie leans forward in his chair, his hands folded in of him on the table. 'So what do you think? It'll do you good. It'll be a change of scenery.'

'I suppose it would be. There's nae scenery around here to speak of, that's for sure.' Frankie senses Jimmy's hesitation. He can see it in the way Jimmy's rubbing his pint with his thumb, the way his eyes are searching the table top for a way to tell his pal he's skint. 'And don't worry about the money. Me and Eileen have got a bit put by for a rainy day,' Frankie says, throwing a neat left to Jimmy's shoulder.

Jimmy shakes his head. 'Naw, Frankie, I couldnae. It's too much, son. A trip to Blackpool maybe, but no Vietnam. It's too dear. I couldnae, honest.'

'Och away. It's no bother. Eileen won the jackpot at the bingo last week. You can pay me back sometime. Forty years, interest free. You can't do better than that.'

'I'll no be here in forty years,' Jimmy laughs. 'I'll be pushing up dandelions.'

'Well, it's a bargain then, eh? You can pay it back on the never-never.'

Jimmy takes a final drag on his cigarette and stubs it out in the overflowing ashtray.

'Here, I thought Eileen didnae like the bingo?'

'Well, she does now.'

Jimmy lifts his pint and nudges it in Frankie's direction. 'Fuck it, why not? Maybe I can tap some money aff my moth-er-inlaw. The auld bag owes me somethin' for doin' up her hoose a' these years. Saigon here we come, eh?'

'Aye, Saigon here we come.'

'See you Jim.'

'Aye, I'll be seeing you the morra Frankie boy. I'm away hame to study up on the Vietnamese.'

'You should start with English first, son.'

'Away ye go, ye cheeky bastard ye,' Jimmy says, putting on his best Glaswegian while feigning a left and a right to Frankie's head.

Frankie ducks and weaves his way into the close and skips up the stairs two at a time, feeling at ease with himself and the world and all of God's wee creatures in it, from the sparrows in the trees to the rats in the canal to all the dogs pissing up against lampposts all over the scheme, if not Glasgow, if not the whole entire sorry grey-and-rained-upon land known as Scotland. It's amazing what several whiskies and half a dozen pints can do for a man's frame of mind. Not forgetting the prospect of an adventure, a temporary respite from the wearisome potato scone predicament known as life.

He pauses at the door to compose himself, smooths down his hair, unsteadily ties one recalcitrant shoelace. He breathes on his hankie and gives the nameplate on the door a bit of a polish. *F. Canyon*. That's a relief. Nothing worse than trying to get in the wrong door at ten o'clock at night. Can have unforeseen consequences.

'Eileen, it's me, I'm back,' he says closing the door behind him and peeling off his jacket.

He is immediately confronted with screams from the kitchen. 'Oh my God! Oh my God! Jesus, Mary and Joseph!'

Assuming there is an intruder in the house and that Eileen is in trouble, Frankie quickly grabs the axe handle he always keeps handy by the door and races down the lobby to the kitchen.

'What the fu . . . '

The kitchen is cloudy with smoke and a faint smell of frying flesh hangs in the air. Eileen is standing by the cooker poking around the chip pan with a metal spoon, tears running down her cheeks and into the hot oil below.

'Aw, my wee Hamish, my wee pet, my wee darlin',' Eileen sobs.

'What is it, Eileen? What's happened?' Frankie asks, relieved she's not being battered to death by a homicidal maniac or one of those mad McCludgie boys from the next close.

'It's wee Hamish,' she weeps, her sobs catching in her chest.

'Hamish? Hamish who? Your Uncle Hamish?' Frankie inquires, his arms now around her shoulders.

'Hamish the budgie. He's in there,' she says, pointing at the bubbling chip pan. 'I let him out of his cage for a wee fly about, you know, and then I thought I'd make you some chips for when you came home from the pub, and when I was cooking them Hamish flew straight into the chip pan and now he's gone.'

Frankie peers in. 'Naw, he's no gone. I can still see him, well, bits of him anyhow. Here give me those tongs.'

Frankie pulls what's left of Hamish from the bubbling oil and gently places him on some absorbent paper on the kitchen bench. Hamish doesn't move or whistle or chirp and Eileen lets out another wail.

'He's dead, Francis. My wee pet. My wee angel. Aw mammy daddy, mammy daddy.'

Frankie holds her and she rests her head on his shoulder and clings tightly to him.

'I suppose that's it for the chips then,' Frankie says, stroking her hair. 'They're all covered in feathers.'

Eileen sniffs, wipes her nose on a tea towel. 'I could open a can of beans. Make some beans on toast. How'd that be?'

'Very nice love. I'll lock the cat in the bathroom, eh.'

All the excitement has got Frankie's heart fair racing along and now he is as sober as a Calvinist judge from the Outer Hebrides, which, on reflection, is a bloody good thing given that he needs to break the news to Eileen that he wants to go off to Vietnam with Jimmy and give Danny a hand. See what they can do to sort things out. Not that there's likely to be any problem. She's always understanding about him going away. She didn't mind when he went down to Merseyside to see the Celtic play Liverpool in a pre-season friendly. Admittedly, he and Jimmy were only away two nights—and it would only have been one if they hadn't got drunk and missed the last train back. She was a bit worried on that occasion. He should've phoned, he knows that, but it's funny how your perception of what's important changes when you've drunk too much for your own good. Important things like letting the wife know you are still alive somehow become less significant than the relative merits of English beer or whether it would be better to buy salt and vinegar crisps as opposed to cheese and onion. But he did spend that weekend up in Loch Lomond with the lads from the work and that was fine. It was just that since they didn't have any weans she did rely on him to keep her company of a night time. Well, they relied on each other, although he didn't mind an occasional bevy and a game of chess with Jimmy. Not that Eileen didn't like a drink, she did. But she hated going to the pub and having to listen to all the men talk about stuff she wasn't interested in. She says men never talk about anything important. They never talk about how they feel. It's all about what they did and didn't do, what they said and didn't say, where they went and what they'd drunk when they got there. Women, football, sex, drink, racing, sex, work, cars, sex. That was it.

But Frankie was different, she knew that. That's why she liked to be at home with him of an evening. They could talk about stuff, share things. He always had his head in a book and liked to talk about the history of Scotland and the evolution of popular music and they could spend hours gabbering on about wild animals and the places they'd like to visit, if they had the money. That Masai Mara National Park in Africa. What a place. Aretha Franklin. What a singer. And he'd cuddle up to her on the couch and tell her that he loved her. And he liked to play games. He wasn't shy like that, repressed. He liked a rumble in the jungle. Like her, he thought religion was a load of shite that fucked you up, did your head in. Promised you a miracle, gave you nothing but an illusion and something to feel guilty about.

Frankie swaddles up Hamish in some kitchen paper and drops him unceremoniously into the rubbish bin when Eileen isn't looking. He covers him up with some potato peelings and wanders into the living room while Eileen puts the beans on. He locates the remote control under the cushion on the settee and flicks on the television. Football replay, crappy Australian soap opera, late news and a documentary about crocodiles. He sits down and watches the documentary for a while before he realises he's seen it. It's the one about the crocodilian family—crocodiles, alligators and caymans.

Eileen arrives with the beans on toast and two cups of tea on a tray, which she places on the coffee table in front of the settee. She hands Frankie his cup and glances at the television. 'Is this the one about the crocodiles and how they only have to eat fifty meals a year because of their remarkable fuel efficiency?' she asks, sitting down beside him and taking the tray on her lap.

'Aye, that's the one. And how they have a well developed sense of smell and a keen ear that readily equips them for a sneak attack.'

They chew and sip and watch, lined up like two peas in a pod. A flamingo stands elegantly in the lagoon like a pink and winged Audrey Hepburn, dipping its long beak into the water in search of something to eat. Suddenly what had appeared to be an inanimate lump of stone reveals itself to be a sixteen foot crocodile which, with one quick lurch, engulfs the unsuspecting bird in its massive jaws before slipping below the surface, two long legs and a twitching wing protruding from its mouth. Around the lagoon, life goes on.

'God, I hate that,' Frankie says, taking another mouthful of beans. 'Those flamingoes have got no idea. You'd think they'd wake up to themselves. They stand there in crocodile-infested waters, like shags on a rock, and expect to get through the day without ending up as somebody's lunch.'

'I'm sorry we ever got that Discovery Channel. It's nothing but death and mayhem every time you turn it on.'

'A bit like here, eh?' Frankie laughs.

'That's not funny Francis. I loved that budgie. He was a good wee pal.'

'Aye, sorry pet, so he was. And I loved how you taught him to whistle "Midnight Train to Georgia". Magic.'

'Aye, you can't go past that Gladys Knight.'

'And those Pips.'

'Wee Hamish loved that song,' Eileen says, feeling teary again.

'That bird had soul, no doubt about it.'

Frankie raises his cup of tea and looks as sympathetic as he can at his distraught wife. 'Here's to Hamish. A budgie in a million.'

'Aye, Hamish. God love him.'

They clink their cups of tea and return to their beans on toast. On the television, the seasonal migration of grassland herds is under way and it takes them inevitably to the water's edge. This gives hungry predators high returns and a crocodile has managed to grab a young zebra by the hind leg and is dragging it under the water. The captive zebra looks pleadingly at brother zebras but, struggling across the turbulent river, they give it a wide berth and clamber up the muddy banks.

Frankie decides it's as good a time as any to tell Eileen about his plans. He wipes the tomato sauce from around his mouth with a tea towel and flicks a stray bean from his trouser leg. 'Well, I enjoyed that and by the way I'm off to Vietnam with Jimmy to sort out this trouble with Danny. Is there any more tea in the pot?'

'No you're not and yes there is,' Eileen says passing him the teapot.

'Look Eileen, I know it will cost us an arm and a leg, but I have to go. It sounds like he's got himself into a right mess. He's been betting on everything that moves—cockfights, football matches, two geckoes crawling up a wall.'

'What's a gecko?'

'A small lizard, common in warm climates. Mind, there was a programme about them last week.'

'Aye, that's right. Prefers to come out at night.'

'That's the one. Anyhow, seems he owes some very bad boys a lot of money. The police as well.'

'The police?'

'Aye. He told me on the phone the other night he has to pay off the police every week otherwise his bar will mysteriously go up in smoke.'

'Listen, Francis, if you think you're going gallivanting around Asia without me you've got another think coming.'

Frankie takes Eileen's hands in his and caresses her fingers. 'Look love, I don't know what to expect over there. Going by what Danny says, these people are right hard cases. It could be dangerous and I don't want you getting hurt.'

'Oh, but it's all right for you to get hurt, is it? What a man. I'll just be the little lady who stays at home alone worrying, will I?'

'You'll have the cat and the fish.'

They both sit quiet on the settee, Eileen with her arms folded across her chest, Frankie head down and peering at the carpet.

'Where's Hamish?' Eileen asks, breaking the silence.

Frankie shifts uncomfortably in his seat. 'I buried him.'

'Buried him where?'

'In the kitchen tidy bin underneath the potato peelings.'

'C'mon Francis, the least we could do is give the poor bird a proper burial. I think you should get a wee box and bury him in the spare ground out the back.'

'Aye, you're right. I'll do that. Listen, Eileen, why don't me and Jimmy go down to Vietnam first and then you can come and join us later on when we've made sure it's safe. How about that?'

Eileen nods, distracted. She knows Danny is in trouble, this is not what she'd expected, and to have Francis going off to a strange country, a country that might be dangerous, is not her idea of a relaxing holiday in the sun. Still, as Francis always says, life's short so you'd better make the most of it because you don't know what's going to happen. Look at poor wee Hamish. One minute he's flying about happy as Larry and the next he's up to his beak in boiling, cholesterol-free oil. The prospect of death makes you feel you want to make the most of life, eh? Vietnam would be an adventure, their own little travel documentary.

'Maybe we should have a party, a kind of going away celebration. It's not every day you get to go to somewhere exotic like Vietnam, is it?' she says, suddenly excited, kissing Frankie on the cheek.

'Good idea. It's about time we had a right good booze-up and a bit of dancing, eh?'

Eileen begins gathering up the cups and plates and Frankie helps her put them on the tray. 'I'm away to bed,' she says.

'OK love. I'll just take care of Hamish and I'll be right in.'

Frankie takes the tray of dishes into the kitchen and places it by the sink. He reaches into the kitchen tidy bin and searches through the rubbish until he finds Hamish. He seemed to have shrivelled even more and now resembled a small octogenarian kipper. He cups the withered bird in the palm of his hand, gently strokes its little frazzled beak, and takes it to the bathroom where he quietly lifts up the toilet seat.

'Au revoir, Hamish old son. Bon voyage.'

Danny slowly rotates his head to release the tension in his neck. His vertebrae crack like twigs underfoot. His head throbs and his vision is blurred thanks to that last head-shaking punch from one of Cam's hard men. He must have been asleep for a while because it is now dark and they have gone, leaving him bruised, bound and bloody. They chose the right time to call on him. Monday night, the only night of the week when the bar is closed. But of course, they knew that.

He lets his head fall back and he closes his eyes and listens to the thunder outside. It splits the sky and rattles his brain. It will rain soon, the thick, gushing rain of Saigon. Where is Mai? She should be back from Nha Trang any time now. If he could just look at his watch he would know long it will be until she walks through the door, smiling, their son in her arms. But the ropes are thick and he cannot shift them no matter how much he struggles.

Even after fifteen years of marriage he misses her when she is away. He is constantly amazed that they are still together, that she puts up with him and his foibles. In his mind he can her now, touch her skin—smooth as freshly-woven silk—taste her lips, like sponges soaked in honey. It doesn't seem that long ago that he first caught sight of her at William Mortimer & Sons. Love among the smallgoods. Who would have thought? Not him.

At twenty-two years old Danny Canyon had never really been in love. Sure, he'd thought he'd been in love, but that was just a confusion of hormones, export lager and loneliness. A quick one in the close after a night out at the pictures or the dancing, fumbling, frustrating and uncomfortable. And there was always something to put him off his stroke right in the middle of it, just when he thought he was getting somewhere. A cough in the dark, the clatter of footsteps on the street, and then he could never get it back in. Not in the right hole, anyhow. He had decided that whoever thought of sex standing up against a wall needed a right good seeing to. Especially if it was in the middle of the winter and you had to deal with two overcoats, gloves, pullovers and a swathe of undergarments. A balaclava even. Other times, he'd been in love with a bevy of women at the same time, whoever he happened to be with at a particular moment, if the truth be known.

But as he strolls into Packing and Dispatch, with Young Bob in full throttle, half way through his introduction to Machinery, Maintenance and Minor Repairs, he finds himself compelled by an invisible, intangible force, to stop and quietly observe a delicate dark-haired young woman methodically packing rolls of Chicken Luncheon Delight into a large brown cardboard box.

Young Bob fails to notice that Danny is no longer accompanying him as he continues into Curing and Preservation, gesticulating away as he explains his five easy ways to dismantle a sausage-meat pump. The words 'outlet valve' and 'rubber gasket' echo through the room as he disappears through the swinging rubber doors like a gunslinger to a date with destiny.

Danny has never seen such a beautiful woman, not outside of magazines anyway. She looks like a girl, but something about her makes it clear she is not. He cannot help but notice how fine her wrists are as she places four rolls at a time into the box, stopping occasionally to tuck a stray strand of long black hair into her white paper hat.

As she bends her head to her task, he sees how her light brown skin glows, luminous in the light from some holes in the roof twenty feet above. It's a warm day and small beads of sweat glisten on her forehead like raindrops on a window pane. Because of the heat and humidity the buttons on the front of her coat are undone and he can just make out the shy swell of her breasts through her T-shirt which has risen slightly above her jeans. He is certain if he cupped both his hands together he could easily encircle her waist with room to spare.

She is surrounded by half a dozen other women, doing the same job with the same ritual movements—taking the Chicken Luncheon Delight from the large steel trolley, placing it straight into the box on the packing table, filling it and taping it shut. But Danny doesn't notice them. They are just a blur of shapes amid one sharply defined vision.

'What are you looking at?' she says suddenly, her dark brown eyes making it clear she is not easily intimidated.

Danny is completely taken aback. He hadn't expected her to notice him, he hadn't expected her to speak. Shit, he hadn't expected her to be able to speak. Danny snaps out of his dream-world like a man shaking off a deep sleep. 'Aw aye, well, och. I'm not sure,' he mumbles. 'You can speak English, then?'

'Yes, better than you it would seem.'

'Couldn't help but notice you there, working away an' that,' he says, nervously fingering a pair of pliers in his side pocket.

'Well, I could not help but notice you, standing there with your tongue hanging out.'

'Aw aye, I'm sorry. I didn't mean to stare. But I couldn't help it, you're so beautiful, if you don't mind me saying so.'

'Oh yes. I bet you've said that to a few girls before. Just like the American soldiers back home.'

'Naw, I mean it. Really, I do,' he says trying to look as sincere as a former bookie's runner can look. 'Where's home, then?'

'Saigon.'

'Saigon? Where's that?'

'Vietnam. Where are you from?'

'Scotland.'

'Never heard of it.'

Danny lowers his head and slips his hands into the cavernous pockets of his overalls, wishing he could hide in there himself. He feels a breath-choking tightness in his chest and he has lost control over his left leg, which is shaking like a mad rattle inside a slithering snake.

She continues packing before straightening up and wiping her hands on her coat. She places them on her hips, fixing her eyes on his. Danny blinks and starts fiddling with his ear.

'What is your name?' she asks, smiling at his obvious nervousness.

'Daniel Barnabus Canyon. My friends call me Danny, my ma calls me Daniel, and my enemies call me other things I won't mention. And what do they call you?'

'Nguyen Thi Mai. I have no friends in this country, my mother is dead and my enemies are back home.'

'What about your father? Is your father alive?'

'Yes, my father is alive. In Vietnam he was a translator with the American journalists but now he lives in Melbourne with me.'

'Is that right? What does he call you?'

'My father calls me Flower. Spring Flower. *Hoa Xham.*'

'Spring Flower. Very nice. Sounds good enough to eat.'

'No, that's spring roll. What does your father call you?'

'Bugger. Silly bugger. That's what he used to call me, anyhow, when he was alive, you know.'

Danny smiles and shrugs and Mai laughs before turning back to her cardboard box. But all heads turn as Young Bob bursts though the swinging rubber doors, his profoundly puzzled eyes darting around in search of his missing companion.

'Bloody hell, Daniel. There you are. Do you want to know how to fix a broken chain without having all the cows fall off or not? Life is short and time is money. Remember that.'

As Danny hurries towards Young Bob, who is scowling at his watch, he glances back at Mai. His heart is full of desire, her hands are full of Special Beef Feast.

Frankie rubs the fog from the inside of the window and peers out at the new day. Saturday morning, the best morning of the week. Two full days of freedom ahead, no bosses, no tools, no getting home at the end of the day completely knackered. Job satisfaction, isn't that what they call it? Ask the old man about job satisfaction. Nothing like getting carried out of the pit on a stretcher with a one way ticket to the great beyond. The football this afternoon. Celtic at home to Motherwell. A doddle. Meet up with Jimmy at the wee shop about half past twelve for a few pints, then into Jimmy's old Cortina and down to Celtic Park for an enjoyable afternoon's entertainment, with maybe a few more pints after the game. Might even have a couple of wee yins to get the blood flowing nicely. In a few minutes he'll get the breakfast on, the full catastrophe—bacon, eggs, fried bread, fried tomato, potato scones, baked beans, sausages, and maybe a sprig of parsley on the eggs for the sake of nutrition and a cheery nod to middle-class cuisine.

It's a rare day for the time of year. The sun is fair belting down and already there's some weans on the street kicking a ball around, pretending it's them that will be on the field this afternoon surrounded by thirty thousand screaming fans. One day it might be them, you never know. You have to aim for something, anything, to get you out of here.

There's a couple of blokes obviously on their way to work for a bit of overtime at time-and-a-half until twelve o'clock, and double time after that. Keeps the weans in clothes and Chistmas presents. Still, five days a week is enough for him. More than that and you're nothing but a machine headed for an early grave. Retire at sixty-five, dead at sixty-five and three months. He's seen it that often. Not much time to relax and play golf then, is there? Not that anybody from around here is going to play golf, mind, strolling from hole to hole talking about business, closing important deals before retiring to the clubroom for lunch. 'You must come to our place in Brittany what grandfather left us when he passed away.' Nothing like inherited wealth to keep people in their rightful place, eh?

There's some boys already out with their bikes, with their sandwiches packed and water bottles clamped to the cross-bar. They'll be off to the Campsies for the day, up past the lochs and up into those rounded hills with their waterfalls and pools of freezing water. Danny Brown jumped into one of those pools once and it was so cold he shat himself. Took him a while to live that down once word got around the scheme. Sat in the corner by himself at the pub for a while as well.

Frankie sees Jimmy coming round by the shops, that big black dog of his in tow, stopping every few seconds to sniff at something that doesn't bear thinking about, and pissing up against anything vertical. Jimmy's giving it a right good tug with the leash, but the thing's so big it might as well be taking Jimmy for a walk. Pets, eh? Shame about Hamish. Not a bad pet, as pets go. Stupid, but. Should have known not to do a kamikaze into the chip pan of death.

Frankie decides to go down and meet Jimmy by the mouth of the close and see how he got on convincing Stella that it was a good idea for him to go to Vietnam with his pal. They're a funny couple, those two, always at each other's throats. Maybe she'll be glad to see the back of him for a while.

Jimmy pulls up at the close looking a bit flushed. The dog's tongue is hanging out almost to the ground and she's dribbling like a sluice gate on a canal, her breathing a raspy steam train chug. Frankie can't help but notice that her underbelly is a mountain range of distended nipples, an upside down Swiss Alps.

'Aye, she's just had pups,' Jimmy says, puffing with some relief on a cigarette.

'Jesus Christ. I thought she'd just had some a few weeks ago.'

'That was last year. She's had more since, the hoor.'

'How many's that, all up?' Frankie asks.

'Eighteen, no counting the ones that didnae make it.'

'That's one fertile dog. What do you feed her, fuckin' oestrogen?'

'Naw, mince and tatties. And chicken noodle soup.'

'Heinz or Campbell's?'

'Heinz. She finds the Campbell's a bit rich, ye know.'

'What do you feed the kids? Meaty Bites?'

'Aye, that and the odd tin of Pal,' Jimmy laughs, reaching down and scratching the dog behind the ear. 'Nothing but the best for this yin though. Isn't that right Blackie, ye auld bag o' fleas.

'How are the weans, anyhow?'

'Same as usual. Glued to the telly. The wee buggers are physically joined to the fuckin' thing. It's like an extra appendage. I'm sure if it got a scratch on it they'd start bleeding.'

'I like a bit of telly occasionally myself,' Frankie says, raising his face to the sun which had just peeked above the roofs of the houses across the road.

'Aye, I know. Lions and tigers and things that howl in the night. But at least you're learning something. I mean, those programmes are educational. But all they do is watch soap operas fae Australia. *Neighbours* and *Home and Away* an' that. I don't know how your Danny managed to live there for so long if they're all like those eejits in Ramsay Street. I kid you not, one of these days I'm gonnae chuck that telly right oot the windae, even if the weans are stuck tae it.'

'Make sure you unplug it first, Jimmy. Electricians charge an arm and a leg, nowadays. How's the wee yin coming along?'

'Wee Estelle? Och, she's a card that yin. I told her to turn down the telly the other day, and ye know what she said?'

'What?'

'Bugger off.'

Frankie laughs. 'How old is she now?'

'Two and a half.'

'That's the younger generation for you, eh? No afraid to speak their mind.'

Frankie and Jimmy stand by the mouth of the close and watch Blackie chasing the pint-sized kids playing football on the street, trying to bite the ball and jumping up on the players who either howl with fear or scream with delight. She licks and slobbers on the faces of the ones who fall over.

'How come you never had weans Frank, if you don't mind me asking?'

'Och, Eileen can't have kids. Fuckin' ironic, isn't it. The most sexed-up woman in the western hemisphere and she can't get pregnant.'

'Maybe it could be fixed. It's amazing what yon doctors can do these days. Artifical indoctrination an' a' that.'

'Naw, we've had all the tests but it's a no-goer.'

'Sorry to hear that,' Jimmy says, dropping his cigarette on the ground and rubbing it out with the toe of his shoe.

'I wouldn't have minded a few you know. Neither would Eileen. She loves kids. But you get used to it.'

'Och, you're probably better off. They'd just be stuck in front of the telly, eating you oot ae house and home.'

'Aye, maybe you're right,' Frankie says, staring into the distance.

'I'll tell you what. You can have wee Estelle. She disnae eat much and she's a right laugh. Really, take her. She's yours.'

'Aye sure. Bugger off.'

They both laugh as they watch the dog squat over the kids' football and pee on it.

'So how did you go with Stella?' Frankie asks.

'She says if I go tae Vietnam not to bother coming back because she won't be here.'

'What did you say?'

'I told her that sounded good tae me.'

Frankie kicks the step with his heel, his hands in his pockets. 'What is it with you two? You fight like cats and dogs, so you do. What's it all about? I mean Stella's a nice enough and you're a nice enough man. For a right bastard, anyhow,' he laughs.

Jimmy takes another cigarette from the packet and lights up, shaking the match vigorously before throwing it on the ground. He sucks in the smoke and blows it slowly into the air.

'Och, I don't know. We're all right when we're no thegither. But put us in the same room and it's twelve paces and take aim.' He shakes his head in disbelief at the situation he's found himself in. How did it happen? 'She says we got married too young. She says she's disappointed with her life, the way things turn oot an' that. As if I'm no disappointed as well. I'd rather be a brain surgeon wi' a big hoose and a big bank account. But I'm no, I'm a fuckin' bus driver living in a shit-hole scheme wi' a wife that thinks I'm a failure. Disnae matter what I do, it's never fuckin' right. Overtime, a part-time job on the side, it's never good enough. We're caught in a trap. We can't get out, son.'

'Well, it's unlikely you're going to be a brain surgeon at this stage in your life, Jimmy, so you might as well wake up and be happy.'

'Drink up and be happy, more like it.'

They watch Blackie biting at the ankles of any boy who has possession of the ball and Jimmy shouts at her to get over here right this minute or she's bloody well in for it. Blackie momentarily raises her head in Jimmy's direction and, ignoring him, continues to bite chunks out of one little boy's sock.

'See that dug . . . '

'Listen Jimmy, I'll get Eileen to have a word with Stella about Vietnam. Eileen's going to join us later on in Saigon after we've sorted out the lie of the land. Maybe Stella could do the same, eh? A wee holiday might be just the thing she needs. Leave all her worries and anxiety behind.'

'Aye, maybe. But I don't think she's ever had a minute's anxiety she didnae want.'

Frankie starts to turn away back into the close. 'Come up to our house the night. Eileen went and got a video about Vietnam. She says it'll be educational.'

'Aye, all right,' Jimmy says, striding towards Blackie who is sniffing away at the back end of old Mrs McLean's west highland terrier. 'Blackie, fucksake, leave that wee dug alone.'

Danny blinks and tries to squeeze the sweat from his eyes. It runs down his forehead and into his eye sockets like a waterfall into a pool. His vision is blurred, a watery mirage. The room is stifling. He tries to take his mind off the heat by concentrating on the ceiling fan struggling and spluttering as it makes another imperfect revolution on its imperfect axis, like a young girl doing the hula-hoop in the playground. He can smell meat frying on the street below. There were times when he had more meat than he knew what to do with, when he was a prince of the slaughterhouse in his blue overalls and his unchallenged access to all areas, like a Rolling Stone at the Filmore East. Jumpin' Danny Flash. The Mortadella Rambler. Sympathy for the Silverside. Yeah. Rock on. Don't mess with me or my main man.

Danny can see Young Bob now, squinting into the innards of a sausage skin winding machine. As he peers in, he explains to Danny the mechanics of how the skins are wound on to a metal spool which is then placed over a nozzle attached to a pump which is, in turn, connected to a container of freshly concocted sausage meat. At the push of a lever the meat is ejaculated through the nozzle and into the skin which, suddenly animated by its new-found substance, writhes in the air like a snake about to strike, before collapsing exhausted and twenty feet long on the banquet-sized stainless steel table.

Ten pairs of rubber-gloved female hands then set upon it with gusto, and twist and turn and bend it into bunches of seven-inch links that are then hung on a hook like bananas on a tree.

'Amazing,' Danny says.

'Yeh, it is. The women seem to enjoy the work, too.'

Danny is having difficulty breathing because of the large white plastic basin of processed pig intestines on the floor beneath him, lying ready and waiting to be wound onto a spool. The woman who operates the machine is perched on her stool and biting heartily into what looks like half a roasted cow stuck between two thick slices of white bread. Danny can't help but notice that she appears to be having no diffi-culty in breathing at all.

'Me and Mai thought we might get married,' he says offhandedly.

Surprised, Young Bob turns to look at the husband-to-be. 'That's pretty quick, isn't it?'

'S'pose.'

'She's not in the club, is she? Hand me that screwdriver.'

'The what?' Danny says, handing his boss a nine-inch Phillips.

'The club. The pudding club. Is she up the duff? Does she have a bun in the oven? Bloody hell, Daniel. Is she pregnant?' Young Bob says, slightly exasperated

'Naw. Naw. Nothing like that. At least, not that I know of, like.'

Young Bob undoes four bolts that attach the sausage skin machine to the metal table and hands them to Danny who places them in a small tin container beside him.

'How long have you been keeping company now?' Young Bob says, giving the machine a hefty tug, trying to free it from its moorings.

'Six months.'

'Six months and you're getting married. Whirlwind courtship, eh?'

'Aye, but we can't see any point in waiting. It's hard to explain, but we don't want to be apart any time of the day or night. It's as if we've just been passing time until we met. Sounds a bit corny to you, I suppose.'

'Yeh, it does a bit. But I don't suppose there are any rules when it comes to matters of the heart. In my day we went out

together for bloody years, mate. Then there was the engage-
ment. More years. Then, after all that, you'd finally get to the
altar. It was a bloody long haul, I can tell you,' Young Bob
grunts, finally managing to free the machine from the grip of
the table. He passes it to Danny who places it on the floor next
to the tin of bolts.

'You must have been desperate for it by the time you got
married, eh?' Danny laughs.

'Ah, mate, you'd be surprised.'

'So you had sex before marriage in the old days then?'

Young Bob winks. 'Before breakfast, lunch and tea, as well.'
He wipes his hands on an old rag, which appears to impart
more dirt onto his hands than anything else.

'How did you meet your wife?' Danny asks.

'At a church dance. Everything happened through the
churches when I was a lad. Or behind the church hall at any
rate.'

'What do you mean?'

'One night Lorna and myself stumbled across the vicar and
Mrs Landsdowne indulging in a hasty bit of extra-marital con-
gress. Mrs Landsdowne played the organ on Sundays.'

'And other days as well, eh?'

Danny and Young Bob laugh as they place the seized-up
machine on a trolley to take it back to the workshop for repair,
strapping it to the frame with a piece of old rope.

'What about Mai's old man? What does he reckon about
this? He'd have to be worried about his daughter marrying a
bloody Scotsman wouldn't he?' he smiles.

'Aye, he is a bit. But I told him at least I'm no English, eh,'
Danny laughs. 'In Vietnam, people go out together for years
before they tie the knot, ye know. But Mai told her father that
they are in Australia now and things are different.'

'And what did he say?'

'He said he wanted her to marry a nice Vietnamese bloke,
but Mai told him she was marrying me and that was that.
She's very strong-minded. She says she's not like other
Vietnamese girls. She says people will think she is a bad
daughter to her father but she doesn't care. She says the war
changed everything for her.'

'Good on her,' Young Bob says.

Danny coughs and runs his hands through his hair. 'The thing is Bob, I was wondering if you'd be my best man.'

Young Bob's face flushes to a pale shade of pink. In the few months he had come to look on Danny as more than his TA. If anyone asked him he would say Danny Canyon was like a son to him. And the best lubricator he'd ever had. No one could wield an oil can like this boy. He sticks his shifter in his back pocket, wipes the palm of his hand on his overalls and offers it to Danny who grasps it firmly. 'Daniel, me boy, it would be an honour and a pleasure.'

Behind them, the sausage skin machine operator finishes the last of her sandwich, picks languidly at her teeth and spits loudly into the tray of pig guts beneath her. But even that can't deflate Danny's sense of excitement about the months, the years ahead with Mai, particularly if the last few months have been anything to go by. They've already made plans to put a deposit on a small house for the two of them and Mai's father. Nothing substantial, perhaps a two-bedroom Victorian weatherboard cottage in Footscray, where more and more Vietnamese people are making a new life for themselves. It's where he and Mai can always be found on a Friday night, at the Viet Rose restaurant, Mai eating spring rolls, sour soup and fried fish with salt and pepper and showered with chilli like confetti at a wedding. Danny is happy to give the spring rolls a go but prefers some steak and chips for his main course.

'Daniel, how will we ever be happy together, if you don't like Vietnamese food?' Mai says, pouring some chilli sauce into her soup.

'It's not that I don't like it, Mai love, it's just that I don't like all of it, you know. You have to remember that where I come from, if you can't cover your dinner in tomato sauce then it's no worth eating. Just give me a bit of time. It took me ten years to get to like brussels sprouts.'

'Yes, well I can understand that. I don't know how you can eat those things. I'd rather eat dog.' She laughs as she recalls some meals back in Saigon . . . 'Well, I have eaten dog.'

Danny grins and gestures with his fork towards the back of the room, where Mai's father sits at the family table of the owner, Le, a former colonel in the South Vietnamese Army. They drink beer and talk about life in Saigon before 1975.

Occasionally, in a concession to their new life in Australia, they may help Le's wife Anh make some spring rolls, filling the rice paper with minced pork, rolling it back and forth and folding the edges to make a neat cylindrical parcel. But more often than not they just sit and reminisce and talk about their children. Of course, Danny and Mai's relationship has been a topic of considerable interest at the restaurant, as has the subject of mixed marriages in general. Le believes it is inevitable that their children will grow up to become Australians and will become less and less Vietnamese as they grow older. For them, people who are not Vietnamese will not be foreigners, they will be Australians, just like them.

'Khai, we must let them marry who they want or we will lose them. And we have lost enough already,' he tells Mai's more traditional-minded father. As each successive Friday evening wears on, soothed by beer and rice wine, Mai's father eventually comes around to his friend's point of view before waking in the morning as uncertain as ever.

'Do you think your father will ever get used to the idea of us getting married?' Danny asks, spearing a chip with his fork.

'Well, he got used to having a daughter like me, so I think he will.'

'But it's a son-in-law like me that's the problem.'

'Maybe, if you eat more spring rolls you will become more Vietnamese,' Mai laughs. 'Maybe when you have made love to me more, your hair will turn black and your eyes will narrow and you will begin to wear a bamboo hat. For sure.'

This is what Danny likes best, to sit and eat and talk with Mai. It's a struggle at work when he's having his lunch with Young Bob, Happy Jack and the others, and Mai is at another table with the women from Packing and Dispatch. Never the twain shall meet, at least in the works canteen anyhow. The men eat with the men and the women eat with the women and it doesn't matter if you're married or engaged or doing it twice a night in the back seat of an EJ Holden, eating sandwiches and warmed-up leftovers constitutes the great sexual divide at William Mortimer & Sons. But at twenty past four everything changes when the great foghorn of a hooter sounds over Smallgoods, Packing and Dispatch, the killing floor, the boning room, vacuum packing, the skin shed, the man in the sentry box by the mighty front gate, the cattle yards and the sheep pens, and everyone downs tools and discards manky blood-stained overalls to begin heading for home, or the pub, or in Danny and Mai's case, a small Italian coffee shop in Barkly Street, a bone's throw from the slaughterhouse.

It is a warm brown place, snug and comforting like the inside of a grandfather clock. Everything is a shade of autumn. The dark wooden tables and display cases with their home-made cakes and biscuits dusted with icing sugar, the coffee beans jammed into tall glass jars, the last breath of afternoon light through the window, the varnished frames of faded photographs of long-gone family members in Palermo, wide-eyed in their dark suits and stiff collars and high-necked dresses frilled at the cuff like a burst of sunshine on a rainy day. Mai says it reminds her of an old French café in Saigon that her grandmother used to take her to, where the waiters wore crisp white aprons that fell to the floor like brilliant sheets of ice and where the croissants and pastries were baked right there on the premises. It smelled like heaven.

Every working day, by a quarter to five, she and Danny are seated at their regular table having their coffee and biscotti and an hour to themselves and their dreams before Mai rushes home to prepare her father's dinner. Sometimes Danny goes with her and helps her make the dishes her father enjoys. He stands by the kitchen window that looks out onto the small back garden and slices a choice cut of Mortimer & Sons pork into fine strips that she marinates in fish sauce, or he chops lemongrass and coriander, onions and ginger, tomatoes and peanuts to fry in a sizzling pan with some tender beef cubes. He peels prawns for sour fish soup. In her kitchen he is surrounded by more herbs and spices than he has ever seen in his life, his nose forever twitching in a jitterbug of new olfactory sensations.

'You know Mai, at our house in Glasgow, my mother had salt and pepper, and tomato sauce and HP sauce. Oh aye, and vinegar. And you used them at every meal, regardless of what you were eating. Never in my life did I expect to be sprinkling herbs on my dinner whose names I cannae even pronounce. Is this why they call Australia a melting pot?'

Mai laughs and tells him he is soft in the head, like the boiled eggs she makes to add to a salad. After dinner they take a few turns around the block, gazing into shop windows and pointing to pieces of furniture they will buy when they have their own home, or they sit on the small rickety porch with its broken planks and tatty old chairs with the stuffing spilling out like a grandad's hernia, and Danny smokes a couple of cigarettes, Mai sneaking a puff when her father isn't looking.

In Vietnam, dutiful daughters don't smoke or marry foreigners, but Mai's life has been changed so much by war and death, and by life in a new country, that the old expectations seem nonsensical and out of place to her, like a woollen scarf on a hot summer's day. There are some things from the old world you should bring with you and there are those that are best left behind, so that you can clear space for your new life. Australia is so different to Scotland and Vietnam, it is a foreign place, no doubt about that. Sometimes they are lost and lonely, but they are trying hard to become part of it. Danny has taken wholeheartedly to meat pies and sauce and Mai has grown to love Australian football. The players leap and run and clash together like giant cymbals in a magnificent orchestra. It's as if they take the spectators' pent-up energy and frustration, their spirit and bubbling excitement about life, and let it erupt on the field like the thunder before the monsoon rain in her beloved Saigon. She screams with delight and anticipation when the siren sounds for the first bounce of the ball, and Danny, Young Bob and Happy Jack gaze at her with a mixture of wonder and embarrassment. 'Garn you bulldogs', she bellows, 'garn you bulldogs', her voice but one sweet note in a great mad roar.

Saigon. Shit. I'm still only in Saigon. Every time I think I'm going to wake up back in the jungle. When I was home after my first tour I'd wake up and there'd be nothing.

Eileen is sitting on the settee comfy and looking forward to the video she's brought back from the shop. *Apocalypse Now.* The man said it was really wild and really out there and was the best film on Vietnam he'd ever seen. A work of art from a great auteur, he said. Well, how can you go past that? She told him that if you are going to travel anywhere new it's best to be prepared and know what lies ahead. Aye, he had said, that was right enough and he hoped she enjoyed the film and that she had a good time in Vietnam.

Jimmy and Stella are occupying the chairs at opposite sides of the fireplace. Jimmy's sipping at a glass of Johnny Walker and she's got a vodka and orange on the side table next to her. Stella seems a bit happier since Eileen suggested they both join the boys in Saigon once they'd made sure it was safe for the likes of them to be wandering about, which she thought was a good idea because the less there is to worry about the better. And she could do with a break, she really could, what with the weans and Jimmy's drinking and the bills that just keep coming. Something to look forward to, eh?

Eileen's got the place nice, with the lights turned down low, and a few sandwiches and snacks on the coffee table, although why Frankie insists on putting out those black olives she doesn't know because nobody eats them except him, and maybe Jimmy when he's too drunk to notice otherwise.

Every minute I stay in this room I get weaker. And every minute Charlie squats in the bush he get stronger. Each time I look around the walls get a little tighter. Everyone gets every-thing he wants. I wanted a mission and for my sins they gave me one.

Frankie strolls into the darkened room carrying a plate of sausage rolls. 'Is that it started?'

'Ssshh,' Eileen whispers. This guy's not looking so well.'

'Oh, I don't know, he looks all right to me,' Stella laughs, winking at Eileen. 'He can put his rocket launcher under my bed anytime.'

In the shuttered daylight of his hotel room, Martin Sheen is naked and lost in a drunken martial arts ballet, each move exaggerated, as if he is dancing in slow motion. The back-ground music by The Doors pursues and haunts him, and as it builds to a thundering crescendo he smashes his fist into the mirror in front of him before collapsing in a pool of bro-ken glass and blood.

'My granny had a mirror just like that,' Eileen says. 'For the life of me I don't know what happened to it. I think my moth-er sold it when granny died. Got next to nothing for it, I bet.'

Frankie leans forward from his spot next to Eileen on the settee. 'Is that Martin Sheen, Jimmy? Did you see him in *Badlands* with that Sissy Spacek? I kid you not, that boy can act.'

'Aye, I think you're right. He's had a few too many though, whoever he is. You should never drink whisky during the day, especially if the weather's hot. Fucks you right up. Gies one ae they ham sandwiches, will ye?'

Stella is into her second vodka and orange as the four of them stare at the screen, saying nothing. They listen to them-selves eat.

Martin Sheen is dragged into the shower and forcibly washed, then fed coffee by two other soldiers until he is in some sort of shape to appear before what looks like a group of senior officers.

Terminate? The Colonel?

You understand captain . . . that this operation does not exist, nor will it ever exist.

Jimmy leaps up from his chair, pointing excitedly at the television. 'Hey, isn't that Harrison Ford there, telling Martin Sheen he has tae terminate the colonel's command?'

Frankie squints at the screen. 'Aye, so it is.'

'Now we're talking, eh. Give old Indiana Jones a hat and a whip and he'll sort out that Colonel Kurtz, no danger.'

'I think this film was made before he became Indiana Jones, Jimmy, so he cannae be Indiana Jones if he hisnae been invented yet,' Stella points out, carefully inspecting the blurb on the back of the video box.

'Oh aye. Well that's just a case of bad planning. Those film makers should have thought ahead a wee bit, got old Indiana Jones in the game in the first place.'

'Have another wee yin, Jimmy,' Frankie says, handing over the bottle. 'I think you need it.'

I was going to the worst place in the world and I didn't even know it yet. Weeks away and hundreds of miles up a river that snaked through the war like a main circuit cable and plugged straight into Kurtz.

Frankie, Eileen, Jimmy and Stella silently pass around the popcorn as Martin Sheen's boat ambles slowly up the river towards the Cambodian border. Eileen jumps when Sheen and his crew of misfits suddenly find themselves under a rain of gunfire from behind the thick blanket of trees lining the banks of the river. Stella screams when Sheen and Frederic Forrest stumble across a tiger in the jungle and scramble terrified back to their vessel. They all struggle to hold back tears when the soldiers slaughter a family of innocent Vietnamese, and they laugh as Sam Bottoms goes waterskiing from the back of the patrol boat.

'No much of a place, is it?' Eileen says, munching on a chocolate digestive biscuit.

'Reminds me of here in the mid-sixties,' Jimmy says. 'Except for the sunshine of course. I'll have one of those sausage rolls, thanks Stella, when you're finished wi' the plate.'

'Go easy on that whisky, Jimmy, or it's you that'll be getting' shot at,' she replies.

'I'll look after myself thanks very much. You just keep an eye on those voddies you're throwin' back there.' 'C'mon you two. My God, look at that,' Eileen says squirming in her seat.

You smell that. Do you smell that? Napalm, son. Nothing else in the world smells like that. I love the smell of napalm in the morning.

'That's Robert Duvall isn't it?' Jimmy says, looking over his shoulder to Frankie who's holding Eileen's hand and rustling about in a packet of cottage cheese and chives crisps.

'I think you might be right there, Jimmy, old son. Christ these crisps are shite. Pass those salt and vinegar, will you, pet?' he motions to Eileen.

'Mind ae him in *The Godfather*? The consiglione? It's not personal, Sonny, it's business!' Jimmy says excitedly, putting on his version of a New York accent.

With Wagner's "Ride of the Valkyries" blasting out from his Air Cavalry gunship, Robert Duvall is pointing out some likely surfing spots to champion boardrider Sam Bottoms. A bridge is blown up, a village reduced to rubble and sticks, and napalm is blithely dropped on the nearby jungle, which instantly erupts in a nightmare of flames and smoke.

'So, that was what it was all about, the Vietnam War. The Americans just wanted to go surfing?' Eileen asks.

'Not quite,' Frankie says. 'But wars have been fought for less.'

'Looks like our kitchen at dinnertime, wi' a' that smoke an' that,' Jimmy says laughing.

'Well you can cook your own bloody dinner from now on, Jimmy Stewart,' Stella says, throwing half a cheese and pickle sandwich at him.

Robert Duvall has taken off his shirt and, arms on hips, is discussing the relative merits of long and short surfboards with Sam Bottoms. The beach around them is a slaughterhouse of dead and dying bodies, of women screaming and children crying as they watch their lives go up in stomach-churning, skin-peeling flames.

'Those poor people,' Eileen says softly.

Slowly they sink into a disturbed torpor as the drink and the food take effect and the patrol boat winds sleepily and interminably up the river. They are caught up in another world. The oppressive heat makes them sweat, the unfamiliar squeals from the jungle make them nervous. They wipe their brows and drink heavily to ease their thirst. Their tongues are as dry as a dirt track in a desert town. Jimmy nods off and dreams he has jumped out of Robert Duvall's helicopter, but his parachute doesn't open and, as he falls, all he can see below are giant red flames that leap into the sky and snap at his feet. He wakes with a start and casts a quick glance around the room, relieved for the first time in his life to be in a housing estate in Glasgow. He takes a bite at an olive but quickly spits it out into the ashtray on the arm of his chair.

'These grapes are off,' he says, wiping his mouth with a tea towel.

The heads? You're looking at the heads? I, uh, sometimes he goes too far, you know. He's the first one to admit it.

Martin Sheen and Frederic Forrest and Sam Bottoms are the only soldiers who have managed to survive and make it to the end of the river. They struggle to absorb what they see around them. Severed heads on poles, thousands of half-naked natives staring malevolently back at them, fire, smoke, mad monkeys ready to bite, Dennis Hopper, draped in cameras and drugged out of his mind. The place smells of evil. It rubs up against their skin.

'I read somewhere that Martin Sheen had a heart attack when he was making this film,' Frankie says.

'Aye, nae fuckin' wonder. I'm ready to have a heart attack myself just looking at it,' Jimmy says, rubbing his chest. 'Maybe going tae Vietnam isnae such a great idea, Frankie. Maybe a bit of advice tae Danny sent through Her Majesty's Royal Mail might be the way to go here. Oh aye, wait a minute Mr Postman, an' a' that.'

'I think things might have changed a wee bit, Jimmy. There's no war on for a start.'

'Well, that's a relief.'

'Look, Jimmy, Saigon's a big city. Seven million people. Things have picked up. It's even got buses, I hear. We'll be fine.'

'You should take plenty of sunscreen though. It looks very hot there,' Stella says, thoughtfully.

'Aye, thanks, Stella. Glad you reminded us. I'd hate tae get sunburnt while some cunt's got my head stuck on a pole,' Jimmy says.

'Sshhhh,' Eileen says, leaning forward from the settee. 'Jesus, Mary and Joseph.'

Martin Sheen is belting the life out of a bloated Marlon Brando, each blow a silhouette against a flickering flame. Outside, the drums are mad and frenetic, and the eyes in the darkness sense the fate of their leader. Martin Sheen falls out into the night and the awestruck crowd parts Red Sea-like as he calmly makes his way back to the boat, collecting a painted and decorated Sam Bottoms on the way.

The horror. The horror.

The video winds slowly to the end and clicks off, the screen a black void, the soundtrack a monotonal buzz. Frankie and Eileen, Jimmy and Stella, sit for a few moments, saying nothing. Eileen clicks her tongue against the roof of her mouth.

'No exactly *The Sound of Music*, is it?' she says.

'I think you're right there, Eileen. I didnae see much in the way of lonely goatherds, did you?' Jimmy replies.

'No, I certainly did not. I'll put the kettle on, eh?'

'Aye, good idea. Better make the tea nice and strong, hen. I think we're goin' tae need it.'

Danny is exhausted and he can barely keep his head from slumping on to his chest. He feels like his neck has gone missing. Still, he can manage a tearful chuckle as he imagines the headline in the *Saigon Times*—'Neckless man found dead above bar, shirt ruined'. Never lose your sense of humour, his father once told him, even in the face of adversity. He can't remember the last time he ate, and here he is tied to a chair with no prospect of wandering down to the street to one of the army of food vendors to buy a steaming bowl of beef noodle soup. He can almost taste the chilli biting into his tongue and the rich peppery broth filling him with vitality. He can feel the crunch of bean shoots, spring onion and mint in his mouth. But all he can do now is wait. And think. He laughs to himself as his mind wanders back to the day of his wedding, the day he and Mai finally made it to the altar with the blessing of her father. Danny Canyon, husband. Wonders never cease.

Danny stands at the entrance to the church snatching anxious glances at his watch as the priest glowers at him over his spectacles. Bloody priests, he's sick to death of them. Back home, that Father McGonigal was always turning up at the house unannounced, with his black jacket fair jumping with dandruff, the place reeking of boiled cabbage, and him in the bath. The good Father was always keen to pop his head in to say hello just as Danny was soaping up. They should've gone for a civil wedding. Or something in the Buddhist line of things.

Where the hell is Happy Jack? What's he doing? He said, 'No, there'd be no problems with the Chevy. Purring like a kitten,' he said. He'd have Mai and her old man there dead on one o'clock. No wuckin furries, mate. So where are they then? It's nearly two and everybody's standing around here like shags on a rock, smoking cigarettes and their tongues fair tickling for a beer. They'll all be thinking Danny's been stood up at the altar, bloody well jilted. That's what they'll be thinking. He feels like an idiot in this kilt. He should never have let Young Bob talk him into it. Nothing like a bit of tradition, he said. Tradition, my arse. The old fella's flapping about under there like a sock on the washing line. The navy suit would have been better. White two-fold cotton shirt, silk tie. Still, that wee dagger in his sock might come in handy for that priest if he gives him one more dirty look . . . Stick this dirk right up his vestments.

Danny's sure Mai has changed her mind or that her father has convinced her she should really marry a Vietnamese lad, when a shout goes up from the assembled wedding party. In the distance, he can just make out the familiar shape and colour of a William Mortimer & Sons delivery truck. As it draws closer, he recognises the distinctive rattle of the diesel engine and can just make out the figure of Happy Jack in the driver's seat tooling down the road like he's in a rush to catch the first race at Flemington.

The crowd moves closer to the edge of the footpath and peers collectively to the right as the van screeches to a halt in a smog of burning rubber and exhaust fumes. Happy Jack leaps from the cabin and runs to the back of the van and yanks open the double doors.

'What happened to the Chevy?' Danny yells above the clatter of the engine.

'Big end bearing, mate,' Happy Jack laughs. 'Bloody big end bearing.'

Inside the van, Danny sees Mai and her father sitting quietly on a few boxes of Mortimer's Chicken and Pork Surprise. Mai helps her father out of the van and Danny takes Mai's hand as she steps down into the street. Happy Jack closes the doors across which is emblazoned 'William Mortimer & Sons, The World's Finest Smallgoods'. A curious onlooker carrying a straw shopping basket asks Happy Jack for half a dozen slices of ham and a pound of sausage mince.

'You're wearing a dress,' Mai says, as they head into the church.

'Aye, and you're wearing trousers,' he replies, caressing the soft silk of her *ao dai*.

'Yes,' she smiles. 'A perfect match.'

Eileen carefully cuts the cream cheese and watercress sandwiches into perfectly symmetrical triangles, the way she'd
seen on that cooking programme on the television, the one
where the two fat women are always working in kitchens the
size of football fields and riding around on a motorbike and
getting plastered on white wine while they whip up a chocolate pudding with custard or crème fraiche or a roast loin of
wild boar with something called 'jus'. Whatever happened to
gravy? They're always taking about all the exotic places
they've been, holidays in the south of France and going horse
riding and drinking bubbly. And how important it is to use
fresh produce. Most of the produce around here is fresh out of
the can, except for this watercress which Frank bought from
some fruit and vegetable shop he knows on the other side of
town, the one that always gives him a pretty carrier bag with
the shop's name and address on it so he can carry his pur-
chases home in style, or know where he is if he loses conciousness among all those exotic fruits and aromatic herbs.

She used to cut her sandwiches straight in half the way her
mother had shown her and the way her sisters still do. They
always say things like 'oh posh' whenever she presents them
with a plate of triangular sandwiches, and they hold them
daintily in the air and take prissy little bites at them to make
fun of her. Gets on her nerves. Always taking the piss out of

stuff they're not familiar with or are afraid of. One day she'll break out a bottle of bubbly as well and see what they have to say about that. They'll probably say something about her being above her station, whatever her station is. Stations are for the police and trains. Frank knows a bloke who can get that French bubbly straight off the back of a truck for next to nothing. Bubbly. What a wonderful word. Makes you feel drunk and happy even saying it. It just chuckles out of your mouth.

Frank and Jimmy are off to Vietnam on Sunday morning, so she thought she'd just have Stella round for a cup of tea and something to eat so they could discuss their plans to join them and maybe sort out a few summer clothes. Not that she has that many of them, mind, given that summer in Scotland these days is just a brief interlude between the rain, sleet, fog and snow. It rushes by so quickly you have to be careful or you'll miss it. Frankie says the Scottish summer is God's cruel little joke. He gives the punters a wee taste of it, then before they can get their singlets off he whisks it away and hands it over to the south of France or the Costa Brava. God's a cock teaser, Eileen thinks.

She arranges the sandwiches neatly on the plate with a bit of chopped parsley on the side. She's bought some ham just in case Stella doesn't like watercress. She's got the portable television on in the kitchen, the one that Frank brought home from the pub. He said it was a bargain, but was reluctant to go into too much detail about its origins. He probably got it from that Sammy McFadyen, the one who sold him the leather thigh boots. He always seems to have a wide variety of goods for sale. He's a regular little department store, that yin. He's got a big van and a garage, so enough said.

She stops what she's doing and stares at the screen as Francesca, the female tiger, and her two cubs wander about the forest somewhere in India. You can tell by the shape of their bellies that they haven't eaten for a while. The mother slips to the ground, her muscles tensing up as she spies a potential target, an inattentive young swamp deer preening itself in the long grass. She keeps low, making herself as inconspicuous as possible. The tiger never chases a target for very long and, true to form, this pursuit is brief and successful. She lets her cubs feed first. They have learned their first important lesson today. Swamp deer are a bit on the tough side. They

take another bite of a hind leg and, as the deep-voiced narra-
tor explains, life goes on in the jungle as it has for a thousand
years.

Eileen shudders when the mother starts ripping the guts
out of the deer. She's never quite gotten used to the raw bru-
tality of life in the wild. Still, that's the way of the world, eh?
You have to take the opportunities when they present themselves. If you want a swamp deer for lunch and one happens
to wander by then you'd bloody well better go and catch it. If
you want a happy life you have to go and find happiness
whenever you can. Ambush it, tie it up with a rope and drag it
back home. That's why she got out of that factory and found a
part-time job working with disadvantaged kids. They're
always so happy to see you and it rubs off. And that's why she
goes to night school twice a week for that course in child welfare. Knowledge is power, that's for sure. Well, either that or a
big bank account and a double-barrelled surname.

She's quite looking forward to Vietnam, now that she's gotten over the initial shock of Frank's announcement. Frank has
to help his brother, he's got no choice. As if she wouldn't do
the same for her sisters. Well, maybe not that little bitch
Agnes. Always moaning about this or that and borrowing
money and never giving it back. Always trying to steal her
boyfriends when they were young. Her and her big tits. And
the fares weren't as dear as she thought they'd be, so that's a
plus. Seems quite a few people go to Vietnam for holidays
these days. The destination of the moment, the man at the
travel agent's said as he handed over the tickets. Enjoy, he
said, enjoy. Don't you worry about that, she'll enjoy it all right,
Sonny Jim.

Eileen puts the kettle on and there's a knock at the door. She
wipes her hands on her apron and lets Stella into the lobby
where she helps her with her thick woollen coat and gloves.

'Hello Stella. How are ye?'

'Freezin', darlin'. My tits are like ice blocks, so they are.
There's a couple of wee eskimos livin' in them, I'm no kiddin'.'

'Och well, come in and I'll make you a nice hot cup of tea.'

They wander into the kitchen where Stella immediately
picks up a cream cheese and watercress sandwich. She
squints and sniffs and turns up her nose like a woman inves-
tigating something unpleasant stuck to the sole of her shoe.

'Got any ham, Eileen?' she asks, placing the sandwich back on the plate with some relief. She turns her attention to the television where Francesca the tiger has her head almost totally immersed in the half-eaten swamp deer's abdominal cavity.

'There's no mercy in the jungle, eh,' Eileen says, noticing her friend wince as Francesca resurfaces, her head a ball of fur, blood and bits of spleen.

'Aye. But there's no mercy here either, darlin'. You know that bloke next door, Charlie Jackson, he just got his marching orders. Thirty-five years on that job and they just gave him his notice, and no so much as a how's your father or a thank you very much. Just leave your overalls and your boots wi' the foreman and collect your pay on the way out the front gate. Cunts.'

'Stella!'

'Sorry Eileen, but it makes me so mad, so it does. I don't know what we'd do if Jimmy got the shove, so I don't.'

'You might have to get a job,' Eileen laughs, nudging her in the ribs.

'There's no jobs around here, sweetheart. I might have to emigrate. We almost nearly went to Canada years ago, before we had the weans. I wish we'd gone. They've got no chance around here. The next generation of thieves and murderers all go to my Kevin's school, I'm no kiddin'. But I suppose it's too late now to get into Canada or Australia. You have to be a fitba' player or a contract plumber who plays the fuckin' cello.'

They carry the tray of sandwiches and the pot of tea into the living room and make themselves comfortable on the settee.

'Love your fireplace, Eileen. Frank box it in, did he?'

'Aye, but he wishes he'd left it the way it was though. He says that wee fan drives him up the wall and it doesn't give out any heat which he says is a major drawback for a fire.'

'Och away. It's a lovely wee electric fire. I've been trying to get Jimmy to do the same to ours, but he ay says he's too busy.'

'Well, no wonder. He does work long hours and on those terrible shifts as well.'

'If he spent less time at the pub, he'd be able to get it done in no time, I'll tell you that right now.'

'Och, you're a hard woman, Stella, so you are.'

Stella finishes off her second ham sandwich and thinks about having another go at the cream cheese and watercress but decides it's too risky. Death by watercress is a definite possibility. She gulps down the rest of her tea and she picks a few leaves from between her teeth with her carefully manicured nails.

'Another cup of tea, Stella?' Eileen asks, pouring herself one.

'What time is it?'

'A quarter to two.'

'Aw good. I'll have a wee vodka and orange.'

'Don't you think it's a bit early?'

'Away, it's after lunch time, isn't it?'

Eileen puts some vodka in a glass and fetches some orangeade from the fridge in the kitchen. She hands it to Stella who makes no attempt at what is generally described as a sip. It goes down her throat like a barrel over Niagara Falls.

'That ham was awfy salty, so it wis. I've got a right thirst on me.'

'Aye, so I noticed.'

Stella dabs at her lips with one of the paper napkins Eileen has thoughtfully provided.

'So you're happy to let those two go gallivanting around Vietnam without us, then?'

'It's only for a few days so they get the lie of the land,' Eileen says.

'That's not all they'll be gettin' the lie of, I'll tell you that for nothing.'

'What do you mean?'

'Those Vietnamese lassies are not too hard on the eye and I bet a few of them would be more than happy to get their claws intae a good lookin' Scotsman so they can get themselves a better life away from all that poverty and squalor, an' that.'

Eileen stares out the window, at the blanket of grey sky and unrelenting drizzle, at the boarded up windows and abandoned cars.

'I don't think any Vietnamese girl will be rushing to Glasgow in a hurry,' she says.

'Maybe you're right. Might be a bit cold for the poor wee things in their silk trousers and straw hats. They'd need more than a bowl of rice to keep them warm on a winter's night, eh? Anyhow, Jimmy wouldn't play around again, he knows I'd kill him.'

'What do you mean again?' Eileen asks, more than curious.

'The bastard was having it off wi' his conductress on the Castlemilk run. Three o'clock in the mornin' and he's parked the bus somewhere and is clippin' her ticket good and proper.'

'My God,' Eileen says aghast. She would never have believed it. 'How did you find out?'

'He came home one mornin' reeking of the slut's stinking perfume and I forced it out of him.'

'How did you manage that?'

'I smashed his face in wi' a poker. I did have trouble making out what he was trying to say though, what wi' his teeth all over the fireplace an' that.'

'For God's sake, Stella. What a thing to do.'

'Och, it wis his ain fault. If he'd put in the electric fire like I'd asked him to there wouldnae have been any poker lyin' around for me to belt him wi', would there?'

'I suppose not,' Eileen says, uncertainly.

'What about your Frankie?'

'No, he's not interested in other women. Says one's trouble enough.'

'Aw aye. I don't believe him. Men have no conscience. They're just dicks wi' legs, that's all they are. They'll go anywhere as long as they can get their end away and they'll have no regrets about it. Unless they get caught, of course. Then they bloody well regret it, especially if their teeth are rattling around their mouths like Smarties in a box.'

Stella lights up a cigarette and exhales deeply. 'They're no the same as us Eileen. They're bloody weird.'

'Francis is different.'

'Aye, maybe. You two do seem happy thegither, I'll give you that. I wish me and Jimmy were the same.'

'Well, going to Vietnam could be a chance to rekindle the flame, eh? A second honeymoon.'

Stella scoffs as she starts on a second vodka and orange. 'A second honeymoon? We never had a first honeymoon. Jimmy was on the early shift. We didnae get home from the reception until four o'clock in the mornin', and he got up at five tae go tae his work. Didnae get to consummate the marriage. Lucky we consummated it before, eh?' she laughs.

Eileen thinks for a minute about how lucky she is, about how she actually looks forward to Frankie coming home from work. She remembers how they met. They were both twentytwo and were minor union officials attending a conference in Edinburgh, so they had plenty in common, plenty to talk about. It may have been a case of up the worker and down with the employers, but they had good reason. The wages some people were getting and the conditions they were working and living in were criminal.

Eileen had never really wanted anybody before she met him, and she has never wanted anybody since. Makes life a lot simpler. 'You two must have been happy at some stage,' she says.

'Aye, we were. But everything changed when we got married. I don't know why, but I wasn't so nice tae him and he wasn't so nice tae me. He was always out wi' his pals and I was always stuck at home in front of the telly. I used tae get so frustrated, once I started punching him in the middle of the night while he was asleep.'

'Jesus Stella, that's terrible.'

'Aye, I know,' she says, hardly able to believe she did it herself. 'Scared the shite out of him though. You should've seen his face. He must've thought he'd died and gone straight tae hell.'

'Did he hit you back?'

'Naw, he just got up and went and slept in the living room. He said if I did it again he'd kill me.'

Stella takes a bite at a Jaffa cake and flops against the back of the settee, letting herself swim in the delicious and soothing warmth of a few glasses of vodka. God bless the Russians. Except for that cunt Stalin.

'I wish I'd had more boyfriends, ye know. I met Jimmy when I was sixteen and thought that was it, he was the only one for me. How wrong can you be? I should've stayed on at the school and made somethin' of myself. But it all seemed so romantic to get a job and get married and get our own wee house. Romantic my arse.'

Stella takes a slow sip of her drink, aware that it's almost finished. 'I can't remember the last time we had sex. I think one ay us was asleep at the time. I can't remember which one though,' she laughs.

She leans forward towards Eileen, her eyes dancing in the fading afternoon light. 'How is it wi' you and Frankie, on the sex front, like?'

Eileen thinks for a while before answering, well aware that telling Stella anything is like broadcasting it to the neighbourhood. You might as well send a press release to the evening news or take an advertisement out in the *Daily Record.*

'I can't say I have any complaints in that department,' she says primly. If only Stella knew, she thinks to herself.

'I bet he's like one of those wild animals in those programmes he's ay watchin'. What is he? A tiger? A bloody big lion, eh? King of the jungle?'

'As I said Stella, I've got no complaints,' Eileen replies, nibbling on a biscuit.

'I bet he's a bloody big stallion, a wild brumby charging across the plains.'

'I'm sure Jimmy's the same.'

'I don't remember. It's been ages since I last seen his thing. By the time he's drunk six pints of heavy, he can hardly keep his head up at night, never mind anythin' else.'

'He's a morning person, is he?'

'Naw, he's nae good in the mornin' either and the only thing I want between my lips at that time is a cigarette and a cup of tea.'

'Well, at least you've got the weans. That's something to be proud of.'

'Aye, if it wisnae for the weans I'd be off like a shot. But it's the weans I feel sorry for, what wi' us screamin' at each other all the time. No way to grow up is it? Not what childhood's supposed to be. What's the word? Idyllic? There's nae idyllic in oor hoose, I can tell you that. No Little House on the Prairie. Just bawlin' and shoutin' and things flyin' through the air and the weans hidin' in cupboards or cryin' under the bed till it's over. Poor wee buggers.'

Eileen takes Stella's hand in hers and squeezes it tightly as tears well up in her eyes. Stella sniffs and shakes her head and shoulders as if to rouse herself from a bad dream.

'Look at me, eh. A regular cry baby. Have you got any more of that ham? I could go another sandwich.'

'No, it's finished. But I've got some Chicken Luncheon Delight. It's from Australia. It's supposed to be very nice.'

'Is that right? It won't hop away when I bite intae it, will it?' she says chuckling. 'Aw, you have to laugh, don't you. If you didn't you'd just cry yourself to sleep of a night. Isn't that right, love?'

'Aye, that's right Stella. That's right enough.'

Maybe they should have stayed in Australia. After all, they had a good life there. It took a few years, but they had managed to save up enough money for a deposit on a house and the repayments were not a problem even though Mai had gone back to school so that she could get into university. That was her dream. She didn't think there was much of a future in Packing and Dispatch.

Danny has an itch in the middle of his back and tries to scratch it by rubbing against the back of the chair but the ropes around his wrist and waist restrict his movement and the itch remains. He breathes hard, his chest rising and falling like the landscape around the Highlands. He wonders what he and Mai would be doing now if they'd stayed in Melbourne. They'd probably have a bigger house, a second car maybe. And Mai would be a lawyer or an accountant or something. She wouldn't be running a bar with him here in Saigon, that's for sure.

If only he'd said no, he didn't want to go to Vietnam, then maybe he wouldn't have gotten them into this mess. They would still be in their home, going to the cinema, sitting in their garden in the evening, swimming in the sea. He can see Mai now, lying on her back in the water and watching clouds like an angel's breath float across the bright blue sky.

Sunday morning at the beach and the wind whips through Mai's hair as she sucks in the salty sea breeze in great gulps that clear her lungs and enliven her spirit. She loves the smell of the sea, the taste of it. Knowing it's there, not too far away. And it's free. Fresh air, fun, and relief from the swelter for everybody regardless of race, colour, class, religion or body shape.

It's a handy beach this one, only twenty minutes down the road from their house. Sometimes, though, if the breeze is right, you can occasionally get a whiff of Danny's work. She could do without that. Mai has made up some sandwiches filled with Pork Surprise, courtesy of William Mortimer & Sons, and there's a flask full of hot jasmine tea, which she likes to drink when she finally gets out of the water after her swim. She quite likes the Pork Surprise as it reminds her of some of the manufactured meats she used to have in a crispy Saigon roll she'd buy from a stall in Rue Catinat. It cost next to nothing, which was just as well because after the Fall of Saigon, or the Liberation depending what side you were on, she and her family had next to nothing left by the time the new authorities were through with them.

It is ten years ago now, but it is still vivid in her mind—she and her father watching from the window of their home in Alexandre du Rhodes Street as the North Vietnamese tanks rushed down Boulevard Norodom, their turrets swinging wildly, towards the Presidential Palace. She remembers how she shuddered and grabbed her father's arm when one tank crashed through its tall cast iron gates that burst open as if they were just a couple of fly-screen doors on the back porch. Because of her father's work with the Americans she knew their lives would never be the same again.

By the time her father returned to the city, after two years reeducation working in the terrible heat of the rice paddies in the Mekong Delta, there was nothing left. Their house, their beautiful old French colonial house that had been in her mother's family for three generations, was gone, given to an army colonel, a designated hero of the nation. How she misses those tall ceilings with the fans whirring away sleepily on hot days. But then every day was a hot day. Not like Melbourne where the four seasons jostle for control of every hour. Hot and cold, rainy and sunny, windy and calm. When she was little she would run madly around the porch with its cool stone tiles, chasing her dog or her imagination, before jumping onto the grass to lie on her back and let warm sun caress her face though the trees.

The room they moved to was smaller than their former kitchen. It was not much bigger than the one mattress they laid on the broken-tiled floor. There was little furniture to speak of. A French clock her mother had managed to save from the old house and a rickety wooden shelf on which sat a silver-framed photograph of her mother in an *ao dai*. A leather strap was nailed to the back of the door, and as her father lay on the mattress in the afternoons, he would pull it to let in some air and allow him to observe the activity on the street outside, the food vendors, the people sleeping suspended in their hammocks, the bird sellers, their captive wares chirping and whistling in their cages. Every hour, the clock would chime to remind them of the life they had lost and her mother would sigh heavily and continue her endless work at the sewing machine.

The decision to leave was not a difficult one, although if they had known what lay ahead, their choice would have been different. All the money they had managed to scrimp together, the family jewellery they had hidden away, all their hopes for a better future, were bound up in that small fishing boat as it chugged out of Vung Tau in the early hours of a dark July morning.

Despite the seasickness, the lack of food and water, and the cramped, stifling conditions, they had enough hope to keep them going. After all, wasn't there a rainbow at the end of the storm? A new and better life in Australia. A big house, a job and maybe enough money to start a business. One day they could bring their family out to join them and share their happy and prosperous life.

But when the Thai pirates boarded their struggling and defenceless boat off the Malaysian Peninsula, the weak and weary passengers could offer no resistance. The pirates stormed aboard screaming and pointing their guns, kicking and punching and battering the terrified Vietnamese. Their eyes mad and blazing with greed and violence, they vowed to kill anyone who did not hand over their money and valuables, their savings and treasures of a lifetime. But when her weep-

ing mother refused to part with the gold chain and cross left
to her by her grandmother, they just ripped it from her throat
and suddenly she was in the sea, flapping her arms, stretching
her head above the water, struggling to stay afloat.

As she floats on her back by the side of the pier, the sun
warm on her brow and the salt a tang on her skin, Mai can still
see the look of surprise and incomprehension on her mother's
face. How did this happen? Why am I in the water? What is
going to happen now? As Mai slowly paddles she can see her
mother slip noiselessly below the surface and sink until she is
no longer there. In only a few terrible seconds, she had
become a memory.

After two years in a refugee camp at Bidong, she and her
father were granted a new life in Australia. And here she is,
swimming, paddling, floating in a sea free of pirates, a sea
where her mother would have been safe, where she could
have learned to swim as her daughter had.

Mai watches Danny standing at the end of the pier, almost
a silhouette with the sun behind him, looking at the kids
doing bombs and throwing each other into the water twelve
feet below. No doubt he also has an eye on the young women
climbing up the rail from the water, their bikinis clinging and
dishevelled, their wet glistening bodies a tangle of bouncing
breasts, ample hips and thighs, firm and tanned and long.
Once up the rail and on to the hot wooden pier, they
rearrange their transparent tops and bottoms, their hair and
breasts, tucking, twisting and pulling, making sure that everything is where it is supposed to be, before leaping back into
the sea and beginning the whole process all over again.

Every summer, this was their Sunday morning ritual, since
they'd been married anyway. Get up early and after a bit of
breakfast, drive down to the pier and, if it's not too cold, dive
straight in. Danny always leaps into the water with his trade-
mark bravado and he emerges laughing and yelping and waving at her to jump right in after him. But even when she finally works up the courage to jump, she still hates the feeling of
her stomach in her throat as she flies through the air to an
uncertain landing below. The thud on the water always comes
sooner than she expects and takes her breath away, like a sudden noise in the dark.

Mai lies back in the sea, her arms spread sideways, her
palms opened upwards. She wiggles her toes and revels in the

cool touch of the water on her body. She remembers herself as a young girl, barely five years old, in the sea at Cap St Jacques where her grandmother had a house. She is floating on her back like now, but her father has his arms underneath her little body, delicate as a flower, brown as a nut. He supports her, telling her that she is safe, that he will not let her drown. Her papa is here.

She sees Danny waving at her to come out of the water. He's probably had enough gazing at the lithe youthful flesh and wants something to eat. They've brought the sandwiches, but she fancies some fish and chips and potato cakes in the park. Maybe even a few dim sims with soya sauce, another element of Australian cuisine that Danny has enthusiastically embraced. Maybe that would be the best time to tell him, when they are lying on the grass in the park and he's hoeing into the flake and chips and everything is right with the world.

When they return from the fish and chip shop Mai spreads out their feast on a blanket. They eat and chatter and joke until they are full, washing down their lunch with ice-cold beer. Mai takes a deep breath.

'Danny, I want to go back home,' she says suddenly, picking at the grass with her fingers.

'Sure, love. I'll just knock off this last dim sim and we'll be off. It's getting a bit hot, anyhow.' Danny wipes his hands on his shirt as he chews the last of the spread before him, and waves his arms frantically at the seagulls stalking the remnants of their lunch. 'Christ, I hate those bloody seagulls. Poor excuse for a bird. It's like God ran out of bird ideas and just threw this one together when he had a hangover or something.'

'No, Daniel,' Mai says, squeezing her husband's hand. 'I don't mean our house. I mean home. Vietnam. I want to go back to Saigon.'

Danny's face freezes mid-chew. He can't quite believe what he's hearing. He swallows and rubs his hands together to shake off the salt and grease, scrunches up the fish and chip wrapping into a ball and throws it at the seagulls who scramble away in a squawking chorus of protest before they regroup and begin frantically pecking at the ball of white paper to dislodge any crumbs. He doesn't know what to say.

'What's brought this on?' he asks, regaining his composure slightly.

Mai feels her eyes water and blinks to keep the tears from running down her cheeks. This is not what she had expected. Once out of Vietnam she assumed she would have been able to settle forever, that she would have been able to leave everything behind her without too much regret or longing for her previous life.

'I don't know. I've just been feeling lost lately, like I don't belong here anymore, like I've woken up from pretending that this is my home. I speak the language and I eat the food and talk and joke with people, but I still feel something is missing in my life. I feel neither here nor there.'

'But you've been happy here, haven't you?'

'Yes, I have. Very happy. It's difficult to explain. I miss the sounds and smells of my country, the way the light is, the way people walk and laugh. How they ride their bicycles. The way the place just is, I suppose. Part of me is still there and I can't bring it here, no matter how many times I go to the football or eat a meat pie or tell myself that I am an Australian now.'

'Aye, I know what you mean about the food. The bacon here, don't get me wrong it's good, but it's not the same as the bacon you get in Glasgow,' Danny laughs.

'Daniel, I'm serious. I want to go back. I want us to go back.'

Danny hangs his head, looking at nothing in particular, thinking of everything that has happened to him since he left Glasgow. Mai says she misses the country where she was born, but Danny's not so sure. He's better off in Australia with his house and his car and his job, and the thought of returning to Glasgow has never really occurred to him. He can't picture himself walking down the wet grey streets swathed in a heavy overcoat with gloves and three pairs of socks to keep out the bone-crushing cold. Sure, he would be able to see his family, Frankie and Eileen, Fiona, Annie, his aunties and uncles. Some of those idiot cousins as well. What was that pub Frankie drank in? A few pints of McEwan's Export wouldn't go down too badly either. He could see his mother every week. Well, once a fortnight. Once a month at least. He could chase up that bastard who virtually stole the Jag from him for four hundred quid. Ripped him off blind, as Young Bob put it when told about the enforced and hurried sale of his most prized possession. But what could he do? He lost a few hundred pounds but he kept his balls attached to the rest of his body. Not a bad result, really.

Maybe he should never have left, what with the family having no money to speak of after his father died. He was needed. Frankie's view of the world is that you always face up to your responsibilities. Negotiate, but never run. If you can't negotiate, retaliate. Get them before they get you. It's a funny business, life, eh? There are so many lives you can lead, could have led, depending on the circumstances forced upon you, the choices you make, the way the fuckin' cookie crumbles. And here he is being presented with another choice, another life to lead. But he loves the life he already has. Why go looking for another one, especially in Vietnam, where they don't even speak English? Not that they speak great English in Glasgow, especially when people have got a few drinks in them, but at least they have a go at it.

'Look Mai, I don't know about us going to Saigon. This country's been good to me. I like it here. I thought you liked it here. You always seem happy enough. I don't know if I want to start all over again. I mean, it was hard enough the first time. Scotland's very different from Australia and there's a lot of cultural differences you have to adapt to.'

'You mean like going from warm beer to cold beer,' she laughs.

'No I didn't mean that,' Danny says, disappointed with Mai's lack of understanding. She always thinks that all Englishspeaking countries are the same. Same skin, same culture, same traditions. So what's the problem about moving from one country to another? 'I've made friends here. You've made friends here. And this is a great country to bring up children. I thought this would be where we would have our children, Mai. And what would I do there? I'm no exactly an employer's dream, am I?'

'We'll think of something. My family still has contacts there. They would help.'

Mai lies beside her husband and takes his head in her hands before kissing him full on the lips for what seems like an eternity. Danny's head swims with images of his past, of wrestling on the carpet with his father when he was young, of his first at the slaughterhouse, of lazy picnics on the sand with Mai, of the first time they made love.

'Kiss me like that and I'll follow you anywhere,' Danny whispers, brushing her hair away from her face as he caresses her cheek.

'Even Vietnam?'

'I don't know. Is it safe? There won't be some bastard waiting at the airport to take you off to prison for a few decades? Stick matches down your fingernails or lock you in a bamboo cage in the river with water up to your neck until they decide they want you to play a wee game of Russian roulette while they place bets on the side? Come to think of it, it sounds like some of the betting shops I used to work in.'

'Daniel, I've told you before, *The Deer Hunter* was not the way the war really was. It was a Hollywood version of the war, like *The Green Berets* was.'

'Hey, be careful what you say about the Duke. If John Wayne was in it, it must've been true.'

Mai shoves Danny in the chest and he falls back laughing, his back on the grass and his legs in the air. He lies back, his hands behind his head, the hot sun on his face.

'Are you sure it's safe?' he asks again. 'They haven't got anything against Scotsmen have they?'

'It's safe, really. The government wants people to come back and open up businesses and make money. Things have changed. And no, they don't have anything against Scotsmen, as long as you don't wear your kilt, anyway. They don't look kindly on men in dresses.'

They let the sounds of the day envelop them, the barefooted kids screaming with excitement as they chase each other around the park, the cruise of the cars along the shorefront, the gentle slap of the waves on the sand, the hum of the heat.

'Well, let's go for six months or a year, eh?' Danny says. 'Get the lie of the land, see what it's like, and if we don't like it we can come back. We can look at it as a bit of an extended holiday. How would that be? That way we could still keep some of our eggs in the basket.

'Mai looks at him uncomprehendingly. 'Eggs? What eggs are you talking about?'

Danny smiles at her and touches her cheek. 'Doesn't matter. Six months, OK?'

'One year?'

'Maybe. At least Vietnam's got better weather than Glasgow at any rate.'

'Everywhere has better weather than Glasgow, my darling.' Mai kisses him again, biting his lip. 'What will you tell Young Bob? You've been partners for so long now?'

'I'll tell him I'm going to be the sausage king of Saigon, the prince of pork luncheon, the master of mortadella, the bailiff of braunschweiger.'

'What is braunschweiger exactly?' Mai asks, puzzled but curious.

Danny takes her arm in his as they head out of the park towards their car.

'Braunschweiger, my love, has a very interesting history . . .'

Beer. Wine. Vodka. Beer. Irn Bru. Whisky. Gin. More Beer. Drambuie. Coca-Cola. The party is going well if the amount of alcohol being swallowed, guzzled, sipped and swilled is anything to go by. And it's still early. No one's collapsed, belted anybody or started singing yet, except for that prick in the corner who came along with Sammy McFadyen. Frankie doesn't mind folks bringing along their pals and relatives, in this case Sammy's nephew who's up from London, but you have to draw the line somewhere. A performance like this might put a dampener on the evening, suck the life right out of it in fact, and given that it's a farewell for him and Eileen, Jimmy and Stella, you really can't put up with this kind of shite. No reasonable man would.

Frankie squeezes through the babbling throng in the living room to where Jimmy is talking animatedly to Big Danny from the pub. The words, 'magazine', 'penis enlargement' and 'Jesus fuckin' Christ', can be heard clearly though the general yelp, chatter and rumble of the party which is in full, hip-swivelling swing. Except for this one spanner in the works.

Frankie mouths a few quiet words in Jimmy's ear. Jimmy nods like a toy dog in the back window of a car, and pushes his way to the corner of the room. 'Jimmy Stewart,' he says, holding out his hand to the young man squatting on the carpet beneath him.

'Hello. Nathan McFadyen, Sammy's nephew.'

'Aye, pleased to meet you Nathan."

'Likewise.'

Jimmy shrugs meekly in mock embarrassment over what he is about to say. 'The thing is Nathan, if you sing one more of those fuckin' Leonard Cohen songs, I've been instructed to ram that acoustic guitar right up your arse. OK?'

Nathan stops abruptly in mid-strum. He stares at Jimmy for a moment, his tongue seemingly lost somewhere in this mouth like a blind mouse in a cathedral. 'Aye. Right you are. No problem.'

Jimmy winks, flashes his gleaming falsies and pats Nathan on his carefully coiffured head. As he turns to take up where he left off with Big Danny, who in the meantime has slipped his arm around that doll Doris MacNamara while keeping one watchful eye on her brawny husband Malky, Jimmy recognises the unmistakable wail of Neil Young's 'The Needle and the Damage Done'. He sighs and turns back to chat some more with young Nathan. Jimmy bends down beside him and pokes him hard in the chest.

'Shut it. I'll no tell you again or that guitar will be playing a duet with your large intestine. All right.' Nathan blinks as Jimmy twangs his g-string.

Frankie sticks on some John Lee Hooker.

'Boom, boom, boom, boom. Gonna shoot you right down. Right offa yo feet. Take you home with me. Put you in my house. Boom boom boom boom.'

Feet start shuffling, heads start bobbing and the room starts shaking like a tin roof in a hurricane.

'Ah, that John Lee Hooker, he's the man, eh?' Jimmy says, doing the one-legged chicken stomp, a dance he invented himself one night after downing half a bottle of whisky and thirteen pints of Newcastle Brown Ale. 'I tell you Frankie, if that Nathan even attempts tae sing anything ever composed by that John Denver, I will personally kick him all the way tae Colorado. Rocky Mountain High, my wullie.'

'Easy Jimmy, son. He's just a boy. But if he starts on any Phil Collins tunes then it's open slather. Show no mercy.'

Frankie wanders about making sure everybody's happy, has got a drink and something to nibble on. He offers Wullie McPherson an angel on horseback but he drunkenly declines, muttering something about badger droppings, and goes for a sausage roll instead. Big Danny is nibbling on Doris MacNamara, and Malky MacNamara is nibbling on Big Danny's wife, Martha, Jimmy's nibbling on the standard lamp and his dog Blackie has somehow managed to sneak into the house and is offering herself to any passing male, irrespective of whether they are members of the canine family or not.

Frankie's done a few curries that are not going down well. Eileen told him not to put in too many chillies, but once he got going in the kitchen he couldn't help himself. After all, what's a curry without chillies? Like a bee without a sting. Pretty much useless. And once you get a good dozen in, it becomes irrelevant how many more you add. As Butch Cassidy said to a terrified Sundance Kid before jumping a couple of hundred feet off a cliff into the raging river below, it doesn't matter if you can't swim, the fall will probably kill you. Same goes for chillies.

Everybody's here. Frankie's side of the family, Eileen's side. There's sisters everywhere. Agnes has got a bowl of garlic prawns on her lap and she's poking at them with a fork like a child pokes at a dead frog with a stick. She's casting around for a place to hide the bowl and finally slips it under the chair when she thinks no one is looking. But Frankie sees it coming and so does Blackie who disentangles herself from around Nathan's left thigh and pushes her snout under the chair and scoffs the lot with a tongue that could easily double as a snow plough. Frankie smiles to himself as Blackie's face registers the new taste sensation known as red hot peppers and watches in amusement as she tries to chew the top off a can of lager. She gives up in frustration and then proceeds to bite her own arse.

'Better not let that dog of yours feed her pups the night, Jimmy,' he laughs. There's weans everywhere, running around, playing games, hiding in cupboards already crammed with years of accumulated detritus, playing dead under the bed and lingering on the edge of adult conversations as if they might discover the secret of acting grown up and being able to talk, drink, sing and smoke at the same time,

The older kids drink anything they can get their hands and lips on, preparing themselves for an evening of head-spinning, gut-heaving bouts of vomiting that will leave them horizontal on the bathroom floor and reflecting on whether drinking alcohol is really an enjoyable pastime only for the average suicidal maniac.

Frankie recalls the parties at his father's and mother's house when the old man was still alive. Parties were different then. Not many people had a record player so people sang more for entertainment. Each person had their own song and it went without saying that you never sang somebody else's, otherwise you'd be breaking the eleventh commandment, 'Thou Shalt Not Sing Thy Neighbour's Song'. Sinatra, Nat King Cole, Billy Eckstine, Dinah Shore, Petula Clark, Gene Pitney, Tom Jones, Cilla Black, echoed down the hall and into the bedroom where he and Danny would sing along under the bed covers, even though they were supposed to be asleep. They loved Johnny Ray songs the best. With all that wailing and weeping they could really put on a turn, like two coyote pups howling plaintively at the moon.

They all sat around the fireplace with the coal fire burning and those who'd already had too much to drink would nod off as their faces flushed red with the sleepy heat. The necessary formalities had to be observed at all times. No talking during songs, no refilling of glasses. Swaying, nodding and the occasional murmur or moan of appreciation were permitted. It was as if they sat in silence waiting for God or Tony Bennett to give them a song and fill them with the Holy Spirit or single malt whisky.

Frankie's Uncle Charlie always took his false teeth out and slipped them into his back pocket before he sang. Then he'd smack his naked gums together and launch into a song he always suspected was a bit on the dodgy side and featured the words 'cock-a-doodle-do' at the end of every verse. Everyone would cackle and titter and break the rules, screaming 'you're terrible Charlie, so ye are'.

As the night wore on, people would get all nostalgic and long-gone family members would be resurrected and the coals of their lives raked over and rekindled till their presence could be felt by all in that small room with its inset bed and cold water sink by the window. Songs would be sung in their honour and people would weep quietly for themselves and their memories of younger and better days, when their whole lives were still ahead of them and death only happened to strangers.

Frankie remembers how his father loved a song himself, the way he'd spread his arms wide as he crooned 'Moon River' to the hushed and attentive room. Sometimes, when he'd come home from the pub, red-faced and beaming, he'd get Fiona up out of her bed to sing 'Over the Rainbow' for his pals, Jimmy McKechnie and Eddie Johnstone. Fiona had the voice of an angel, he always used to say.

When his father was drunk he would reminisce about his own parents, Eddie and Margaret, already dead when Frankie was born. They'd died young, Maggie of tuberculosis and Eddie from too many years working in the flour mill. He had enough flour in his lungs to keep Glasgow in sliced bread for a year, his father would say.

Frankie feels a nudge in his ribs and Jimmy is swaying in front of him like a palm tree in the wind, muttering something about Sammy wanting to say a few words to wish them good luck for the trip. Frankie is not keen, having witnessed Sammy's oratory on many previous occasions, but before he can say anything Sammy is up on a chair and clearing his throat and wildly waving his arms at the people in the room. They glance in his direction but are disinclined to pay him any attention, especially in the middle of 'Dancing in the Street' by Martha and the Vandellas. *'Are you ready for a brand new beat?'* they sing in unison, except for Jimmy, who is warbling 'Are You Lonesome Tonight' to nobody in particular, complete with hand gestures and microphone in the form of a bottle of Gordon's gin.

'Aw, eh, can ah have your attention please, ladeez and genelmens,' Sammy shouts from up high on his chair.

'Summer's here and the time is right, for dancin' in the street', is the only response he can muster.

'Aw c'mon, fucksake, just shut the fuck up a minute, I'm no kiddin,' he wails in exasperation.

The room keeps shaking and the pictures on the wall rumble on their hooks. *'Doesn't matter what you wear, just as long as you are there'*, they yell, arms waving in the air and drinks spilling onto Eileen's new carpet.

Frankie takes pity on him and turns down the volume to a collective protest of 'what the fuck . . . ?'

Sammy wipes his brow with relief. He wasn't quite sure how long he could stay upright on the chair. He clears his throat

again, sounding like a foghorn with the flu. 'Ladeez and genelmens, youse all know why we's here.'

There is a pause while Sammy consults his nephew about
why he is here. 'We are here, as we all know, to wish Frankie
and Eileen and Jimmy, you too Stella love, all the best for their
trip to Venezuela.' Big Danny whispers in Sammy's ear. 'Sorry,
Vietnam. We're gathered here to wish them all the best for
Vietnam, a safe journey and a safe return. We'll be thinking of
you, Frankie, Jimmy, Eileen . . . ' Sammy takes a long swallow
of his beer and forgets what he was saying. He stares at the
carpet for a while before his eyes light up like a bulb in a sock-
et. 'You too Stella darlin'. So in summation, for what we are
about to receive we truly thank you Lord . . . Aw, wait a minute,
that's no it. Could youse all raise your glasses and be upstand-
ing. I give youse the bride and the groom. Naw, wait, wait. Aye,
I've got it now. I was just kidding youse on. I'd like to wish
youse all a happy new year.'

Lost in his own little festive season, Sammy's eyes fill with
tears and his chin recedes into his neck as he begins to sing.
'*Should auld acquaintance be forgot and never come tae mind,
should auld acquaintance be forgot for the sake of Auld Lang
Syne.*'

Frankie throws back his whisky, shakes his head and turns
on the stereo again as Stella wobbles over to Sammy and with
a quick flick of her arm, pushes him off the chair. 'You're a
fuckin' eejit, Sammy,' she slurs, trying to remember where she
left her vodka and tonic.

The night shakes on in a haze of cigarette smoke, rambling
chatter and various forms of creative choreography. Sammy
McFadyen has his head out the window and is vomiting into
old Mrs McLean's garden three floors below. Young Nathan is
trying to glue his guitar back together after Big Danny took
matters into his own hands when the lad got three lines into
the first verse of 'I'm Being Followed by a Moonshadow'. The
McCludgie twins have somehow managed to find their way
into the party, but after a warning from an axe handle-bearing
Frankie, they promise to behave themselves and appear to be
content to sit on the settee and munch away on three fish
suppers and six deep fried Mars bars. Fergus, the younger boy
by a minute, examines each individual chip like it is a strange
creature from another planet. Satisfied it is fit for human consumption, he drops it into his open mouth like a penny into a

wishing well. Frankie's got Marvin Gaye on the stereo and Eileen and Stella are dancing cheek to cheek, moving slowly across the carpet, their eyes closed in a drunken and blissful other place, their bodies a tee-pee of support, lest they fall over.

Doris the Doll has one arm around Jimmy's eldest, Andrew. With the other, she's caressing his downy cheeks and singing "I Loves You Porgy", three inches from his face, which is as crimson as a tropical sunset. The boy smiles and tries to look at the ceiling but Doris jerks his head back whenever his eyes wander from her lustful gaze.

Later, when the evening is at an end, Frankie thinks about picking up a few empty bottles and cans, or emptying a few overflowing ashtrays, but surveying the wreckage, decides against it. The scene before him resembles the aftermath of the Battle of Culloden. There are bodies everywhere in various states of conciousness and any minute now the peasants will be rummaging through their pockets and chopping their fingers off to get at their gold and silver rings. He turns off the lights and opens a couple of windows to let in what passes for air in this part of town. He stumbles into the bathroom, his eyes half closed, to find Jimmy asleep in the bath, an empty bottle of vodka clasped to his chest. Blackie is spreadeagled on top of him, her great serpentine tongue coiled around his neck like an anaconda around the bough of a tree. They are both snoring.

It's been a party to remember. People went home happy or drunk, or both, or with people they didn't expect to go home with at all. No marriages broke up, although Stella did go off and leave Jimmy comatose in the bath. 'Dog fucker', she slurred before bouncing off the walls in the hall and falling out the front door.

No one ate the Thai curries except for Blackie. But what the hell, he'd enjoyed making them. It's not his fault if these people think all fish are born pre-battered.

Frankie yawns and slips off his shoes and socks and pads into the bedroom in his bare feet. A pale blue scarf is draped over the bedside lamp imbuing the room with a faintly surreal hue. Eileen is standing next to a wooden chair wearing a bus conductress' uniform. Her peaked cap is slightly askew and tilted forward over her eyes, her dark serge skirt is thigh length and tight, and the top of her black sheer stockings are just visible below the hem. A leather satchel is slung crosswise across her naked breasts and a small metal ticket machine hangs from a thick leather belt around her waist. In one hand she is carrying a small bell. Routine Number Eight.

Frankie smiles to himself and takes up his position on the chair by the bed.

'Where to love?' she asks matter-of-factly.

'Saigon.'

'That full fare or pensioner?'

'Full fare.'

Eileen sets the dials on her machine and punches out the ticket. 'There ye go. Change buses at Carntyne. Number 13's the one ye want.'

'Thanks very much.'

Frankie casts an eye around the bus. 'Quiet the night, eh?'

'Aye. People are home in their beds this time ae the night. I wouldn't mind being in bed myself, if ye know what I mean.'

'Aw, aye. It's getting late, right enough.'

'Off home are ye?'

'That's right.'

'Do ye live by yerself?'

'No, I live with my mother.'

Eileen moves closer till her right breast is level with his mouth. She licks her finger and slowly circles her nipple, which glistens wet and becomes hard. 'This nipple is right out of control the night. Can't do a thing with it. I push it down and it pops right back up again. Like a Jack-in-the-box, so it is.'

'Aye, I know the feeling.'

Eileen laughs and the coins in her satchel tinkle like bells on a sleigh. 'Do ye get out much, living with your mother, an' that?'

'No I don't actually. She's eighty-three and takes a lot of looking after.'

'Aye, I suppose ye do at that age.'

'She thinks she's Shirley Bassey. Keeps launching into "Hey Big Spender" all the time. Gets very embarrassing at the supermarket, you know.'

'Shame. No an easy song to sing, that yin. Have you got a girlfriend?'

'No. Not at the moment, anyhow.'

'I don't suppose you get much sex, then?'

'No, it has been a while, as a matter of fact.'

'How long's a while?'

'Well, never. I've never done it.'

'Away!'

'No, it's true. Swear to God.'

'Let's keep God out of this, eh? He has a tendency to spoil things of this nature. A real stick in the mud, so he is. Look, do you mind if I sit down next to you. My feet are killing me and this satchel weighs a ton.'

'No, not at all. Please do.'

Eileen takes off her satchel and pulls up another chair, lying back on it and resting her legs on each of Frankie's shoulders. 'Ah, that's better, it's nice to get a load off, eh? Now the first thing you have to learn about women is how to please them.'

'Is that right?'

'Absolutely. Keep a woman satisfied and she's yours forever. Well, a while, anyway.'

'Sounds good to me. So how do you please a woman?'

'I thought you'd never ask. The first thing you have to know is how to use your tongue, and it's not for talking either.'

Eileen pulls Frankie's head down between her legs and wraps her thighs around his back, letting her head fall over the edge of the chair, her long wavy hair tumbling across the floor. 'Just pretend it's a toffee apple, sweetheart. That's it. Take your time. And don't mind me if I ring this bell. I like to ring the bell sometimes. I'll let you know when it's time to get off.'

'Whaa . . . bow. . . cush . . . ma . . .,' Frankie mumbles from below.

'What?' Frankie raises his head and grins. 'What about the other customers?'

'They can take the train.'

Mai sits quietly with her aunt on a wooden bench on the promenade at Nha Trang. The ocean is bright blue and calm and in the distance she can make out the shadowy outline of Bamboo Island through the late afternoon haze. To the north, the brightly painted fishing boats are leaving the safety of the river estuary and making their way out to sea. To the south, she can just distinguish the ochre-coloured villas of the late Bao Dai, the holiday retreat of the former king of Vietnam who is now just a meaningless blip in the communist version of her country's history. As her elderly aunt dozes beside her, she watches the young men play soccer on the beach, barefoot and shirtless. Their energy seems boundless as they dash across the sand in clamorous pursuit of the ball. Children tear into the water, whooping and somersaulting, their little bodies sleek and brown like magical sea creatures at play. Families sit on deck chairs, crunching steamed crab and prawns and drinking beer poured over glasses of ice.

She laughs as she remembers her first holiday by the sea with Danny. He had rented a caravan by the beach at Ocean Grove, half an hour from Geelong. She couldn't believe it. A house on wheels! She had never seen such a thing in her life. It had everything inside, a television, a little sink with running water, a gas stove and a kitchen table that folded down into a double bed. Some people in the caravan park had even planted daisy bushes and grass on their sites and they sat there all day and drank beer and ate barbecued chops and salad. Their children had brought their bicycles. It was their home away from home. A few people couldn't even be bothered walking across the sand dunes to the beach. Too much like hard work, they said. But she and Danny swam every day in the freezing water and some young boys taught them how to body surf. She felt exhilarated, like she was a dolphin shooting through the waves. Sometimes she was dumped by huge breakers and she tumbled along the seabed as if she was just a pebble in a whirlpool. When she emerged, battered, frightened, her mouth full of water and sand, she'd be in two minds about jumping back in. This was the sea that had taken her mother, but was also the sea that had set Mai free. In the end, Danny would haul her back into the water, whooping and yelping, as effervescent as the sea crashing around them.

But here, sitting on this beach, Mai thinks about Danny. She doesn't like to leave him on his own, as he's always saying how much he misses her when she's away visiting various members of her family. And lately, he's been distracted, anxious about the problems he's having with the local police. He does work long hours at the bar and he rarely takes a day off to relax. Mai knows he's tired. Sometimes she thinks it was easier for him at the slaughterhouse. He may have been surrounded by blood and death and intestines but at least he got the weekends off. Still, they've been lucky in Saigon. Since 1975, by some miracle, her aunt had managed to keep a building in the city from the sticky fingers of the new communist government and she was happy to lease it to her niece for a small rent and some good French wine whenever Danny and Mai could get hold of it. The government was keen to attract more tourists, and especially their tourist dollars, to the country. She and Danny convinced the authorities that their proposed bar would be good for tourism and they were given a licence. There were few customers at first, but when *Lonely Planet* mentioned the Blue Moon in their guide to Vietnam, it wasn't long before it became a popular spot on the tourist itinerary. Some of the local expatriates also made it their regular watering hole and could be seen propping up the bar and playing pool four or five nights a week.

It's so different now. When she escaped all those years ago, the government had closed down all the restaurants. They were capitalist ventures, it proclaimed. There was hardly any meat, and even rice was becoming difficult to get hold of in any quantity. Now there are restaurants and cafés everywhere in the city, some of which are owned by the army or the police or the People's Committee. Mai laughs to herself. The communists find capitalism a useful way to supplement their meagre incomes so that they can afford to educate their children in Australia or America. Communism's all very good in theory, but it doesn't get your kids a good job in a big foreign company.

Mai closes her eyes and breathes in the salty air. The smell of seafood makes her mouth water. She slips off her sandals and rubs her feet in the sand, delighting in the sensation as it crunches between her toes. She decides that when she returns to Saigon she will put Benny in charge of the bar for the night and take Danny out on the town. She might even wear her grandmother's silk *ao dai* and together they will stroll around the corner to La Fourchette where Monsieur Pilois will beam and inquire after their health and then usher them to a table by the window. He will serve them a complimentary aperitif. And why not? How many nights did they while the hours away there before their bar became as popular as it is now? They would sit at the same table and Danny would marvel at the life in the streets outside. His conversation was one long streak of exclamation, of amazement, of disbelief. He couldn't get over the things he saw, the aromas he savoured, the sounds he heard. The beggars, the shoeshine boys, the young girls selling chewing gum and lottery tickets—he would rush from his chair and give them all money to stop them peering dolefully through the glass.

After they have eaten and drunk more wine and cognac than is good for them, they will take a cyclo to the Rex for a night of dancing. It was Danny who taught her to dance the foxtrot, the evening three step, the rumba, the waltz. He'd been forced to take dancing lessons at school in Glasgow and it wasn't until he met Mai that he was grateful for them. He had first eased her around the floor at a Footscray Football Social Club dinner dance, gently nudging her this way and that with the touch of his hand on her back or the inclination of his hips, Young Bob and Lorna, Happy Jack and Nancy gliding expertly beside them. When they can dance no more they'll take the elevator up to the roof garden with its sparkling fairy lights and topiary, and watch the world below cruise by in an endless stream of bicycles and motorbikes. Maybe they will take to the streets and join the throng, ambling down Nguyen Hue Street to the Saigon River to watch the glittering restaurant boats, lit up like giant birthday cakes, shimmer upstream to Anh Phu. Perhaps they will just sit on the embankment and eat chocolate ice cream, if she can convince Danny that it's safe. He still believes street food is a conspiracy to poison foreigners.

Mai chuckles to herself, momentarily disturbing her slumbering aunt who opens her eyes briefly before sighing softly and returning to sleep, her head resting against Mai's shoulder. Maybe she'll book a room at the Caravelle so that after their long, wine-drenched dinner, they can walk the short distance to the city's best hotel and spend the night in each other's arms or, as Danny likes to put it, do the business. In the morning they'll wake late and have a long languid breakfast by the pool, occasionally glancing through *The Herald-Tribune* for items of interest.

Mai gestures to a passing coconut seller. He takes a young coconut and with his machete chops the outside of the fruit into a shape like a miniature hut with a sloping roof. He slices off the top and inserts a straw. Mai sips the cool refreshing juice from inside and wonders what Danny is doing now. It's his day off, the only day of the week the bar is closed. Perhaps he's swimming in the pool at the Saigon Centre, where one of his regular customers is the manager and lets him use the facilities free of charge. He'll swim his twenty laps in that curious style of his, a frenetic splashing he calls the Glasgow crawl, and have a club sandwich and a beer by the pool. He'll shower and change and go to De Tham Street to buy some new CDs to add to his already encyclopedic music collection. At a dollar each, Danny buys them by the dozen, trying not to worry too much about the pirate producers plundering recording artists' musical endeavours without even the slightest nod to the concept of copyright. The only right they are concerned about is their right to make a living, and if Bono or Paul McCartney lose a few dollars in the pursuit of this then that's just too bad.

But just as likely, Danny will be down in the cellar, conducting an inventory of the stocks of beer, wine and spirits, his usual activity on his day off if she's not there to make sure he gets away from the place, at least for a few hours. Either that or he'll spend the day playing pool or darts with Benny. They might go out for a bowl of pho at Pho Hoa, Danny's favourite soup place in Saigon.

Mai worries that the decision to return to Vietnam wasn't the right one for Danny. It was the right one for her, no doubt about that. Saigon is her home, these are her people. The strength of the attraction, the longing for her past, surprised her. But for Danny it is still a foreign place. The smells, the sounds, the talk, the history, the very *being* of it all. He jokes that it's almost as foreign as Edinburgh. But they have been happy here, there's no denying that. It has been a challenge, especially at first—so much bureaucracy to do battle with, so many people to bribe, so many customs to adapt to. But Mai's extended family has been a godsend, always eager to help, smoothing the way whenever they can. They still know some people in high places. And her mother's sisters have brought something of her mother back to her. The curve of her nose, the shape of her eyes, the sound of her voice singing an old song. And Danny is happier now that there are more foreigners living and working in the city. He has more people to speak English with, to laugh with and to tell jokes he knows they will understand, although some of his friends complain that the Glaswegian version of English he speaks is more difficult to comprehend than Vietnamese.

Mai watches the sand take flight as the late afternoon breeze rolls off the sea. Umbrellas flutter and rumble and pieces of paper race across the beach. The crab- and lobster-sellers clasp their conical hats to their heads as they squat on the beach scanning its length for one last customer.

'Come Auntie, it is getting late. Soon my bus will be here. Come, take my arm,' Mai whispers, and they head along the sandy path through the pine trees to Tran Phu Street.

Frankie presents himself for inspection in front of the bathroom mirror. He blinks and squints and stares and stretches his pink-rimmed eyelids as far north and south as they will go. He rubs his palms over his cheeks and chin, a prickly scrub of black and white stubble. He sticks out his tongue and leaves it exposed and drooping like a drunk displaying his pickled member to a couple of grannies on a late night bus. He notes with interest that his tongue has a texture similar to that of a dirty shag-pile carpet. He scrapes it with his upper teeth and immediately regrets it as the bitter taste makes him involuntarily wince and shiver. His head descends slowly under the tap like a spider drooping from the ceiling on a silken thread and he noisily rinses his mouth out until it tastes vaguely normal. He shouldn't have drunk so much last night. He knows that now and he knew that then when he was throwing those single malts down his gullet like a performing seal guzzling fishy rewards at the circus. So why did he do it, he asks himself, placing his hands on the sink to steady himself. He has no fuckin' idea. Was he searching for poetic oblivion, a temporary respite from all life's woes? Or did he just feel like getting completely scunnered because it felt good at the time? It's a mystery and at this time in the morning he has no answer to it. Why do we do what we do even though we know before we do it that we will regret it afterwards? It defies all logic. Perhaps we haven't come so far from the apes as we think we have. Or perhaps it has more to do with the logic-inhibiting properties of whisky and gin.

His balls ache. His dick has a migraine. He glances down to its foreshortened and wrinkled detumescence and gently lifts it up and down and tilts it this way and that. There are no bruises or abrasions, but it is certainly red and a touch swollen, a brave wee soldier on the battlefield of love. Once Eileen had got that bus conductress' uniform on she was loath to take it off and kept insisting on one more turn around the block. When he woke and dragged himself out of bed, he left Eileen clutching her ticket machine to her breast, her peaked cap hanging cheekily over her peaceful brow. He can hear her now, snuffling and giggling to herself in the bedroom and occasionally tinkling her little bell. Frankie has never known or heard of a woman who can laugh in her sleep and is in constant wonder of it. If you can laugh in the lonely darkness of the night, surely it gives you a head start in dealing with the world in the cold and anxious light of day?

Frankie runs his fingers through his hair, registering the increasing presence of grey within his naturally black and fecund locks. Old hair, Jimmy's daughter Estelle calls it. He remembers that by the time he died, his father had hair like a drift of snow. When he arrived home from the pit he'd lean over the scullery sink and scrub himself down with carbolic soap. Face, shoulders, arms and hair. So perhaps he'd just sandpapered the colour out of it. Hair care was never at the top of his old man's list of priorities. Certainly, he doesn't recall seeing any body-building protein shampoo around the house or any vitamin-enriched conditioner, for that matter.

He parts the hair on his chest. He thinks he looks like a zebra. Perhaps he's been watching too many documentaries on the Discovery Channel. Are his regular viewing encounters with African wildlife turning his chest hair a greyer shade of pale? Is this the insidious influence of television that those cultural watchdog academics from Glasgow University are always writing about in the paper? He again lowers his gaze to his crotch and shakes his head in disbelief. Age, it just comes out of nowhere. Like a lion stalking a baby antelope, it suddenly bursts out from the long grass and before you know it, it's got its teeth into your scrawny tree-bark neck and suddenly your pubic hair glistens with curly filaments of silver.

He doesn't remember ever getting a look at his father's nether regions so he doesn't know whether it is an inherited trait. Throughout his childhood and early adolescence Frankie had only ever known his father with his trousers on. And he couldn't really make any inquiries about this subject with his mother since, as far as she was concerned, all things sexual and physiological were best left undiscussed, packed in a lead-lined box and hidden at the back of the coal bunker under one hundredweight of large brown lumps of fossil fuel. Christ, when his sisters first got their periods they thought they were dying and screamed the house down. What a racket! His mother hadn't bothered to tell them anything about what would happen to their pubescent bodies so when they were confronted with blood, *their* blood, dripping down their milk white thighs it all came as a bit of a shock to say the least. She just handed them a napkin, told them to stick it between their legs and warned them to stay away from boys. It took them some time to work out the connection between men and menstruation and, by then, it was too late anyway.

Frankie turns on the taps over the sink until it fills up with hot water, a translucent balm to soothe his aching head and cleanse his smoke and alcohol-choked pores. His skin feels like an old cloth that's been used to wipe the kitchen floor. He lowers his face into the water and closes his eyes. He holds his breath and pretends to be a hippo trotting bouncily along the riverbed, a four ton ballerina that's had a few too many fish suppers. He concludes he must still be a wee bit pissed. But as he wallows in this soothing little ceramic water hole, dreaming of a wild life on the African plains, he is overcome by a sudden attack of panic. His chest muscles constrict and he feels short of breath. What's going on? What the fuck is he doing? A few more hours and he and Jimmy will be away down the track to a date with destiny soon to be followed by Eileen and Stella. Saigon. The other side of the world. Christ, the only time he's been overseas was when he and Eileen went to Ibiza and the place was full of Scotsmen and English-style pubs and fish and chip shops run by blokes who used to live in Parkhead. Not what you would call an exotic foreign clime. There was nothing culturally or physically challenging about it. It wasn't too hot, it wasn't too cold, it didn't give you altitude sickness. It was safe to go out at night and walk the streets.

They ate potatoes there. It was a home away from home with castanets and olive oil.

But Vietnam, Christ, that's another packet of crisps altogether. Danny says the weather's steaming, that it's almost human in the way it treats you, one moment welcoming and friendly, the next evil and contemptuous. He says people there don't think the way we do. They're Buddhists and believe that when you die you get to come back for another life, a shocking concept for most residents of Glasgow who think that one life spent in that particular city is more than enough. Besides, with the kind of food they eat and the amount of alcohol they drink, most Glaswegians are in no condition for a repeat performance anyway.

It must be an alien place, this Vietnam, Frankie thinks to himself. It's the East, for fucksake, and he knows nothing about it except for what Francis Ford Coppola and a dog-eared, barber shop edition of *National Geographic* have told him. It's not his territory, his stamping ground, and if there's one thing Discovery Channel has taught him it is that it's best to stay on your own turf, for outside lies danger and strange beasts whose only aim in life is to rip you apart with their bare and terrifying teeth and, once they've had their fill, leave the remnants of your torn and bloody carcass to the hovering vultures and skulking hyenas. Most people don't even speak English there, not like Spain where it's a second language. How can he reason and negotiate with people when they can't understand a word he's saying? Danny didn't say whether he speaks Vietnamese or not. Frankie learned a smattering of Gaelic at the night school, but that's not going to do him much good is it?

Frankie lifts his head out of the water, shakes it hard, and his hair falls like a sodden mophead over his face. He pushes it back and is surprised to sees his eyes shot with fear and uncertainty. He looks tired and worn, his skin feels tight across his cheeks. What has he been thinking of? Going to Saigon seemed like a good idea at the time. But maybe he's just been carried away by the momentum, the perceived romance and adventure of it all. It's something to look forward to, isn't it? Well, at least he thought it was. Now he's not so sure. He should never have got Jimmy involved. He can't afford a new pair of shoes never mind a plane ticket to

Vietnam. Jimmy's a good pal, and he'll do anything to get out of the house and away from Stella for a few days, but maybe this is the wrong time, the wrong place, the wrong situation.

What if he pulled the plug now, announced to everyone that the game's over? Time to trudge home to their beds and forget he ever mentioned Vietnam. What would people say? What would his father say if he were still alive? That Danny was always a silly bugger and that he got himself into this mess and he can bloody well get himself out of it? That Frankie should just stay home and look after his ain? He wipes his face with a towel and remembers his father lying on the carpet wrestling with all his weans on a Sunday afternoon, pushing and pulling them and tickling them and tipping them upside down on their heads till their faces went purple. They all jumped on him and screamed with joy and elation because it felt like the best time they ever had, all the weans together, and they didn't want it to stop. Maybe that's it, Frankie reflects, maybe you have to try not to let it ever stop, the memories and the exuberant innocence of those childhood years.

But what choice does he have but to go? You can't wipe your hands of your own flesh and blood even though you might kid yourself on that you can. Blood ties, blood brothers, blood that's thicker than water, perhaps it's just all fuckin' blood. He and Danny might not be the best of friends any more, shite he's got closer pals at work and around the scheme, but there's a family bond there that goes beyond friendship. Maybe it's irrational, maybe it's spiritual, maybe it's because you laughed with each other and got tired and sweaty and excited when you were weans kicking a ball around the back until it was dark and late and you didn't want to go in, even though your mother was hanging out the window threatening all manner of terrible punishments if you didn't get your little arses home and into bed this minute. Maybe it's because you watched *Top of the Pops* together on a Thursday night, propped up on the couch, jiggling your feet while your mother did the ironing. Maybe it was because you loved each other, although it was never something you thought about or even knew it was something you *could* think about. Maybe it was because you just took it for granted that you would always be there for each other, to lend a hand with the wallpapering, or to put a new clutch in the car, or mind each other's weans while you went out for a well-deserved night at the pictures. Whatever it is, it doesn't seem to go away. Frankie had never imagined travelling to the other end of the planet to help his brother out, but the principle was the same as stopping up the next close to say hello and make him a cup of tea because he's in his bed with the flu. There's no mileage limit on responsibility.

Frankie combs his wet hair slick and tight against his scalp. He wonders what John Shaft would do in this situation. Would he plunge into the dense dripping heat and intimidating uncertainty of Vietnam, not knowing what dangers lay ahead of him? Damn right, he nods affirmatively to himself in the mirror, you're damn right he would've. They say that cat's a bad mutha. Frankie closes his eyes, and in his mind his poky little bathroom with its floral wallpaper and pale green vanity basin explodes with the sounds of a guitar so funky you can chew on it, violins that keep company with the angels and a thumping anthemic line of brass that would not be out of place at the Messiah's second coming, and he begins to sing. Softly at first, he builds in volume and conviction with each inspirational phrase. 'Who is the man that would risk his neck for his brother man? Shaft! Can you dig it? Who's the cat that won't cop out when there's danger all about? Shaft! Right on!'

Frankie is lost in the music dancing around in his head. He is being cleansed, set free, dispatched on his journey, when a faint and tuneful whimper creeps like misery from behind the shower curtain across the bath.

'He's a complicated man, no-one understands him but his woman.'

Frankie whips back the plastic curtain. Jimmy is singing away to himself, his arms wrapped around Blackie in a fond embrace. Frankie smiles to himself and reaches for the taps on the wall below the shower head.

Mucky tracksuit pants. Gravy-stained jacket. T-shirt splotched with tomato sauce. Worn brown slippers. No socks. The man is a walking stain, viscous and uncertain of direction. A threadbare cap encases his head, like a night cover over a canary's cage. He is dribbling slightly from one corner of his mouth, which is ringed with three-day silver stubble. Rocking back and forth at the edge of the platform, his puddle-like eyes struggle to focus on the two men staring back at him through the window of the three o'clock train from Glasgow to London, now stopped at Berwick-upon-Tweed, the last station before it crosses the border into the land of the pork pie and chips.

'That'll be us in a few years, Frankie boy,' Jimmy says, pointing at the crimson-faced drunk, who is slurping from a bottle concealed in a crumpled brown paper bag. 'Nae money, nae prospects. Ruined by a fateful journey tae the wilds of Vietnam. Two men who turned to the drink to try to forget what they had seen in the jungle, like yon Colonel Kurtz, eh. The horror, the fuckin' horror.'

Frankie laughs, nodding in the direction of the drunk is now peeing against the side of the train and all over the top of his slippers. 'No way. You'll never catch me wearing tracksuit trousers wi' a tailored jaikit. And you, for fucksake, you turned to the drink years ago.'

Jimmy takes another swig from the carton of orange juice which he carefully laced with vodka before they left Glasgow Central earlier in the day. 'I suppose you've got a point there. I hivnae started peein' all over myself yet like that eejit, but. That's somethin' that might be on the horizon. I'll get back fae Saigon sufferin', what dae ye call it, post-traumatic stress thingamay, and that'll be it, I'll be dribblin' like a leaky tap, and mumblin' away tae myself at train stations, singin' dirty songs and trying tae feel up a' the young lassies.'

'You don't need post-traumatic stress disorder for that Jimmy, you just need old age and some bad luck. There's a very thin line between comfort and catastrophe. For all we know, that poor bugger was a bank manager who got laid off and his wife left him and took the weans and the car, and he lost the house as well, and he ended up a sad old wreck of a man with nobody to talk to except himself. Maybe he just woke up one morning and the day was just too much for him, just pushed him over the edge. Could happen to any of us, Jimmy son.'

'Aye, maybe you're right. If it's gonnae happen, it's gonnae happen, never mind what goes down in old Saigon, eh? Que sera, sera. What ever will be, will be.'

'Mind, he could just be a no-good shite who drank his wages away every Thursday night at the pub and left his wife and weans to starve with no a bite to eat in the house or a pair of shoes among them.'

'Aye, serves him right,' Jimmy says, looking at the dribbling drunk with palpable disdain. 'Away ye go, ye bastard ye. Away and fa' under the train. Ye should be ashamed ae yersel. Yer poor weans.'

Frankie sits back, closes his eyes and savours the rumble and sway of the train as it pulls out of the station and rollicks along the track. He listens to the dark bellowing echo as it chugs throatily through a tunnel, the ear-splitting screech of the brakes as it pulls up to a station. He watches the country-side roll by. It seems to him that life looks pretty much the same everywhere down this line. People just go about it with a different accent. Same life, same shops. Bingoland, Furnitureland, Gardenland, Foodland, Liquorland, Crazyland. One big happy, well-fed, bunch of dedicated consumers lolling about the garden in a comfy swing with a floral awning bought for fifty per cent off. Life's a bargain in this green and pleasant land. As long as you're getting your end of the deal, anyway.

But crossing the Clyde and the Tyne, big rivers once teeming with industry that had provided jobs for generations, Frankie couldn't help but notice that they were now home to shopping malls and tree-lined walkways and plush chrome-filled bars that served tapas all hours of the day and night and charged three pounds fifty for a pint. Grilled chorizo sausage on call, that's progress for you.

Glasgow, Newcastle, Durham, York, Peterborough. Stone walls become hedgerows become stone walls become hedgerows again. The world is a brilliant acrylic paint splash of green. The bushes and trees by the sides of the track are full and effusive, bursting to break free of their railway cutting existence and head into the open fields and shake their trunks and rattle their branches and watch their leaves float away in the big blue summer sky.

Frankie looks at Jimmy, takes him in, with his head slumped back and his mouth open wide, asleep and snoring, his nose sucking up the air. The air is sucked up his nose like a Hoover draws the dust from a carpet. That's what two pints of vodka and orange will do to you. And the state of him last night. Parafuckinlytic. Frankie had had to drag him out of the bath this morning so he could get ready for the trip. But Blackie wasn't keen to relinquish the cosy warmth of his master, and growled and snapped like some bugger was trying to steal his bone. In the end, Frankie had had to turn on the shower full blast which got them both moving quick smart. Sobered them up as well. As for Eileen, she was strolling around the house, smiling to herself and whispering 'fares please' any time Frankie came within range. It's amazing they managed to get out the house in time to catch the London train. Especially when Jimmy insisted on having a big fry-up before he would go anywhere. He said he needed it to soak up the alcohol which was still coursing through his body like a stretch of white-water rapids.

Soon they'll be there. Paddington Station, then into the city for a bit of a gander and a drink, then onto the Heathrow Express for the big flight to Saigon. Up, up and away. Frankie pulls out the book he's been reading from his bag. *Broken Stairs*. The compelling tale of one woman's dark inner life and her torturous journey to self-discovery and fulfilment. Written by a twentysix- year-old student of mixed race at Harvard. 'A startling accomplishment', *The Sunday Times* says on the back cover. 'A haunting debut', *The Guardian*. 'Stunningly original', *The Scotsman*. 'A brilliant new voice', *The Independent*. 'A load of shite', Francis A. Canyon. He should have known when it said the book was full of wry humour—not a laugh in it, in other words. He'd bought it on the back of the effusive endorsements from the cosy club of salivating self-obsessed literary critics on the jacket. Seven pounds and ninety-nine pence down the bog. It was a book full of perfect sentences, like hair with too much spray, where everything is held in place, with not a stray curl or strand, not a whiff of life anywhere. Dead on arrival. Still, the writer's a doll, he thinks, appreciatively inspecting the little photograph on the inside back cover. She definitely looks a treat in that black turtleneck pullover.

Frankie chucks the book back in his bag with a dismissive flick of his wrist and tries to rouse Jimmy, who's singing away to himself in his sleep. "Let's Get It On" by Marvin Gaye.

'You've got no a bad voice when you put your mind to it, Jimmy,' Frankie smiles, still shaking him.

Jimmy yawns and rubs the sleep out of his bloodshot eyes. Smacks the top of his mouth with his tongue. 'What, was I singin' again? Jesus Christ. It wisnae Julio Iglesias wis it?'

'No, Marvin Gaye.'

'Thank fuck for that.'

'Do you often sing in your sleep?'

'Aye, a' the time. Some people sleep walk. Me, I sleep sing. On a good night I can get through most of *Otis Redding's Greatest Hits*.'

'Next time, could you do me something by Sinatra?'

'Aye, nae bother. Before or after he recorded wi' Capitol Records?'

'Post '53, thanks pal, if you don't mind.'

'Aye, goes without sayin'.'

Frankie flicks a few pages of the magazine Jimmy was reading. 'You seemed to be having a very nice dream there. You were getting right into it.'

'Aye, so I wis. I was in this shop, lookin' tae buy a new mattress and the shop assistant was a right cracker, wi' long red hair and big blue eyes, ye know, and a wee bit ae a lisp. Dead sexy. Anyhow, she asks me if I would like her tae demonstrate how good the bed is. So right there and then she starts bouncin' up and down on it. Up and down, up and down. Then she invites me tae sit next tae her and then she gets on top ae me and starts daein it tae me right there, wi' people walkin' by an' a' and testin' the mattress wi' their knuckles an' that, and they were askin' me if it was soft or hard, ye know. And then Stella came in and she sees me, so she comes over and she says "whit's it like?" and I says "whit?" and she says "the mattress", but I couldnae speak, I just grunted and moaned.'

'Did you buy the mattress?'

'Naw, it wis a bit on the soft side. Wi' my back I need somethin' wi' a bit more support, ye know.'

'What happened then?'

'We took the escalator up tae bathroom fittings.'

'Did you get anything?'

'Aye, an ensuite bathroom. If you don't have an ensuite bathroom these days, folks think ye don't have a brain.'

Frankie shakes his head in bewilderment, but taking note that he must tell Eileen about the dream. She'd appreciate it.

'Better gather up your stuff, Jimmy. We're nearly in London.'

'Aye, right ye are.'

'Where did you get this magazine anyway?' Frankie inquires, turning over a few more pages, pausing briefly at a series of instructive photographs on how to get 'fab abs' in only six weeks.

'Found it underneath the seat. It's no a bad yin. There's a good article about how to age gracefully, ye know, keepin' yer body in shape and yer mind active.'

Frankie laughs. 'There's no problem about keeping my mind active son, but the body's a different matter all thegither. I tell you, I used to look pretty good when I woke up in the morning. Now I don't even recognise myself. My face is all puffy and wrinkled. It takes the rest of the day for it to reconfigure itself into the shape it's supposed to be, and then it's time for bed again. There's no such thing as ageing gracefully, not when your teeth fall out and your toenails go purple.'

'Aye, I know what you mean, pal. See my hair, it used to be that thick, ye know. What do they call it in yon shampoo ads on the telly? Luxurious. Fuckin' luxurious, so it wis. It used tae bounce when I walked aboot the place. Now look at it. It's like a patchy fitba' pitch. I've got hair sprouting oot my ears and oot my arse, but can I get it tae grow out my head? No fuckin' way, Jose. I'm tellin' ye, I never thought my body would turn out like this. I'm sure it belongs to somebody else and I've got it by mistake. It's a cruel joke.'

'Aye, I know where you're coming from, Jimmy. But these men's magazines are a load of shite, so they are, with their perfect pecs and gut-busting exercises, and their secrets to sexual staying power and poncy articles about sexuality.'

'What the fuck's sexuality anyhow, eh? Sexuality's for women and poofs. Working cunts like us just have small dicks and backache.'

'I couldn't have put it better myself, Jimmy. You might want to keep this fold-out poster, though, on twelve sexual positions every man should master. It might come in handy some day. Could be just what you and Stella need to get the fire going again.'

'I think she'd be happy wi' wan or two and a cup of tea in bed of a mornin'.'

'I suppose that's what you'd call ageing gracefully, eh?'

'Aye, I suppose so.'

Jimmy turns the pages to an article on how women can really get to know their man, what makes him tick. 'Here, do ye think women can really know us Frankie, what goes on inside our heads an' a' that?'

'I don't think so. They think they know men, but really they only see themselves as reflected through what they think we are. But I suppose they know as much about us as we know about ourselves.'

'Which is bugger all, eh?'

'Got it in one, son.'

BLAB! That's what it said in the magazine. London's coolest bar. The brainchild of two East End brothers who'd been in the club game for fifteen years ('It's in our blood, guv,' they told *The Sunday Times* weekend supplement), it was decked out to look like the kind of place the Kray twins might have owned in the fifties, with small lamp-lit tables and cosy, upholstered booths along the walls. Perky girls dressed as bunny rabbits sold cigarettes and Havana cigars from trays draped around their shoulders. Aspiring actors and actresses had been hired especially to play the parts of the legendary gangsters and molls of the London underworld, giant images of which decorated the walls like centuries-old frescoes in a Florentine chapel. They looked upon the guests with contrived suspicion and mumbled away about jobs, and fit-ups and rumbles. Strictly kosher this, strictly kosher that. Not surprisingly, it had become the meeting place of those who fancied themselves as something other than they were. People who worked in the media. Fashion designers. Public relations consultants. Award-winning newspaper columnists. Film people. People who wore square-toed shoes. The business.

Frankie and Jimmy are suited up and lingering uncertainly outside the bar they are assuming to be BLAB!, although there is nothing to indicate that it is. No neon sign, no discreet brass plaque, no tuxedoed muscle-bound bouncer on the door refusing to catch their eye while fawning servile-like over people he's seen in some eye-glazing sitcom set in the East End.

'Are you sure this is it, Jimmy?' Frankie asks, peering over his pal's shoulder at the entertainment section of the magazine.

'Well, this is the address. BLAB! Every visitor to London should go here at least once in their lifetime. "Wicked", it says here.' Jimmy looks around nervously. 'Let's go to the pub.'

'Away. Come on, it'll be an experience. See how the other half live.'

Three leggy blonde women in groin-length skirts and a tall well-tailored black man swagger and chuckle their way to the charcoal-grey door, all gleaming teeth and expressive dancing fingers.

'Eh, excuse me,' Jimmy says. 'Is this BLAB!?'

One woman answers without breaking her stride or lowering her cigarette from the proximity of her right earhole. 'Yes, darling, of course it is. Of course it is.'

'It's just that there's no sign or anythin'.'

'Signs are passé, darling. They're so vulgar don't you think?'

'Och, I don't know about that. I quite like them masel because then ye know where ye are, is that no right? And if there's nae sign how do ye know if you're in the right place?'

'One just knows, darling. One just knows,' she beams, as she and her friends stride confidently through the door which swings open as if by magic from the inside.

Jimmy nods and Frankie shrugs his shoulders and they saunter in after them. They perch themselves at the bar, a crescent moon of highly polished endangered rainforest hardwood. Hand-blown glass bowls of tropical fruit hang from the ceiling. As people talk and move to the music, they reach up and scoop up a lychee, a guava, or a kiwi fruit and bite into the succulent flesh, moaning with pleasure as the juice spills sensuously down their faces.

'Pint o' heavy, thanks pal,' Jimmy says to the elegantly attired bartender who, with one eye, is carefully assessing himself in the large gilt mirror on the opposite wall. He licks his index finger and lightly smooths down one perfectly-coiffured eyebrow.

'No heavy here, mate. You'll have to go back to Jock-land for that, my son.'

'Right ye are. What have you got then?'

'What haven't we got mate?' the bartender states with a cocky wink of his eye.

'Well, pints o' heavy for a start.'

'Yeah, well, you've got a point there, eh?' he laughs. 'Good one. Well, let me see. We have a very fine selection of cocktails. You can have a Jack the Hat, a Gangster's Moll, a Chicken Soup, a Reggie and Ronnie, a Barbara Windsor, a . . . '

Jimmy interrupts, raising his hand like a traffic policeman at a busy intersection. 'Got anything resembling beer?'

'Yes, sir. We have a wide range of international lagers. Stella Artois, Heineken, Beck's, Holstein, Corona . . . '

'Corona, what's Corona?' Jimmy asks.

'It's from Mexico. A very fine beer, sir. Imbued with the spirit of old Meh-hee-coh,' he grins, displaying two rows of perfectly straight pearly-white ivories.

'Is that right? We'll have two of those then.'

The two dainty bottles of pale liquid are presented with a ritualistic flourish of hand, wrist and elbow manoeuvres.

'Senors. Enjoy!' the bartender grins in a flashy, Mexican kind of way.

'Muchas grassyarse pal,' Jimmy replies as he sidles up next to Frankie and whispers in his ear.

'That prick's stuck a lemon in my beer,' he says, poking at the slice of citrus wedged in the neck of the bottle. 'That must be the way they serve it in Meh-hee-coh,' Frankie laughs.

'Is that right?' Jimmy says, lighting up a cigarette. 'Maybe back hame we should slip wee slices of black puddin' intae bottles of McEwan's Export. Or potato scones. Whit dae ye think?'

'I don't think it'll catch on, Jimmy.'

'Oh aye? Listen, if folk will eat deep-fried Mars bars they'll fuckin' eat anythin'.'

'Well maybe you're right after all. The depths to which the average Scotsman will sink when it comes to food and beverage consumption have yet to be truly plumbed.'

'Aye, and they'll eat and drink any auld shite as well.'

Frankie and Jimmy sip at their beer and decide it's not so bad, even if it does have lumps of fruit in it. They move to a booth away from the dance floor and, just for a laugh, they order a couple of Nancy Boys as well, which turn out to have a certain bleach-like flavour. They observe the goings-on with amused curiosity. A garrulous couple, dressed as if for an evening's ballroom dancing, pour themselves into the booth next to them.

'I don't audition any more,' the man says, running his fingers through his short, forward-combed hair. 'Can't be fucked. Why should I? I've been doing this for fifteen years. Why should I audition for those pricks, who've done what? Fuck all. And all for a few measly grand minus tax. Sixty-three pence in the fucking pound. Why do that when I can go to the States and get half a mill for a few days' work. Why? Answer me that.'

'I don't know why you bother with them at all, darling, really I don't,' his anorexic female companion says, shaking her head sympathetically and blowing perfect smoke rings into the air, her crimson lips pursed like a fish peering out from a bowl. 'You're too good for them. And it's their loss, it really is.'

He leans towards her and caresses her cheek and gazes into her eyes. 'And tell me about you, my sweet. How *are* you?'

'Oh darling, I've got to start eating. I'm losing weight again and it comes straight off my tits.'

'I know the feeling sweetheart. When I was fourteen stone I had an eleven-inch dick. Now I'm down to eleven and a half, it's the size of a cocktail frankfurt.'

'I'm sure we can do something about that, darling,' she smiles conspiratorially. 'Do you want to go to the poetry reading on Saturday night?'

He exhales a thick plume of smoke and picks out some stray tobacco from between his teeth. 'I don't think so, sweets. I'm not convinced by poetry.'

'What do you mean?'

'I don't think it's relevant any more.'

'What? Do you mean it's passé?'

'Yes, exactly. It's a redundant form of communication for the twenty-first century. It's been overtaken by cyberspace and it needs to reinvent itself.'

'Like with sound effects and accompanying three-dimensional visual images, that sort thing?' she says.

'Exactly. Poetry for the new millennium. E-poetry. Poetry with attitude.'

'I think you've got something there.'

They kiss passionately with accompanying sound effects, reminiscent of an evening spent in a Soho cinema for men with some time on their hands and raincoats on their laps.

Frankie nods in their direction as they saunter out the door, still joined at the mouth. 'There's some folks you just want to have a quiet word with down a back alley or up a dark close, eh.'

'Aye, and let yer fists dae the talkin'. Speakin' of which, Frankie, son, have you got anythin' that might resemble a plan for when we get tae Vietnam, an' that?'

Frankie drains his third Corona, smacks his lips and places the empty bottle precisely in the middle of the coaster. 'Aye, I definitely want to try some of the soft-shelled crab they have there.'

'That's no what I meant.'

'I know. There's nothing more that I would like to have at this particular moment in time than a plan. A carefully thought out, meticulous, crafty plan that takes into account all possible outcomes and has various contingency arrangements should we encounter the unexpected. A Robert the Bruce of a plan. A Jock Stein of a plan, a fuckin' Sean Connery of a plan. But all I've got is a St Mungo of a plan.'

'And what does that mean?'

'What that means, Jimmy boy, is that we have to get down on our knees and pray that when we get there we know what the fuck we are doing.'

'Right,' Jimmy says, more uncertain than ever. 'We could always go hame now, ye know. Catch the last train back tae Glasgow. Tell the women Vietnam's shut for the foreseeable future. Sounds like that might be a good idea, if ye ask me.'

They stare at each other in silence. Frankie looks at his watch and nods at the door. 'We'd better skedaddle or we'll miss the plane.'

'Christ is that the time? Right, we'd better vamoose, eh. I'll just get a kerry oot though, you know for the journey. Just tae see us right till we get tae Saigon.'

Jimmy turns to face the bar and yells to the barman, who is vigorously polishing his nails with a bar towel. 'Hey, muchacha, gies twelve bottles of yon Mexican beer, eh. And haud the fuckin' lemon.'

When Mai arrives home from visiting her elderly aunt in Nha Trang she doesn't expect to find Danny strapped to a chair in the apartment above their bar with his face bruised and swollen and with blood all over his shirt collar. It looks like it will stain, she notes. At first, she thinks she is seeing things. After all, it has been a ten-hour bus ride from the central coast and she is exhausted. The bus kept breaking down and the driver seemed to spend hours underneath it banging and cursing while the disgruntled passengers slept or sat by the side of the road, smoking cigarettes and talking in the darkness. She'd smoked a couple herself, shocking the Vietnamese men. But as Danny always says, bugger them.

The sight of Danny in the chair is so unexpected and out of context that it is almost beyond comprehension. When she's gathered her wits about her she realises it is definitely him, asleep or unconscious, his head drooped on his chest and his hands tied with thick rope behind his back. For a moment she suspects he may have been indulging in some weird sexual game with one of the women who hang out in their bar, trying to tempt any westerner with fifty dollars and a hard-on into a taxi and off to the nearest hotel for an hour's worth of beer-soaked sex. But she knows better. Danny has a few vices but playing around with other women isn't one of them. As he well knows, she'd kill him. She'd kill him twice. In fact, he doesn't really like the working girls coming to the bar at all, but what can he do? The men would just go somewhere else if they couldn't get what they wanted within easy fondling range.

Despite her confusion, she just calmly proceeds to try and untie the rope around his wrists and arms. By the time she works the rope loose, Danny is beginning to wake up. He moans and twists his neck around as if trying to free himself from a bad dream. He slowly raises his head from his chest and smiles at her, realising he isn't dead after all and that the beautiful woman looking anxiously at him and caressing his cheek is his wife.

'Hello, love. How was the trip? That mad auntie of yours still sending you out to catch frogs for dinner?'

'Daniel, for God's sake. What happened? Who did this to you?' Mai pleads, on the verge of tears. 'Look at your face and your shirt,' she says, looking more closely at his puffed-up and discoloured right eye.

'A guy asked for Scotch and Dry and I gave him Scotch and Coke. He seemed to take exception to that.'

'Danny, please, no jokes. What's going on?'

Mai doesn't really need to ask. She already knows but just wants her suspicions confirmed or her fears allayed. Maybe, just maybe, it is something else. Maybe it is all a mistake. But then, it isn't as if she didn't know this was coming. She was in the bar with Danny a few weeks ago when the police threatened him that if he didn't start paying them a weekly cut of the takings again they couldn't promise that his bar would remain open or that his personal safety could be guaranteed. Saigon can be dangerous in the early hours of the morning and anything can happen, they sneered. He could wake up one morning and find his legs missing. Danny had tried to explain that business was down. Many of the foreign companies had pulled out because of the economic crisis and their staff, his customers, had gone with them. So he was having a bit of an economic crisis of his own and couldn't really afford what the thugs were asking for. What would be the point if he had to close down, he asked them. Ten per cent of nothing is nothing. They might as well get ten per cent of something. Surely they could see that?

But they couldn't, or didn't want to. Big Minh's was still making its weekly donation to the Police Welfare Fund, they said. So were the Mekong Bar, the Rolling Thunder and the Five O'clock Follies. Danny tried to point out that these were much bigger operations with a different clientele. Big Minh's was five times the size of his place and was basically just an oversized knocking shop with ear-splitting music. They were making money hand over tit so it was no wonder they could still afford to slip a few hundred dollars every month to the forces of law and order. Sex pays, no doubt about that. But the police were not what you would call sympathetic. They just shrugged and commented on what a pretty face Mai had and that it would be a shame if it wasn't pretty any more. Mai felt faint as she watched the two off-duty policemen wave and smile as they breezed out the door.

Mai hated the police. She shook inside whenever she thought of them. So much had changed since the old days and so much had stayed the same. The police were on the take then and they are on the take now. Corruption was killing this country and it made her mad. The same old people were making the money, the party officials and their families, the People's Committees, the lucky Vietnamese managers of State-owned companies. And of course, the cops. Even the traffic police were doing well, with their pristine cream-coloured uniforms and flashy motorcycles, pulling over whoever they felt like, whenever they wanted, for some trumped-up traffic infringement which would evaporate as quickly as it was fabricated when the appropriate amount of cash was sitting snugly in their well-lined pockets.

Some people in the country were trying to live on a dollar a day or a dollar a week, and in Saigon whole families were sleeping on the pavement or under bus shelters in the heat and the rain. Meanwhile, these bastards were living it up in their nice houses in District 3 and going to the beach to drink beer and stuff their faces with shrimp and crab. There was no doubt about it, most people were better off now, but not as better off as they should be. Except for a few, of course. Like those fat policemen. They got plenty to eat that's for sure, and not just soup either.

Mai helps Danny up from the hard wooden chair and across to the soft couch by the doors to the balcony, which she opens to let out the unsavoury smell of sweat and cigarette smoke. Why do these men always have a cigarette hanging from their mouths at all hours of the day and night?

'Was it the police?' she asks, propping a pillow behind his head.

'No, not this time. It was the boys from District 4,' Danny says, leaning back and tentatively touching his swollen eye.

Mai stops making Danny comfortable and looks straight at him. 'What do you mean, the boys from District 4? What boys?'

'The boys I owe money to.'

'*They* want money from you as well?'

Mai sighs and sits down next to him on the couch. 'You've been gambling again, haven't you?'

'Christ, this eye's killing me. I could do with a nice piece of steak to drape over it. Shame I'm no working at the meatworks any more, eh. I could get a slice of porterhouse from the boning room. No charge. Do you know what that would cost here?'

'More than your life's worth if you don't tell me what's going on. Please, Daniel.'

Danny takes Mai's hand and strokes it with his thumb. 'I'm sorry, love. I have been placing a few bets, aye.'

'Oh, Daniel,' she says, leaping up from the couch. 'You promised me you had left all that behind you. You're so hopeless. I would strangle you if someone hadn't beaten me to it.'

'Look, I just thought I could win some money to help get us out of this mess with the police. Pay them off, like.'

'What have you been betting on?'

'Cockfights.'

'I'm assuming you lost.'

'Aye, well, it's hard to pick the form of a chicken, you know. All the ones I seemed to bet on were only good for soup.'

Mai walks slowly over to the balcony, her arms folded across her chest. 'How much did you lose? How much do you owe those people?'

'Twenty thousand dollars.'

'My God, Daniel. Twenty thousand dollars. How could you lose so much money on cockfights?'

'I don't know. You can't exactly back them for a place. They either win or they're dead. There's nothing in between. When these birds win by a short half head it's because they've bitten it off and eaten it. Some of that's interest though. Aye, and they want a slice of the bar takings as well.'

District 4. Mai knew of it, of course, but had never been there herself. Even though it was just a mile or so away across the Ben Nghe Canal, she'd never had any reason to go there. If she stood on the roof of her house she could just make out the cranes at the port, outlined against the evening sky like giant shadow puppets. She'd heard the stories about the gang fights over territory and protection money. The people who lived there controlled much of the heroin and prostitution trades, and what they euphemistically called 'security' at the discos, bars and restaurants all over town. If you paid up you stayed open for business, if you didn't then somebody would close you down by whatever means they thought necessary, even if it meant dropping you in the river with your throat slit and gaping.

But it wasn't just the gangs and standover merchants who called District 4 their home. Some of the city's poorest people eked out a miserable existence in their tumbledown wooden shanties along the canal, a black and rubbish-filled waterway that they used as their bathtub, water supply and toilet. You could see them in the blue darkness of the early morning, the cyclo drivers and lottery ticket sellers and food stall vendors, already on the streets, hawking their wares, cajoling potential customers, beginning another long and back-breaking day for little return.

District 4 was convenient for them all, the place to be. Just a bridge away from District 1 where the tourists were ripe for ripping off or where they could collect their hard earned graft. It was a good place to hide from people who may not have your best interests at heart or from the authorities who wanted to send you back to the countryside where they thought you belonged. No registration papers, no life in the big city. And it was close to the docks where all sorts of wondrous booty from around the world could be lifted with ease if the policeman or the guard on duty was given his due.

Mai had read in the weekly police newspaper that much of the crime in Saigon had some connection with District 4. The word was that the men who stabbed those two policemen thirty times outside the Harbour View Hotel were from the back alleys by the river. And they did it for fifty dollars, the going price for an assassination. The cost of one night with a middle-ranking whore.

A friend had told her that ten Chinese who had been lured to Vietnam on the promise they would be taken to a western country and given work, had been chained up and tortured in District 4 and told that if their famlies back in China didn't cough up for their release they'd be posted back to their home country in bite-sized bits.

Danny gets up from the settee and goes off to the bathroom to soak his aching face and get some sticking plaster for the cut below his chin. Mai takes the opportunity to open the secret drawer in the old wooden cabinet where she keeps their meagre savings out of harm's way and slowly counts out the onehundred- dollar notes. But before she's finished she knows that whatever she has, it is not going to be enough.

'These people. When did they say they'd be back?' she asks, placing the money back in the drawer and quietly locking it.

'Next week,' Danny says wearily, his exhaustion now over-whelming him. 'The police and those bastards from south of the river, they both said they'd be paying us a visit next week. They said they were looking forward to it. I can't say the same for myself. I hate it when people drop in unannounced. I pre-fer it if they ring first, don't you?'

'What are we going to do?'

'That's the twenty thousand dollar question, love, and I can't say I have the answer. How does South America sound to you?'

'Daniel. Please. Did you telephone Francis and talk to him about all this, like I suggested?'

'Aye, I did.'

'And?'

'He said he'd catch the first bus over.'

'Danny, you know very well that . . . '

Danny laughs. 'I know darlin'. I'm just joking. He's coming by aeroplane.'

'That's good,' Mai says, relieved.

'Aye, all the the trains were full.'

They feel as if they have walked into a brick wall. The heat invades their being and attacks from all directions. It crushes their heads and shoves its long sweaty tentacles down their throats and fills their lungs with what feels like the devil's scorching breath. It prises open their pores and unleashes torrents of moisture that gush onto their skin, soaking their clothes and plastering their hair to their scalps. It engulfs them in a sauna of a mouth and swallows their every gasp, refusing to release them from its merciless grip as it pushes and shoves and wrings them into submission.

After the dour, grey-infused skies of Glasgow and London, the scalding sun stings their eyes and they squint into it, instinctively and defensively lowering their heads in a vain attempt to see what lies ahead of them. Through the glare they can just make out a seething silhouette of people, pushing against a long metal barrier just outside the arrivals terminal, yelling excitedly, grinning and pointing, holding out extended fingers to loved ones returning home from their travels. They flick their fans and wave their hands as if to ward off the thick tongue-shrivelling air. Some are clad in their Sunday best, others stay cool in their silk pyjamas, their conical straw hats outlined like pyramids in the first light of the desert day.

It feels to Frankie and Jimmy that at any moment the world will collapse on top of them and they will be lost in a choking crush of heat and sweat and bodies heavy with excitement and anticipation. The noise batters their ears, tunnelling into their skulls and beating out strange hypnotic rhythms that echo around their heads like distant drums in a strange dark jungle. Planes take off and land. Taxis come and go. Luggage scrapes on concrete. Strange faces await them as they drift along the corridor created by the barrier, catching their eye, smiling, beckoning, holding others at bay to give them room to move, to manoeuvre their way into the car park. How considerate, Frank thinks. People push and pull at him. Let me help you. Sir, this way. You want taxi? Where you go? Where you from? How much? It's up to you. Maybe fifteen dollars. City very far. I do cheap for you. No problem. Frankie feels lost, a fever-stricken man stumbling directionless in a predator-filled swamp. The taxi drivers surround him and Jimmy like would-be assassins. Crocodiles in the waterhole. At any moment they will seize their opportunity and strike the two men down and relieve them of their luggage and their lives. He's certain of it. Any minute now and it will all be over. Jimmy sips on his bottle of Corona as if it could be his last as he and stops and sings 'South of the border, down Mexico way' to a smiling elderly woman, whose face collapses into one large walnut of an enveloping wrinkle, broken only by a crenellated row of stumpy teeth stained a deep ochre by a lifetime of chewing betel nut.

'Use more toothpaste, darlin', more toothpaste,' Jimmy says, making a circular motion with an imaginary brush.

A hand reaches out and grabs Frankie's suitcase and beckons to Jimmy to follow and they do without question, not quite knowing why, to a battered Citroen with the words 'Blue Moon' painted on the side doors.

Jimmy collapses into the back seat while the small Vietnamese stranger loads their cases into the boot of the car. Frankie leans back against the car door and takes in the mayhem before him. 'It's a bit like Blackpool in the fair fortnight, eh?' he says, wiping the sweat from his forehead with a sodden hankie.

'Aye, except for the fact the sun's shinin',' Jimmy replies, squinting at Frankie from inside the car.

Frankie also gets into the back seat of the car, his sweat-soaked shirt clinging to his back like wet leaves to the ground.

Jimmy yawns, leans back and stretches his arms behind him.

'That last Corona's done my head in. All I need is one ae yon big sombreros and I'd be away havin' a wee siesta.'

'You've quite taken a shine to that Mexican beer, haven't you?'

'Si, senor.'

'OK. We go,' says the small man in the driver's seat, as he turns the key in the ignition and the car moves slowly forward towards the exit.

Jimmy turns towards Frankie, and pointing at the driver, shrugs his shoulders. 'Aw, sorry Jimmy, this is Benny Le. He works for Danny at the bar.'

'Pleased to meet you, Benny. How's it goin', all right?'

'Very good, Mr Jimmy. We go twenty minutes and can be in the bar.

'Where is Danny anyhow? I thought he might have come out to the airport to meet us, like,' Frankie asks.

'Mr Danny, he go out to find Madam Mai's dog. Somebody, he steal the dog and want money to give him back,' Benny says, both eyes on Frankie in the rear-view mirror and none on the road. A young woman on a motorbike brakes sharply to avoid a collision and her yellow cotton hat flies through the open window of the car.

Frankie and Jimmy look at each other in disbelief. They've been in Vietnam for less than an hour and already somebody's nicked the sister-in-law's pet and they've managed to abscond with a complete stranger's head gear.

'So you're telling me some bastard's kidnapped Danny's wife's dug and wants a ransom to gie it back?' Jimmy asks.

'Yes. Is very terrible, mate. Madame Mai, she very sad.'

'Fucksake.'

'So how will Danny get the dog back?' Frankie inquires.

Benny swerves to avoid a man on a bicycle who has at least fifty upside-down chickens and a handful of quacking white ducks strapped on his bike.

'Mr Danny, he go to dog market and talk to the man he bought the dog from in the first place. Him probably steal the dog back and now want more money. It happened same before.'

'What you mean this isn't the first time?'

'No, it happen two time already. Doggy kidnapping very big business in Vietnam. Many people like have little dog for pet. For sure.'

'I'd like to see the cunts kidnap Blackie, eh?' Jimmy laughs.

'Aye, she'd either eat them or fuck them to death. They'd pay you to take her back.'

'Aye, that'd be right. She's a dug and a half, that yin. Here, they won't eat the dug, will they, these kidnappers? I hear people eat dugs in Vietnam,' Jimmy says, slightly disturbed at the prospect.

'No, no. No worries, mate. They different kind of dog. Bred special for eating. Not fluffy little white dog, mate.' Benny laughs.

'Have you eaten dog, Benny?' Frankie inquires, wondering what sort of sauce it would take best. Bearnaise? Madeira? In its own juices, perhaps?'

'Yes, mate. I eat the dog. Very good.'

'I suppose it tastes like chicken,' Frankie says.

'No, it taste like dog.'

'I wonder what your Blackie would taste like, Jimmy.'

'A dirty big lump ae black puddin' I would think. Wi' HP sauce.'

'And chips.'

'And mushy peas.'

'Sounds pretty good, eh Frankie. I might take a bite oot ae Blackie when I get hame.'

'Aye, well you'd better put her on the leash first, Jimmy. Otherwise she'll be having you for breakfast.'

As they head down Nam Ky Khoi Nghia Street Jimmy nods off, his head lolling back and forth against the side window. Frankie watches this strange new world unfold before him.

In some ways, it reminds him of Glasgow in the old days before the council tore the life out of it by demolishing the tenements and sentencing people to life imprisonment in the new schemes. Not that it looks the same, mind. There are no Victorian sandstone buildings or people in overcoats and balaclavas. But it feels a bit the same. It's full of life and bustle, people going places or just having a natter, and the streets are lined with shops selling everything you could ever possibly want to get your hands on. People live in these streets, like they did in Shettleston when he was a boy. It's not like the schemes now where people just exist, where the life has been sucked out of the place, where the streets are sad and empty. It's a bit like the old Glasgow speeded up, like a record player that's been clicked on from thirty-three to seventy-eight. Look at these people go. And in this heat!

There aren't many cars right enough, but it's as if all the world's motorbikes have come to Saigon for a convention, a dirty great big love fest for 100 cc engines, all droning away like the highest notes of a harmonica. Occasionally, an accelerating tenor screams out of the traffic before disappearing again into the mass up ahead. There doesn't seem to be much of what would traditionally be described as a Highway Code. People drive on the side of the road that suits them, unconcerned about the prospect of a fatal collision with the oncoming traffic. Cyclos give way to motorbikes, which give way to cars, which give way to trucks. The overriding principle appears to be not to stop at any cost, followed by trying to fit as many people onto the one motorbike as possible. Mum, dad, kids, granny, pets, farm animals.

'There don't seem to be many traffic lights here, eh Benny?'

'No, just a few,' Benny laughs, turning to face Frankie. 'People here, they no like traffic light.'

'There's an awful lot of motorbikes in Saigon, eh?'

'For sure. Seven million people and two million motorbikes. Big trouble, mate. Many accident.'

Frankie sits back in his seat and grips the armrest as Benny goes within inches of collecting a cyclo carrying what appears to be several tons of building materials and a barrel of beer.

And the people are wee, like everybody he knew when he was growing up in Chester Street. His pals, his aunts and uncles, the neighbours, everybody was a bit on the short side, except for the polis maybe, and come to think of it that Auntie Annie who was tall and built like a double-decker bus with a home perm. Bad food, bad houses, bad jobs, bad health, no money. Stunts your growth every time. But these people look healthy with their nice tanned skin and shiny black hair, although every bloke seems to have a cigarette dangling from the end of his lips. Not the women though. Funny that.

What will Danny look like after all these years? He was always a good-looking boy, and could talk the leg off a chair. The bookmaking game was right up his alley, no doubt about that. Tailor-made. What'll Danny the man be like after the good life in Australia, with all that free rump steak from his work and swimming at the beach? And it can't be such a bad life here either, him being his own boss and being married to Mai, who looks a right doll if the picture Danny sent over is anything to go by. And he says they have a woman who does the cooking and the washing and cleans the house. How good is that? Lord and Lady Muck, the two of them. Danny said most people have a maid, but. Still, most people or not, it's still a cosy arrangement. The food's good too, apparently. Lots of fresh vegetables and they don't hold back on the chilli. Perfect.

Jimmy stirs. He yawns and stretches his arms out above his head and peers out the window at a woman having a pee on the footpath, her arse bared to the passing traffic. He rubs his eyes and decides he must still be half-asleep.

'You know, Jimmy, I reckon Danny probably has a pretty good life here,' Frankie says.

'Aye, I'm sure he does, except for the fact that some people want to do him in and throw his mutilated body in the river. Some people might think that would affect his quality of life, as they say in *Vogue Living*.'

He's got a point there, Frankie thinks to himself. After all, that's why they're here, to see if they can help sort this problem out. He must have got carried away by the heat, the excitement of being in a new and exotic place, for him to forget that. Funny the way the mind works. Avoid confronting reality, pretend things are all right, have a nap and things might be all right when you wake up.

'OK, we nearly there,' Benny says, pointing to an imposing piece of 1960s architecture set in an expansive garden behind large metal gates. 'Presidential Palace, mate. When communists, they come to Saigon, they drive tank straight though the gates and they capture the place and win the war.'

'There would've been a lot of damage to those gates, Frankie, what wi' a tank crashin' right through them. Big weldin' job tae repair them, eh?'

'Aye, a week's work at least.'

They turn left into Le Duan Street, past the park with its tall acacia trees planted by the French. Along the perimeter, food vendors are selling everything from hot noodle soup and sticky rice to ice cream and bread rolls with sliced pork or pâté. Inside, on the grass, elderly men and women are enthusiastically doing their exercises, jumping up and down, their arms and legs spread wide. They jog on the spot and touch their toes, serious about the business of keeping fit and healthy.

Frankie can't help but notice the women seated by themselves on stone benches around the park, some with their faces masked by handkerchiefs, others smiling encouragingly at passers-by.

'They the hookah,' Benny says. 'Five thousand dong for the hand-job. No worries mate.'

'That's about twenty pence,' Jimmy says, in disbelief.

'Aye, five for a pound. A bargain in any currency,' Frankie says.

'But them girls no bloody good, mate. They cheap whore. Cyclo driver whore,' Benny says.

'How good dae you have to be for that particular service?' Jimmy laughs. 'There's no a lot tae it, if you know whit I mean.'

'But they ugly, mate. Terrible ugly,' Benny replies, narrowly avoiding a potentially fatal collision as a soup cart is pushed across the busy boulevard by its ambling owner who must be blind or fearless or both.

'You seem to speak English with an Australian accent, Benny,' Frankie says.

'Bloody oath mate. Many Aussie, they come to the bar and they teach me speak Aussie. No fuckin' worries. Aussie, Aussie, Aussie, Oi, Oi, Oi.'

'Is that right?'

'Sure. Mr Danny, he can speak very good Aussie also. Fair suck of the sav, mate.'

'Are you from Saigon, Benny?' Frankie inquires, curious about their voluble guide's background.

'No. I'm from the country, from Camau. I'm a country pumpkin, mate,' he says suddenly pointing to the left. 'Look, over there, very big cathedral. Notre Dame. Many Catholics go there.'

Frankie is surprised. 'I thought people here were Buddhists?'

'Not everybody. Many people, they Catholic. The French teach them. What about you? What religion you have?'

'I'm a Celtic supporter, Benny.'

'Aye,' Jimmy laughs. 'He goes to Parkhead Cathedral for ninety minutes every Saturday afternoon.'

Benny laughs with them out of politeness but has no idea what they are talking about.

'We come to the bar now,' he says as they turn left from Dong Khoi Street into Mac Thi Buoi Street. 'Over there.'

As Benny attempts to do a U-turn, scattering cyclo drivers, food vendors, street children and stray dogs in all directions, Frankie takes in the familiar, if older, form of a young man he once knew, bent double, straining to raise a metal grille that protects the double-doored entrance to what he can only assume is the Blue Moon. His hair appears to have kept its same strawberry blond blush, although from this distance it's difficult to tell whether it is flecked with grey or not. The face, the features, are much the same, but chipped and imprinted with life's experiences. His eyes still flash with life and betray his readiness to leap into the unknown, to take a chance on anything that might come his way, a family trait, though the choices may differ. He is stockier perhaps, but a slight Glaswegian frame still underpins these few extra pounds. He hasn't changed that much, Frankie thinks, and the games of football they played out the back together as short-trousered and scuff-kneed boys don't seem that long ago now. It's as if he can taste the chill air of a cold winter's night with their mother's voice piercing the darkness, telling them it's time they were in their beds. Frankie watches him flick back his fringe, sweeping it away from his eyes. He calls to the nearby Vietnamese woman caressing a curvaceous lump of barking fluff and flesh and points to the car.

As he pulls the grille upwards in one long, fluid haul, Danny turns to watch Benny ill-advisedly attempt another doomed Uturn and the shoeshine boys move down the pavement out of harm's way. The sun dazzles his eyes, making it difficult to see into the car, but there's no mistaking his brother in the back seat, languid and self-possessed, taking it all in but giving little away. Quiet warmth or a tactical manoeuvre, it was always hard to tell. But a smile from Frankie was worth a thousand from anyone else. He looks fit. His face is taut, nothing has subsided, the varnish has just aged. No doubt he's still eating more than his fair share of vegetables. He should move to Australia, he'd like it there. Danny watches him sit higher in his seat. His shoulders are still their father's, a bequest from twenty years hacking at the coal face. He sees Frankie lean to the man beside him and point out the window.

The right front wheel of the car is perched on the pavement and the rear is sunk in the deep tropical storm gutter when Benny finally pulls the car to a halt and yanks enthusiastically at the handbrake. Frankie squeezes out the back door and Danny moves forward from the now open entrance to the Blue Moon.

'Hello Francis. All right?'

'Aye. A bit hot. You?'

'Not bad, mate. Could be better.'

'I see you got the dog back then?'

'Aye. At a price, but. The little bugger is costing me a fortune.'

'Well, you got him back, that's the main thing.'

'I suppose so. You look well, Francis.'

'You too.'

'Yeah, maybe. A bit older, you know. How's Eileen? Annie and Fiona?'

'They're good. They send their love and say a wee letter now and again wouldn't go astray. They want to know if you've got a tan.'

Danny laughs and holds out his hand and Frankie shakes it firm and long.

'Thanks for coming,' Danny says. 'It's good to see you. It's been a while, eh?'

'Aye, it's been a while, right enough.'

'You'd better come in,' Danny says nodding in the direction of the bar. 'It's hot as buggery the day.'

'I think some more introductions would be nice,' Mai says, moving towards the two brothers, clutching the prodigal pooch.

'Aw, Jesus. I'm sorry Mai. I don't know what I was thinking. Forgive me. Frankie, this is my wife Mai and Mai this is my brother Francis.'

'Pleased to meet you,' they both say at the same time.

'I have heard many good things about you,' Mai says.

'I wouldn't believe a word of it if I were you,' Jimmy exclaims, leaning against the side of the car. 'He's a right prick, I can tell you that for nuthin'.'

Frankie laughs. 'This is my pal Jimmy. Jimmy Stewart. Bus driver extraordinaire and collector of discarded reading material.'

'And connoisseur of the world's finest ales,' Jimmy adds, pointing towards the bar. 'Speaking of which, it's like an oven oot here. Any chance of something cool and refreshing?'

'I think I could manage that,' Danny laughs.

'You don't have any of yon Mexican beer, do ye?'

'Corona? Aye. A few cases, I think.'

'Good man,' Danny says rubbing his palms together.

'Do you like it with a slice of lemon?'

'No senor. Cold and wet is good enough for me.'

The Blue Moon is cool and dark inside and bathed in a shuttered half-light, the air dancing with a confetti of illuminated dust particles. It smells of the night before, of alcohol and cigarette smoke, of laughter and animated voices, and the table where they sit is still sticky to the touch. It is not a big space, but it has atmosphere and you can tell that at night it would be a good place to be. The bar dominates one corner of the room, a crescent of dark wood and mirror-backed glass shelves groaning with bottles of all shapes, sizes and colours, like an old-fashioned chemist's shop. Frankie counts at least half a dozen different kinds of malt whisky and is pleased to see there is Heineken and Tiger Beer on tap, beers he's only ever had from a bottle. High in the corners above the entrance, two televisions peer down like giant eyes on a three-quarter-size pool table, a darts board and a mixture of tables and chairs and stools of different shapes and dimensions. Cricket, Australian Rules football and rugby memorabilia hang from the walls along with a variety of musical instruments that have seen better days. Two saloon-style doors afford a view of the heads and feet of passersby.

Jimmy is gulping down his bacon and eggs and toast, rustled up in the bar's kitchen with the help of Benny, to whom Jimmy has given a quick lesson in the art of cooking a good Scottish fry-up. He's proved to be a good student, despite his tuition being hampered by a lack of black pudding, potato scones, baked beans and a decent lump of lard.

Benny also works at night, Frankie is told, playing pool and darts with customers, fetching drinks, joking around and generally making it an enjoyable night out for them, more enjoyable hopefully than an evening spent in any of the other bars in downtown Saigon. A Benny of all trades, Danny calls him.

Frankie, Danny and Mai sip iced lemon juice, catching up on developments in their lives, recent and past, the stories they had never shared, their joys and disappointments, their successes and failures, their fears and dreams. The stuff that made them what they are. Frankie cannot help but notice how much Mai and his brother are wrapped up in each other, the looks they share when their eyes meet, despite whatever difficulties Danny's sporadic but intense bouts of gambling might have caused them. He sees how their eyes linger, how they know there is no better place to be than with each other. Devoted is the word that immediately comes to mind. He can feel it. It's definite, a statement of fact, rather than a possibility, and he's glad. When you love someone, and they love you back, you can rescue some meaning out of what could be a meaningless journey, a one-way ticket to nowhere in particular. A horrible waste of time. He wonders how Eileen is getting on without him.

'So I came home from my auntie's house in Nha Trang and there was my Daniel tied to a chair, with blood on his face and his eye all black. I was very scared for him and very angry with these stupid men,' Mai says, stroking Danny's cheek.

'And I couldn't get the blood out of my shirt. It's ruined. Pure cotton it was too.'

'Aye, a man should only wear nylon when he's about to get the shite beaten out of him,' Frankie says in mock seriousness. They all laugh.

Danny goes to the bar to make some more iced lemon. Jimmy is asleep, slumped across the table, his head cradled in his arms. Mai takes Frankie's hand in both of hers and strokes it with one long and delicate finger. 'I am so glad that you could come here to Vietnam. Not just for this business we are having with these crazy men, but because of Daniel. He needed to see you, to talk with you. He feels he let you down when he had that trouble in Scotland, with his job you know, and then when he ran away to Australia. He feels bad about this. But he was just a young man and young men do stupid things. And since the birth of our son, he has come to realise how important his family is to him.'

Frankie leans back in his chair and spreads his arms, amazed. 'Your son? What do you mean your son? Danny didn't say anything on the phone the other week. You'd think you'd mention something like that.'

'Yes, you would. But I think he wanted to keep it as a surprise for you. Would you like to meet him?'

'Defin-*ately.*'

Mai disappears upstairs and returns with a baby boy, his arms encircling his mother's neck and his head buried shyly in her bosom. Mai coaxes him to look up, talking softly in his ear, kissing skin like silk, the colour of milky tea. He wriggles and snuffles and slowly twists his head to reveal eyes as dark and luminous as the sea at night and a thicket of hair the colour of hay gathered in the field. His features are a perfect blend of those of his parents. The first Scottish-Vietnamese wean in the family.

'Hello, my wee darlin',' Frankie coos, gently tickling his chin with one flickering finger. 'Are ye all right?'

'Robert, this is your uncle Francis, from Scotland,' Mai purrs, drawing her son closer to her face, savouring that distinctive baby smell, an intoxicating perfume of milk from the breast, soft blankets and the sweet honey breath that whispers from his mouth like a gentle summer breeze.

'Robert. That's a good Scottish name, eh sweetheart. You're a wee cracker,' Frankie says, taking his nephew in his arms.

'How old is he?'

'Eleven months.'

'Hey Danny, you've done well here son. He's a wee champion,' Frankie says to his brother, who is still at the bar, stirring some sugar and ice into the lemon drinks.

'Aye, I know. So is his mother.'

Jimmy yawns, reminding Frankie of an old hippo emerging from ten minutes underwater, and stretches his arms skywards before ambling over to the three adults gathered around a small bundle of something that looks to him suspiciously like a child. 'Jesus Frankie, it looks at lot like you. That was quick work pal. You've only been in town a few hours and already you've gone forth and multiplied.'

'He looks a lot like me, dunderhead, because he belongs to Danny, who you might remember, is my brother and as such we do share a certain family resemblance.'

'Oh aye. Mind, he's lovely though, eh. Here, geez a wee haud.'

Frankie carefully passes Robert to Jimmy, who lifts him up high, whereby an enormous raspberry reverberates from his puckered and plumped-up mouth on to the baby's naked tummy. Jimmy shakes his head from side to side while conversing with the baby's belly button. 'Wubba, wubba, wubba, wubba, wubba wump!' Robert looks shocked, his eyes somehow larger. 'Doodly, doodly, doodly, doodly, doo!' Robert cranes his neck, desperately searching for his mother, who smiles reassuringly at him. Robert decides to smile too, then giggle, then wriggle madly like a ticklish worm.

'You certainly have a way with the weans, Jimmy,' Danny says. 'No doubt about that.'

'Aye well, as my granny always said, if you see anything under one foot tall and wearing baby clothes, tickle it.'

'A sound, if not enlightened approach to child care, Jimmy,' Frankie laughs.

'Well, it seems to work,' Mai says. 'I will have to do this myself. Jimmy can give me lessons.'

'Aye. Nae bother, hen. You'll pick it up in nae time.'

'Hey, wait a minute,' Danny says. 'I'm no having a man I hardly know burying his mouth in my wife's stomach, thanks very much.'

'Oh Daniel, we will practise on Robert, not me,' Mai laughs, giving her husband a playful shove.

'I know, darlin'. I'm just kidding you on.'

'Eh, this wean needs attention in the nether regions,' Jimmy announces, suddenly conscious of a familiar odour in the air, a forewarning of things to come.

'Here, give him to me,' Mai says.

'Naw, it's all right. Just geez a nappy and I'll fix him up. Nae problem.'

'Vietnamese babies don't wear nappies,' Mai says.

Jimmy is dumbfounded. 'So what happens when, he, ye know, has a wee accident?'

'Well, we try to take evasive action by putting them on a potty every half an hour or so, but if we don't get there in time the maid cleans it up,' Danny says, smiling.

'Is that right? We used to dae that when Blackie was a pup. Then we'd gie him a skelp on the arse so he'd know better than tae pee on the carpet.'

'We don't go quite that far,' Mai says, looking concerned.

'Naw, I suppose you don't. I'll take him anyhow and super-vise the forthcoming event.'

'Are you sure?' Mai says.

'Aye, nae bother.'

'Jimmy's got four weans of his own,' Frankie says. 'He's wiped more bums than he's had pints of lager.'

Jimmy looks at his friend square in the eye and raises his eyebrows like a man about to confess all to the parish priest.

'Well, almost as many,' Frankie coughs.

Jimmy and Mai head upstairs to attend to the baby, leaving Frankie and his brother alone in the bar as the hot morning sun pushes hard through the windows and the ancient copper fan overhead splutters into life with one tug on a rope thick with the grease from a century of sweaty palms.

'So,' Danny says, expectantly.

'So,' Frankie replies, turning his gaze to the busy street out-side.

'What would you like to do?' Danny inquires. 'I could fill you in on what's going on or you could have a bit of a lie down. You must be knackered after the trip from Glasgow. It's a bloody long way.'

'Look, if you don't mind, I might go for a walk, stretch my legs, get some fresh air. You know, clear the head.'

'Aye, fine. Tell you what. Why don't I meet you in an hour or so at the Café Givral and we can have a cup of coffee and a bit of a talk.'

Danny rustles through a drawer behind the bar and pulls out a map of the city which he spreads out. He circles various points of interest while explaining to Frankie the whereabouts of places he might like to go and how to get to the Givral.

'Now off you go and don't talk to any strangers, OK,' Danny laughs.

Not wishing to look like an obvious tourist, Frankie folds the map and slips it into his pocket, gives the bar doors a push and steps almost confidently out into the street. He stops for a moment and squints into the sun. Left out the door, straight ahead, turn right at Dong Khoi and left into Le Loi and that'll get you to the Ben Thanh Market, Danny told him. Go past the Rex Hotel. And don't stop at the Rex, it'll cost you a fortune for a cup of tea.

'The Rex is just for tourists.'

'But I am a tourist.'

'Aye, well. Don't go in there anyhow.'

Frankie edges and swerves and nudges his way past the community of food vendors, and shoeshine boys, people sitting by child-sized tables sipping tea and coffee or eating soup with chicken feet in it, shop owners sitting or dozing on chairs by their premises, smiling and beckoning him to come and have a look inside. This place, it's so *alive*. Everybody's doing, buying, selling, making or eating something. The place just *goes*.

The late morning heat is intense and before long his shirt is soaked with sweat. He finds he is forced to walk mostly on the road because the pavement appears to be reserved for commerce, conversation and for parking motorbikes. But he doesn't mind as he can get a better view of the upper storeys of the old French buildings with their shuttered windows and peeling stucco walls. You can say what you like about the French, and there is much to say, Frankie reflects, but the bastards certainly knew how to build a handsome city. Trees, parks, boulevards and elegant architecture all over the place. They certainly leave their mark wherever they go. But then, if they're not feeding their colonial subjugates coffee and croissants they're shooting them, locking them up or forcing them to slave away on rubber plantations. Danny says the place is full of French tourists now, returning to reassert their cultural superiority.

Frankie turns right at Dong Khoi and strolls up past the Grand Hotel. It says on his annotated map that Graham Greene used to frequent this street when it was known as Rue Catinat. Wrote a book here. *The Quiet American*. Not many of them around these days, unless they are six feet under, and even then you can't be sure they're not all blethering away to each other about fried chicken, high taxes and how the spirit of the Lord is still alive within them.

'You!'

Frankie turns to see a cyclo driver across the street, his brown legs heavily muscled with sinews like ship's ropes, waving and bearing a smile suggesting many years of intimate acquaintance. Frankie watches him turn his shiny carriage and pedal to his side of the road.

'You. You remember me? I talk with you yesterday.'

'I don't think so, pal,' Frankie says, surprised.

'No shooah, I talk with you.'

'Is that right? That might have been difficult as I was in London yesterday,' Frankie replies, still walking. 'And I don't remember seeing you or talking to you on your mobile phone.'

'Shooah?' the driver says, his face a picture of puzzlement.

'Aye, I'm sure.'

'How long you been Vietnam?' the driver says, nonplussed and still smiling.

'Three hours.'

'Ah. Very good. My friend, you want massage?'

'No thanks. I'm just out for a walk.'

'Make you very happy.'

'I'm pretty happy already, thanks very much.'

'Twenty dollar. Number one massage. Girl very prehtee. No problem.'

'I'm OK at the moment, thanks pal,' Frankie says, his smile becoming more of a strain than a pleasure.

'Where you go? One dollar we go round Saigon. One hour.'

'I'm just walking.'

'Where you go?'

'To the Ben Thanh Market.'

'Ah, I know. I take you there. We go round.'

'I want to walk, thanks son.'

'The walk no good Saigon. Very hot. You get very tired. What you buy?'

'Fruit.'

'What you want? How much you pay? I buy for you. Dragon fruit. Banana. Mango. Potato.'

'Potato's not a fruit.'

'What?' the cyclo driver says, looking perplexed.

'Doesn't matter.'

'Where you from? England? America?'

'Scotland.'

'Scot-land?'

'Aye, it's near England.'

'Ah England. Manchester United. David Beckham. Very good.'

Frankie walks on in silence, the cyclo driver still trailing behind him like a small boy following his dismissive older brother.

'Where you go now? I take you pagoda. One hour. We go round.'

'As I said before, no thanks. I'll see you later, all right.' He stops abruptly and turns to the surprised driver, poking him in the chest with his rolled-up map. 'One, you're driving the wrong way up a one-way street and that's dangerous. There could be weans about. Two, I don't want to go anywhere with you and I don't want any fuckin' massage. Three, I know you're just trying to make a living, but be nice and go away or I'm going to have to do something to you that you won't enjoy. Do you understand me?'

Frankie strolls on, trying to remain calm. It's always best to be polite until no other course presents itself. As he nears the corner of Le Loi Street, he hears a familiar voice yelling from some distance behind him.

'You! You want massage? Massage very good. Boom boom, number one!'

Frankie looks back at the cyclo driver who is smiling and waving at him and optimistically gesturing towards the vacant seat of his two-wheeled chariot.

Frankie laughs and walks on, shaking his head in wonder and admiration. These people, they've certainly got balls. He can't get over the way everyone smiles at him, how they smile at each other. They're always laughing, holding hands, touching each other on the shoulder, being friendly. They'd probably even talk to you in a lift. And after all they've been through with the French and the Americans, and getting the shite blown out of them by bombs and being fried to a crisp by napalm, and all in their own country too. You've got to give them credit, no doubt about that.

Frankie stops at the corner of Nguyen Hue and Le Loi and checks his location. Opposite is the Rex Hotel, a saccharine art deco cake of a building where, according to his map, foreign journalists were briefed by the American forces during the war at what became known as the Five O'clock Follies.

His attention is caught by a building on the other corner which appears to be some sort of shopping centre. Inside, he finds a three-level bazaar selling the useful and the useless, the genuine and the fake, from tools and toys, clothing and footwear, to sunglasses and hand-embroidered tablecloths, cheap CDs, intricately assembled miniature sixteenth-century Spanish galleons, and a small Silicon Valley of electronic goods. Frankie stops in front of a flashing bank of at least thirty televisions, some of which are tuned to *The Bill*.

'That Matthew. He number one man. He like flirting the ladies,' one of the young shop assistants says, giving Frankie a knowing thumbs up.

But Frankie's mind is elsewhere. Up on another screen, three male lions from the wrong side of the tracks are attempting a takeover of Scarface's pride in the south of the Likulu National Park. The young males are five years old now and are looking to get their leg over on a regular basis and seem to have decided that this particular pride is as good as any. Seeing the bachelors approach, the pride males roar to proclaim ownership of the territory. But the bachelors' challenging responses stop the pride males in their tracks. During takeover bids, male lions often kill each other. Reviewing the situation, the reigning two lions flee because, after all, three against two is no contest and should they stay to defend their territory they would face almost certain death.

'Men. They're all the same, regardless of whether they walk on two legs or four—they're always fighting over women,' Frankie says to no one in particular.

Frankie thinks it wise to check the time, particularly since the talkative cyclo driver has slowed him down, but finds nothing on his left wrist but freckles and hair. Where is his watch? He is sure he was wearing it when he left the Blue Moon. Fuck it, Danny will soon be waiting for him at the Givral. He'd better get a move on. He turns to leave Matthew and 'The Bill' to their old tricks when his passage is blocked by two Vietnamese men in suits, looking not unfriendly but not as if they are planning to invite him out for a cup of tea and a blether either.

'Mr Canyon?' asks the taller one with the wispy moustache. 'Mr Frankie Canyon?'

'Who wants to know?' Frankie says, wondering why it is that facial hair always gives Asians a sinister air.

'Saigon police.'

'I might be. Why?'

'We would like you to please come with us.'

Frankie notices that he is attracting attention and has drawn a crowd. Even the shop assistant has abandoned the contrived action of the 'The Bill' in favour of the real life intrigue unfolding next to him.

'Our chief, Mr Hoanh, he would like to talk with you.'

'About what exactly?'

'That is for him to tell you.'

'Look, I'm a bit tied up at the moment. I'm out for a walk and a wee bit of shoppin', you know. Then I have to meet my brother. So you can see how it is, eh. Busy, busy, busy.'

The policeman emits an impatient sigh. 'If you don't come with us, I'm sorry but we will have to arrest you.'

'On what charges?'

'We can think of something, shooah,' he smiles, exposing a disquieting row of ragged teeth, stained yellow and brown by years of sucking on cheap cigarettes.

Frankie quickly glances around the market, searching for a way out, but he is hemmed in by curious shoppers, beggars, shoeshine boys, cyclo drivers and a vendor trying to sell him a Barbra Streisand CD. 'No thanks darlin', I cannae stand that woman,' he says, distracted.

The CD seller pushes it towards him, presses it against his chest, her eyes wide and smiling. 'No, she very good. Number one. I sell you very cheap, no problem.' She takes a deep breath and starts singing "The Way we Were", spreading her arms wide and raising her head high as if she is extracting the lyrics from the heavens.

'Aye, that song's so bad it would make anybody weep,' Frankie says, grimacing at the sound of it. 'That Barbra Streisand should restrict herself to singing in the shower. Precious as fuck, so she is. She should enunciate herself to death, that yin, so she should.'

The woman continues, not dissuaded by the withering look of distaste on Frankie's face. She is possessed by Barbra. He feels like he is going to be sick and decides anything is better than this.

'All right, let's go then,' he says, and the taller policeman motions towards the open entrance. 'By the way, how did you know who I am and where to find me?'

He smiles. 'This is a communist country, Mr Canyon. We know everything.'

Frankie nods at the other policeman who is engrossed in 'The Bill'. 'That Matthew's a very naughty boy, eh?'

'No, he very strong man, the ladies they like him good,' he says, nudging Frankie towards the door.

Frankie glances back over his shoulder to the CD seller who, encouraged by the crowd's enthusiastic response and her own sense of being possessed by the very spirit of the diva herself, bellows the final disembowelling verse. Frankie gags, feeling his breakfast rise bitterly to his throat and, with considerable relief, accompanies the canny local constabulary out into the sweltering bedlam of the Saigon streets.

Danny is halfway through what looks like a pound of cream sandwiched between two wafers of flaky pastry when Frankie strolls in the front door of the Givral. The place is busy with tourists and well-to-do Vietnamese and their teenage children, who are beautiful and slim and well dressed with clear middle-class skin that must be impervious to the virulent acneinducing properties of cream and sugar consumed by the bucketload. Frankie can't help but notice how confident they seem, this generation of young Vietnamese who have not known war, only the new-found prosperity of their parents with their high level government jobs, and factories and their import and export licences. They wield their mobile phones as if they are extensions of their own flesh and blood and each flick of their perfect hair is executed in the knowledge that it will settle naturally to the place where it will exhibit their delicate features to the best possible advantage. They know the future of this new Vietnam belongs to them and they are ready to grab whatever part of it they can get.

'Hello,' Danny says, looking up from his corner table by the window and looking slightly anxious. 'Did you get lost?'

'No, I got picked up by the polis,' he replies, pulling up a chair beaming. 'They said they'd been following me since the airport. Somehow they knew I was coming to see you.'

Danny is visibly shocked and quickly surveys the room for any official-looking faces that might have followed his brother. He's been followed before himself.

'Getting picked up by the police here is nothing to laugh about, Francis. Believe me, I know. It was probably the same police who've been putting the heavies on me. What did they want?'

'Well it wasn't, and it was more a case of what I wanted, Daniel. More of a case of what I wanted.'

'I don't understand,' Danny says, confused.

'Well, put it this way, those police bastards who've been giving you a hard time won't be giving you a hard time any more.'

'Oh aye? I don't get it. What did you do, shoot them?'

'No, but something just as effective. You know me, Danny, avoid violence at all costs. A word in somebody's ear can be a powerful weapon,' he says, pointing to his brother's morning coffee. 'That looks good. I think I'll have one myself. Waiter!'

As Frankie eats his cake and sips his drink, he explains to an incredulous Danny how he had come to make the acquaintance of one of Saigon's most senior policemen and how, over a cup of tea, they had discussed Danny's predicament and how, coincidentally, Hoanh was preparing to embark on a major crackdown on corruption within the force. The two policemen who had been harassing your brother, the chief assured him, would be dealt with.

'And what did this Hoanh want?' Danny asks, still suspicious, having been in Vietnam long enough to know that everything comes at a price.

'Well, he does want one thing.'

'I knew it,' Danny says, shaking his head. 'And what might that be.'

'He wants to meet Mai. He thinks he and she are cousins.'

'And that's it?'

'No, there's something else.'

'And what might that be?'

'I don't know, but I could feel it. There's something else going on,' Frankie says. 'I'll figure it out. I just need a bit of thinking time.'

Danny shakes his head in exasperation. 'Look Francis, I'm grateful that you came here, and I know you mean well, but it's not that simple.'

'What do you mean?' Frankie says, disappointed at his brother's response.

Danny sighs. 'What does Mr Hoanh get out of this, eh? If he's police inspector then he only got there because he's as corrupt as everybody else in the force. You don't get to that position if you're not on the take, if you're not playing the game like everybody else. C'mon Francis, didn't the old man tell you to always be wary of the polis?'

'Aye, he did and right enough too. And you're right about Hoanh. He said he's taken plenty of backhanders in his time. But he said things are changing, that there's a big crackdown on—what did he call it?—social evils.'

Danny laughs derisively. 'I've heard that before, the old campaign against prostitution, smuggling, drugs and embezzlement. You don't understand, Francis, the Government guys who came up with this campaign will be skimming off the top for all they're worth. They are masters of lining their own pockets. And the polis, that's how a lot of them make their money. They run women, they sell drugs, they stuff their pockets with other people's hard-earned cash. Why would a guy like Hoanh cut himself out of the action?'

'I don't know, Danny, I've only been here for a few hours for fucksake. All I know is what he told me.'

'And what was that?'

'That he's sick of the whole bloody mess. That it's time for things to change if Vietnam is to get anywhere. He talked about tourism and the global economy and . . .'

'Jesus Christ,' Danny says dismissively. 'The global bloody economy. I'll believe it when I see it. Fucksake.'

The two brothers sit silently, a wall of memories and rivalries between them. Danny stares out the window at the coconut seller on the corner. Frankie fiddles with his spoon, dipping it in and out of his coffee.

'So what is it they put in the bottom of this coffee, anyhow?' Frankie asks, breaking the ice.

'Condensed milk,' Danny replies abruptly.

'Jesus. I thought it tasted funny. Why don't they use real milk?'

'Because they haven't got many fuckin' cows, Frankie, that's why,' Danny says, exasperated, before reluctantly acquiescing to a shared grin.

'OK Danny, how long have you got to pay these bastards from District 4?'

'Three days.'

'Well, maybe we should pay them a visit tomorrow, you know, have a wee talk with them.'

'We can if you want, but they won't listen. These are pretty mean guys, Francis. They don't like to be fucked with.'

'Well, neither do I. So, how much do you owe them anyhow?'

'Twenty thousand dollars.'

'Jesus Christ, Danny, how did you manage to be into them for that much? I bet it wasn't marbles this time, eh.'

'No,' Danny laughs. 'Cockfights. I had a bad run. You know me. Can't leave it alone if I'm on a losing streak. The next one is always the one where I'm going to get my money back. But some of that's interest ye know, for the payment being overdue.'

'Aye, well, you always did all right at the two-up back at the school in Glasgow. But cockfights, Danny, fucksake. Didn't Sammy Skelly tell you never to bet on poultry?'

'Not that I remember.'

'Well, he should have. Stick to animals with four legs and preferably ones without beaks,' Frankie laughs.

'Thanks very much, but it's a bit late for that kind of advice, Francis.'

'Aye, maybe. Another cake?'

Short. Tight. See-through. The working girls trying their luck at the Blue Moon adhere to a uniform of sorts. Their long legs, all silky brown thighs and thin ankles, are draped languidly over stools by the bar, barely crossed on a chair by the window, or splayed by the side of the pool table when going for a difficult shot off the side cushion. Abundant black hair tumbles over bare shoulders. Small breasts, a triumph of moulded padding and the latest uplift technology, promise more than they can deliver. Lips thick with colour and gloss suggest a certain flexibility of use, small brown nipples betray an interest in any fascinating new male companions and perky buttocks jive like two juicy pears on sticks. Jimmy, for one, is entranced.

'Don't leave much to the imagination these lassies, eh Frankie,' he says, seated on a stool by the bar, fondling a bottle of Corona, his eyes like a barn owl out hunting at night.

'You could say that. You wouldn't get anything like this down at the Tollcross Arms.'

'A bloody good thing too. Some of those blokes would look pretty fuckin' terrible in a mini-skirt and a thong.'

'Aw, I don't know, a dozen pints and they'd start to look pretty good, I think,' Frankie laughs.

Frankie watches his brother behind the bar, pouring beers, mixing drinks, chatting to the customers with a well practised air of joviality and concern. He was always a good talker, was Danny. The clientele is mostly Australian with a sprinkle of Brits and other Europeans, so the televisions are always tuned to the Australian Rules football or the rugby, depending on what night of the week it is, tennis if there's nothing antipodean on. Danny also tends to the music, choosing the track and the volume according to the mood of the clientele and the direction in which he would like the evening to go. Laid back, convivial, party time, a riot. There's a lot of stuff Frankie hasn't heard before, mostly Australian, but Danny promises he'll put on some Muddy Waters later on to keep him happy, but for now it's AC/DC shaking the speakers off the wall with 'Dirty Deeds Done Dirt Cheap'.

Frankie leans over the bar and nods to his brother. 'Danny, these girls, they look a bit on the young side. They should be home in bed. By themselves I mean. Where do they come from?'

'Some of them come up to Saigon from the country, ye know, from the Mekong Delta. They're here to make some money for themselves and their families back home in the village. Some of those people in the countryside are trying to live on a dollar a day and a bit of rice. It's a disgrace. That's why I let a few of these girls come in here. As long as there's no hanky panky on the premises they can chat up a few of the customers and it's up to them what they do after that. As long as they do it somewhere else I don't mind. They're decent girls in a bad situation. But be careful, they're no as young and innocent as they look. They're very streetwise.'

'I imagine some of the customers don't mind them coming here either.'

'Some don't, no. The girls want money, the men want sex. But, after a while, these men begin to treat all women like whores, ye know. Other blokes don't like it, they just want to be able to have a game of pool and not get hassled.'

Frankie is momentarily startled as he feels a light caress on his back and turns to see a girl who could be anywhere between sixteen and thirty smiling at him as if she has been waiting for him to come into this bar for most of her life.

'Hello. What's you name?' she asks, taking his hand.

'Frances. Frank. Frankie. Take your pick. What's your name?'

'My name Ngoc,' she says, laughing at his tongue-twisting attempts at pronunciation. 'Where you from?'

'Scotland.'

'Scot-land?'

'Aye. It's near England.'

'Ah, England!' she says excitedly, clasping her hands together and pressing them against her well-aired breasts. 'Ryan Giggs!'

'Well, he's Welsh actually.'

'What?' she says, looking puzzled, her brow suddenly furrowed.

'Doesn't matter. No problem.'

'How old you?'

'Forty-two.'

'Ah, *bon muoi hai tuoi*. Very young.'

'Not so young, not so old,' Frankie says, finding it surprisingly difficult to suggest she return to sit with her other light-lyclad friends. 'How old are you?'

'I nineteen.'

'You're very beautiful.'

'No-o-oh, I ugly. I have very sad life. My mother, she die when I eleven year old. She too young. This life, I no lucky. Maybe next life.'

Frankie takes her hand and squeezes it softly, amazed at how small and delicate it is and how it almost disappears completely within his. 'I'm sorry to hear that love, very sorry indeed.'

'Thank you. You very kind man, very handsome.'

'I don't think so, sweetheart,' he quietly protests, thinking she'd change her mind if she saw him first thing in the morning.

'No, shooah. You buy me one drink?'

She breathes softly into Frankie's ear, moving her hand to his thigh, slowly making circles on the cloth with the long penetrating nail of her index finger. He watches the crimson polish slowly revolve its way closer to the epicentre of his trousers.

'Sure,' he sighs. 'One drink. No problem.'

She nods at Benny behind the bar, her finger fiddling with the top of Frankie's zip.

'Him wake him up,' she purrs.

Frankie looks into Ngoc's twinkling eyes, at her mischievous smile, at the inventive things she is doing with her tongue without it leaving her mouth, and reflects on the brevity of life, on the opportunities that present themselves and the processes by which a decision is made to pursue them or not, the factors one has to take into account before one acts. The pros and cons. Why we choose to go this way or that. However, fools do rush in, so they say. Look before you leap, that's what his granny always told him, and keep your thingamy in your trousers. But then again he read somewhere that a man with an erection is in no need of advice. Frankie prepares to sink into the realm of the senses, but is suddenly blinded by the bright light of reason and responsibility. He sighs the forlorn sigh of a man in possession of a conscience.

'Aye, him wake up but him should go back to sleep or him wife kill him,' Frankie says, removing her hand from where he knows it shouldn't be. 'Thanks anyhow, darlin'.'

Benny serves him another beer and places a milky looking drink tinkling with ice cubes before a disappointed Ngoc.

'Cheers,' he says, with an apologetic shrug.

'Cheeah,' she replies, her mouth a full blown ruby pout.

'What's that you're drinking?' he asks, curious.

'Saigon Tea.'

'Doesn't look like tea to me,' he says, squinting into the glass.

Ngoc laughs, slapping him on the shoulder. 'Not real tea! All bar girls in Saigon drink Saigon Tea. A little Jim Beam and much milk. Girl drink many and not get drunk and Madam, she make customer pay fifty thousand dong for one drink. Very funny. Madam, she make a lot of money.'

'Saigon Tea? Nothing's what it seems in this town, eh Ngoc. I'll have to remember that.'

'Mr Frankie! Telephone,' Benny yells, his hand cupped over the mouthpiece, trying to muffle the thumping flow of Led Zeppelin down the line.

'Hello,' Frankie says, sticking a finger in his ear.

'It's me. Eileen. The goldfish are dead.'

'What? Who's dead? Your uncle Hamish?'

'No, the goldfish.'

'Ah, the goldfish. How did that happen?'

'I was cleaning the bowl and I put in some fresh water from the kettle, but I forgot I had the kettle on a few minutes before to make a cup of tea and what with the heat and that, the fish leapt right out of the bowl on to the floor.'

'Did you try and pick them up?'

'No, the bloody cat was in there like a flash and ate them. And I'd just fed it as well. A whole tin of salmon it had.'

'Salmon! You're feeding the cat salmon now! Christ, I hope you gave it a glass of white wine as well.'

Eileen ignores him. 'Oh Frankie, it's no fair. First the budgie now this.'

'Oh aye,' he says, the distinctive aroma of fried feathers suddenly fresh in his mind. 'You've had a bad run with the domestic pets, Eileen, no doubt about it. But at least the cat's still alive.'

'It won't be for long when I get a hold of it.'

'Don't do anything rash, Eileen. It was just following its natural instincts.'

'Well, my natural instinct's to give it a right good battering with the frying pan.'

'Well, just restrain yourself,' Frankie says, picturing his wife chasing the cat around the house while wielding a large cast iron skillet. 'How are the preparations going?'

'No bad. I'm just cleaning out the cupboards.'

Frankie sighs. 'Eileen, why are you cleaning out the cupboards when you're supposed to be packing to come here?'

'I'm no leaving the house wi' dirty cupboards. You should see the state of them.'

'Nobody's going to be looking in the cupboards while you're away.'

'Well, you never know.'

'Eileen, fucksake,' Frankie says, reminded once more that sometimes his wife is a complete mystery to him. So is that why you rang, love, just to tell me about the cat and the fish?'

'No, of course not. Have you seen my white canvas shoes?'

'The one's with the matching bag?'

'Aye. That's them.'

'They're in the hall cupboard. Maybe you'd better give that a clean-out as well.'

'No, I can't the now. Stella's coming for lunch. I'd better go, she'll be here in a few minutes. See you in a couple of days. Give my love to Danny.'

'What about me?'

'You? I've got a surprise for you, big boy.'

Frankie hands the phone back to Benny and turns to find Ngoc beside him, a coy smile on her dolls' house face.

'I sit with you, so you should give me tip.'

'Try and get to bed before eleven, sweetheart, it's better for the metabolism.'

Frankie sees his brother gesturing towards the door. Time to go. The meeting with the boys from District 4 has been arranged somewhere on their patch and it probably wouldn't be a good idea to be late. Always scrub behind your ears and be punctual, that's what his granny always said. But then she sat in the kitchen in front of the coal fire all day wearing her gas mask from the war and talking to herself, so things have to be kept in perspective.

Danny says these lads are right hard cases, but he's never met a man yet who won't listen to reason if given the opportunity for considered reflection. Failing that, there's always an axe handle or other large blunt instruments. The highly persuasive properties of a shared bottle of single malt whisky also cannot be ignored in situations like these. A few glasses in the right light and old grievances can be forgotten and bitter enemies can become the most devoted and sentimental of friends who enjoy nothing more than singing a few old tunes together in the drunken early light of the new day.

Benny says some of the streets in District 4 are crowded and too narrow for cars, so they should take the Citroen down to Rue Calmette, leave it there and walk over the bridge across the Ben Nghe Canal. From there, they can head down to Doan Van Bo Street where they are to be met and taken to an as yet unknown house.

Benny knows some of these people, so he says anyway. When a bar owner falls behind in his protection payments or has trouble paying off his gambling debts, they will usually suggest the bar be used as a place to deal drugs from, and in time the debt will be paid off. No problem. And if you refuse? Benny says the Flying Dragon gang sent two of its hard men to Australia where they kidnapped the son of a wealthy Saigon bar owner, slit his throat and dumped him down a storm water drain. The man had another son studying there so he paid up before the two thugs had boarded the return flight home.

Hoanh had also told him that much of the gang trouble here was about heroin. Apart from introducing nice buildings and baguettes, the French also ran the opium monopoly in Indochina, and when they left the CIA took it over. Now, with their hard won independence, the Vietnamese could supply the heroin themselves, seven kilograms of which are sniffed, smoked and shot up on the streets of Saigon every day. You could see them in the morning, seven or eight children lined up like sardines in a can, being injected by a kid not much older than themselves. One needle, no hope. While it was easy to help his brother with the two policemen who were trying to supplement their meagre income from Danny's takings—a posting to some remote mountainous town near the Chinese border would do nicely—Hoanh said the gangs were a different matter altogether. They were strong, ruthless and had connections with the forces of law and order who themselves were undermined by collusion and corruption in the ranks. If you pay them peanuts, don't expect them to perform miracles. But he'd said it wasn't impossible.

'Right, we're away then,' Danny says, slapping Frankie on the shoulder.

'What about Jimmy? He looks pretty happy there wi' that young lassie,' Frankie says, nodding in his pal's direction.

Jimmy has his arm around the shoulders of a pretty, if muscular, young woman, a short feather boa coiled loosely around her neck.

'She's no a lassie, she's a *pe de*,' Danny says, smiling.

'A what?' Frankie asks.

'A lady boy, stacked up top *and* down below.'

'Whatever she is, she looks good in feathers.'

Frankie catches Jimmy's eye and he reluctantly waves goodbye to his new-found friend. The four men head for the Citroen, leaving Mai to run the bar. She blows Danny a kiss and mouths the words 'bugger them' as they swing out the door.

The city is buzzing as giggling families and young enraptured lovers on their motorbikes cruise the Saturday night circuit of Dong Khoi Street, Ton Duc Thang, Le Loi and Nguyen Hue, from the cathedral to the river and back again. Round and round, up and down. Ten thousand smiles, a few hundred collisions.

Frankie gazes out the window, wishing he was out there riding a motorbike with the rest of them, feeling the warm air on his skin, Eileen behind him, her arms around his waist, her face buried in his neck. They would ride and ride, free of any concerns about fried budgies and boiled goldfish and the depressing thought of getting up for work in the morning.

'Danny, tell me, I've never come across people who smile so much. Why is that?' Frankie asks, amazed at the general joi de vivre before him. 'They're always beaming. You walk down the street and complete strangers smile at you. You go to a shop and they smile at you. What are they on?'

'They're not on anything, that's the amazing thing about it, especially if you think what they've been through. They've been bombed to buggery, napalmed, millions of them were killed and still they can walk about the streets holding hands and laughing. They're an extraordinary people. I only hope the government doesn't let them down because they deserve better than they're getting.'

'And they're no bad tae look at an' a',' Jimmy adds, obviously pleased with himself. 'That lassie I was playing the darts wi' was a wee cracker.'

'Aye, so he was,' Frankie smiles.

'You're right though, Jimmy,' Danny says. 'They're the most beautiful looking people you're ever likely to see. All the rest of us look ugly and clumsy by comparison. It's as if God made them first and all the rest of us are just poor imitations. But don't get too romantic, Francis. Some of them are just out to get whatever they can, especially from foreigners. They'll rob you blind given half a chance.'

'He? What do you mean *he*?' Jimmy says, it suddenly dawning on him what Frankie had said. 'Is there something you're no tellin' me? Well is there?'

'OK, we here already,' Benny announces, pulling into a dark side street near the bridge. 'Everybody follow me, it's very terrible here. We have to be careful.'

The stench of the water is thick in their nostrils as they walk slowly over the Cau Calmette. Frankie peers over the side at the rubbish floating on the filthy water, a floating graveyard of bags and bottles. An old woman washes clothes from the edge of her dilapidated houseboat, a frenzy of rusty corrugated iron, scarred wooden planks and torn sheets of plastic. He watches her carefully pour some water on the row of flourishing plant pots beside her, their leaves trailing into the canal like fingers in a pond. As in Glasgow, being houseproud appears not to depend on the quality or location of the home in question.

The bridge is not long and they are quickly over it and across Ben Van Don Street and into Doan Van Bo. They walk slowly now, alert for the presence of their unknown guide who may be lurking somewhere in the shadows or who could suddenly emerge from the crowded streets.

Danny suddenly notices a young man leaning casually against a wall, a cigarette dangling limply from the corner of his mouth. A quick shift of his eyes and Danny knows he's their man. 'I think we're on, lads,' he says, nodding in their new friend's direction.

They follow him off the main street and into a maze of narrow alleys that bustle and flow like veins through the neighbourhood. Theirs are the only western faces and people stare at them from windows, from shops and houses, as they push and edge and muddle their way through the throng. One small street is a mouth-watering feast of barbecued, boiled, fried and fresh food. The spicy aromas tease their appetites as they step around the cooked chicken, pork, fish and quails, newly plucked and splayed and set out haphazardly on the ground like a madman's picnic. They quicken their pace and hold their breath as they pass a tub of pigs' intestines, all except Danny whose years at the slaughterhouse have rendered him immune to all stomachchurning odours. The women smile, the men laugh among themselves at the group of white people so stupid as to venture down these streets as darkness is about to fall.

The narrow alleyway is a sauna and they are sweating heavily, except for Benny who seems accustomed to it. Two ancient women, brown and brittle, smile with what's left of their tobacco- and betel-nut-stained teeth from within their modestly stocked shop, mysterious and dark as a temple. Cigarettes, dried fruit, snake wine, razor blades and a handful of plaster pigs are displayed uninvitingly in a wooden cabinet that is more scratch than polish. In the corner, a solitary candle flickers by an altar the colour of sunset. The smell of fried pork and fish sauce hangs in the air like a fog. Children, ducks and dogs squabble for control of territory in a carnival of barking, quacking and screaming. A small boy is rocked to sleep in a hammock by his elder brother. The family washing hangs on a chicken wire fence.

The street winds on like a meandering stream, close and overbearing. Men huddle in intimidating cliques, bare-chested and picking at their teeth or just staring at whatever takes their fancy. Some ease the hours away in small cafés that are just a clutter of child-sized chairs and tables, drinking sweet black coffee or iced tea or beer. A voice unexpectedly startles them. 'You! Where you go? Can I help you?' Boys shake and swerve and swear in rundown amusement parlours, a weary collection of a few scratched and worn machines that have seen better days. Still, they beep and whirr and hoot, fulfilling their duty to the satisfaction of their juvenile pilots. The barbers' shops and beauty parlours are filled with customers having their hair cut and permed and dyed, their aching shoulders and necks soothed by the magic hands of a sympathetic masseuse. Caged birds sing sweetly in the half light.

The heat catches in their throats. It's difficult to breathe. They are close to the port, Frankie can feel it. He can smell the river, feel the mist rising from the murky water, hear the groaning of the cranes as they haul huge containers from the ships and dump them with a massive thud on to the docks below. Some of the contents find their way back to the very streets they are in now, free of charge, no duty, no tax, no problem. That's what he's heard anyway.

Frankie looks around, amazed and disbelieving. What is he doing here? It's a long way from Shettleston, from Dennistoun, from the stinking scheme he calls home. It's so *foreign*. The smells, the sights, the sounds, the touch of the air on your skin, the feel of the ground beneath your feet. The very taste of it. Yet, there's something of himself in these strangers in their sandals and pyjamas and straw hats, their cheap trousers and loose white shirts, their fifty cent haircuts and eternally simmering cigarettes. They're just trying to get a life, one that might be better than the one they've got.

A knock on a metal door built into a brick high wall, the bark of a wary dog, the rattle of keys and the rumble of bolts and they are in a garden, a garden full of the soothing sounds of water running over smooth stones, a garden full of the soft light of wooden lanterns, a garden full of peaceful grottos in which to sit and quietly contemplate, a garden full of mean-looking fuckers who seem ferociously unhappy with the world around them.

Except for him. No gun, no attitude, no scowl, no fear. No sweat. Seated alone at a large rectangular wooden table, his smile is as broad and long and bright as the fine white sand of an Australian beach. It is a smile that says nothing, betrays no emotion, gives no clue to what lies underneath it. A grin for all occasions. His suit is the warm pale blue of a tropical sea at dawn, his shirt the colour of fresh snow, his hair black as the Devil's heart, thick and unruffled, a perfect follicular edifice. He spreads his arms like a priest about to bless his congregation, indicating the vacant chairs around him.

'*Xin chao*,' he says. 'Please, sit. Can I get you something to drink, some tea, perhaps, some beer, some ice-cold water? Anything you like, I have.'

'Tea,' Benny says, nervously.

'Water is fine for me,' Danny says, folding his hands in his lap.

'A nice cold beer would be good,' Frankie says, looking straight into the eyes of this fountain of charm.

'Aye, same for me thanks,' Jimmy says, adjusting his weight in his chair. 'Eh, you don't have any of that Corona stuff, do ye by any chance?'

'Ah, the beer with the spirit and flavour of old Meh-hee-coh,' he laughs.

'Aye, that's the one. So you've seen the advertisement as well then?' Jimmy inquires.

'Of course. I have the satellite television. Twenty-four channels. You like with the lemon or not with the lemon?'

'Nae lemon, thanks pal. I prefer my beer without fruit. Have you got any peanuts?'

'We have many peanuts,' he says, his smile brighter than ever. 'Many, many peanuts.'

The drinks arrive without any apparent instruction from the man in the suit, who continues to beam like a full moon on a cloudless night while they are served. He closes his eyes and taps out a Latin beat on the table with his fingers as if he is somewhere else, a place where the music is played on conga drums, and where the women are tall and chocolate brown and wear scented flowers behind their ears, where their ripe and luscious breasts are a perfect pillow on which a man can rest his weary head at the end of a long and difficult day.

'Do you like music, Mr Daniel? Can I call you Daniel?'

'Aye, Daniel's fine, Mr . . . '

'Cam. Nguyen Nam Cam.'

Danny feels Benny shiver next to him. 'What's the matter?' he whispers.

'Nam Cam,' he says, breathless. 'In English, "nam" mean five and "cam" mean orange. He is Mr Five Oranges. Very famous. Very terrible man. Big trouble for you.'

'I myself, I love music,' Cam continues. 'I love the Latin music the best, from Cuba, from Argentina, from the Brazil. I love to r-r-rumba! I love to tango!' he laughs, swooning from side to side on the dance floor in his mind, his black patent leather shoes flashing as he moves to the sensuous beat. 'But here we are in Vietnam, Mr Daniel, with our little problem, very far away from the rum and the Coca-Cola. What can we do?'

'Aye, what can we do right enough?' Jimmy says, with a philosophical shake of his head, his second bottle of Corona almost empty. 'That's the big question, eh? Just get up in the mornin' and go out blinking into the light, eh? See what the day holds for ye. Ye cannae dae more than that.'

'Ah, but you can, Mr . . . ?'

'Jimmy. Jimmy Stewart.'

Ah, like the movie star?'

'Aye, but no relation.'

'Yes, a shame. But Mr Jimmy, you must wake up and attack the day, make it your own, bend it to your will. The day is yours to do with what you want. That is why I am where I am today. That is why I am a rich man. That is why I have Mexican beer. When I first came to Saigon after the American war many years ago, I had nothing. But now I am a success. I am cosmopolitan! I have the new Armani suit, the new car, the new woman, the . . . '

'The new hair,' Frankie interrupts, smiling knowingly at his voluble host.

'Ah yes, I have also the new hair,' he says proudly, gently patting into place his sculpted quiff.

'Is that hair weave or hair plugs?' Frankie inquires.

'Hair plugs. Individual strand replacement.'

'Very fiddly,' Frankie says.

'Very expensive,' Cam replies, laughing. 'But what is money? You cannot take it with you when you die, but you need to it to make you happy when you are alive, eh, Mr Francis? Anh noi that. I speak the truth.'

'You know my name?'

'Of course. I know everything Mr Francis.'

'Call me Frankie.'

'I know everything, Mr Frankie. I know everyone. I know when a new ship arrives at the port. I know when a new shoeshine boy sits on a corner in Dong Khoi Street. I know when a girl from the Delta fucks a tourist at the Caravelle. I know when someone comes to Tan Son Nhut airport from what do you call it, Bonnie Scotland. I know when someone speaks with Mr Hoanh of the Saigon police. I know when someone owes me *money*!' he screams, banging his fist hard on the table and sending glasses and bottles tumbling to the tiled courtyard floor.

When the silence breaks, when the sounds of life outside the wall slither back into the courtyard like a snake from its hiding place, Cam slowly brushes some imaginary crumbs from his trousers and smooths down his hair. His voice is a grating rasp, a gritty exhalation of iron filings. 'There are no secrets in Saigon, my friend.'

'Well, so it seems, Mr Cam,' Frankie says, wiping some beer from his shirt. 'So it seems.' For some reason he can't get that Beatles song out of his head now, "Do you want to know a secret?" Remembering 1963. He and Danny watching 'Thank Your Lucky Stars' and wearing their plastic Beatle wigs. 'I bags to be Paul.' 'I bags to be John then.' Both of them standing in front of the television, legs apart, miming away and strumming their bits of wood and string knocked together to resemble guitars, and their mother laughing away at them while she's at the sink doing the washing. Fucksake, it was only yesterday, only yesterday, and here we are with Danny looking like he wants to leap up and give Mr Five Bloody Oranges a swift uppercut to the gob. Thirty-odd years have gone by in a snap of the fingers. What's going on? No one said life would just disappear like this. Whatever happened to those Beatles wigs anyhow? Where do childhood treasures go?

More drinks arrive and, as if nothing had happened, Cam once again lets his charm run free, like a dog bounding off a leash. He sips at a Cuba Libre, beaming at the head of the table, like a proud host presiding over a grand and sumptuous dinner with his beholden guests around him.

'My friends,' he says, savouring the tang of the rum and lemon, 'we have a small problem, a problem that is an irritation to me and a problem we must deal with. I must apologise for not having taken the time out to meet you before, Mr Daniel. But, you understand, sometimes I have to—what is the word?— delegate. I am a busy man and I know you are too. I have many places to go, important people to see, and you, my friend, have your little bar to run.'

He turns to Frankie, his smile a sudden torchlight flash. 'And you, Mr Frankie, do you have children? No? *Anh buon.* I am sad. A man should have children. I have children, two sons, and I must look after their interests. You see, the money that your brother owes me is money that one day will belong to them. And you know, children, they can cost a lot of money.'

'Aye, never a truer word was fuckin' spoken, Cam, old son. See ma weans . . . ' Jimmy says, before deciding a discussion about the financial burden imposed by one's progeny is not appropriate at this particular moment in time.

'My sons, my dear sons, they study in England. It's good for the business. So let us get this little matter of a few thousand dollars out of the way and then we can listen to some beautiful music together. Perhaps the Afro-Cuban Allstars. Ve-rr-y good! What do you think, Mr Frankie from Scotland?'

'Well, I'm a soul and blues man myself, Mr Cam. Ray Charles, James Brown, Gladys Knight and the Pips, that sort of thing. But, hey, I'm always willing to give something new a go. But you know, there's one thing that sticks in my craw, if you know what I mean.'

'Craw? Craw? The large perching bird with glossy black plumage?'

'No, that's a crow, Mr Cam. What sticks in my throat is that my brother Danny here is an honest man, just trying to make an honest living, you know, like most working people, wherever they may be, whether it's in Scotland or Vietnam or fuckin' Peru. But everywhere you go, there's always someone trying to take their hard-earned money away from them. People who do not have the moral right to do so. In Scotland, it was always the English landowners, or the landlord in the tenements, or the bookie, or the big factory owners—the system, Mr Cam, the system. My point is, while my brother is happy to pay off his gambling debts, it is a matter of principle that he can't give you a slice of his takings, or this so-called interest on what you say he owes you, otherwise he'd be perpetuating the kind of exploitation suffered by the Scottish worker for a thousand years. Do you get my drift?'

Jimmy begins to applaud, but an icy glare from Frankie sees him quickly return to his fourth bottle of Corona. He shrugs and swallows a handful of peanuts.

'Exploitation? You talk to me about exploitation. What do you know about exploitation? For one thousand years the Chinese ruled our country, and the Chinese, Mr Frankie, they do not, how you say, fuck around. They made life very miserable for us. And then the French, they made us slaves in their rubber plantations and they put us in prison, they fucked our sisters and they murdered us and they try to make us little clones of themselves. And they bring their Catholic God to Vietnam with their Father, Son and Holy Ghost. And they expect us to take this seriously? We have to go to mass every Sunday morning. Very boring, Mr Frankie, very, very boring. And the priests, they like the little boys, I think. Sure. So, don't talk to me about exploitation. We *know* all about exploitation.'

'So why do you perpetuate it then, Mr Cam? Why do you take advantage of my brother?'

'Because it is what I do. It is how I have chosen to live. It is how I pay for these men around us, it is how I buy my beautiful clothes, it is how I buy beautiful women with the lovely big tits, it is how I buy satellite television with twenty-four channels. I do it because I can. I do it because someone has to. I do it because if I am not the one who exploits then I will be the one who is exploited. And besides, sometimes it can be a lot of fun and you get to meet interesting people.'

'But holding knives to people's throats, Mr Cam. Not very civilised, is it?'

'The possibility of once again being a poor peasant toiling in the field makes a man less concerned about being polite, Mr Frankie.'

'Aye, and so does being ripped off and threatened, Mr Cam.'

Cam claps his hands like a mandarin signalling the end of an audience and a servant appears out of nowhere to ease his chair from under him.

'My friends, it is time for me to leave you. I have an important appointment with my favourite programme on the television.'

'And what's that, Mr Cam? *Who Wants to Be a Millionaire?*' Frankie inquires.

'No, my friend. *Wild Africa* on the Discovery Channel. Tonight it is "The Scavengers of the Kalahari".'

'Ah, the one about the hyenas.'

'You know it?' Cam says excitedly.

'Aye, I do. It's a very good programme as a matter of fact. Did you know that despite their appearance they make very loving and attentive parents? They also have jaws that are capable of crushing bones. They're very interesting animals overall.'

'I didn't know that. So you like the Discovery Channel, Mr Frankie?'

'Aye, you could say that.'

'A man after my own heart. In the jungle it is a case of every man for himself, is it not?'

'Aye, Mr Cam, I suppose it is.'

'So, my men will come to the Blue Moon in three days to collect our money,' he says, heading inside to what appears to be a spacious and luxurious residence. 'Please don't disappoint me. Help yourself to more beer, more peanuts. I have many, many peanuts,' he says, laughing like one of the hyenas he is about to watch on his giant-sized screen.

The four men look at each other, uncertain of what their next move should be.

'One more beer for the road, boys?' Jimmy says, his throat suddenly parched.

'No, I don't think so,' Frankie replies. 'There's a phone call I have to make.'

Sammy McFadyen has just finished unloading eight boxes of black pudding that he picked up for a song from a bloke who works part-time in a butcher shop in Paisley, and he's looking forward to his dinner. Making a quid, honest or dishonest, on the mean streets of Glasgow is getting harder, no doubt about it. And he isn't as young as he used to be, no doubt about that either. Humping boxes of processed offal all over the place is doing his back in, so it is. The wife is away to the bingo and she's left his dinner in the oven. Chops, mashed potatoes, peas, gravy. Four slices of buttered white bread sit neatly on a side plate on the table, like an offering to some strange Celtic god with a liking for carbohydrates. Fuckin' magic, Sammy says to himself, rubbing his chubby hands together in joyful mouthwatering anticipation. As he raises the first morsel of mid-loin lamb to his gaping mouth the telephone rings in the living room. 'Fuck,' he says. 'Fuckin' fuck.' He shoves the meat into his mouth anyway and stomps to the phone. 'Hello,' he yells, chewing away like a cow on the cud.

'Sammy?'

'Aye, this is he. Who's that?'

'It's me, Frankie.'

'Frankie boy!' Sammy shouts excitedly, bits of lamb and mashed potato spraying across the room like shrapnel from an exploding bomb. 'Where are ye? Shite, are ye in yon Venezuela then?'

'Vietnam,' Frankie says quietly on the other end of the line, forever disappointed in Sammy's powers of recollection.

'Aye, Vietnam, that's right. God, ye sound so close. That's amazin' that, so it is. Ye could be just around the corner, so ye could.'

'Aye, it's the wonders of modern technology, Sammy.'

Sammy proceeds to tell Frankie about a consignment of white enamelled, genuine antique-style telephones he'd picked up a while back and how he'd had no problems getting rid of them because the women around the scheme thought they were right classy. 'I've never seen anything like it, they were virtually runnin' oot ae the back ae the van. Nae kiddin', I coulda done wi' another hundred. But dae ye think I could find them? Naw. I looked everywhere. Hunted high and fuckin' low, so I did. Christ I was cursin' masel' . . . '

Frankie knew there was a price to pay when you rang Sammy. The cunt could talk the horn off a rhinoceros, but he had no choice. All you could do was hang on the phone and hope dementia didn't set in.

'Sammy! Sammy! Fucksake, this is costing me a fortune here,' Frankie yells, finally running out of patience.

Sammy reluctantly ends his tale of what, as far as he is concerned, was one of the greatest transactions in the history of Scottish commerce. 'Sorry Frankie, phone calls fae Vanuatu must be awfy dear right enough.'

Frankie takes a deep breath and continues. 'Listen, Sammy, yon nephew of yours, Nathan, he works with the Civil Service down in London, is that no right?'

'Aye, that's right.'

'Well, do you think he could do me a wee favour?'

Sammy coughs, wheezes and whistles his apprehension and uncertainty down the line. 'Eh, I'm no sure Frankie, ye know, what wi' Big Danny smashing his guitar the other night an' that. Nathan wisnae very happy, no very happy at all.'

Frankie makes apologetic noises. 'Aye, that was a bit out of order, Sammy, I know. But he was singing Cat Stevens songs. At a party, for fucksake. That's taking liberties.'

Sammy dwells on this for a moment and thinks about his dinner going cold on the kitchen table. 'Aye, you're right there. That wis a bit beyond the pale. Look, I'll see what I can do. What is it that ye want exactly?'

'What I want, Sammy, is for your Nathan to find out where a couple of Vietnamese lads are doing their studies. They're at university in England somewhere, but I don't know where specifically.'

'Aye, sure, Frankie. Whit's their names?' Sammy says, plucking a stub of well-chewed pencil from behind his left ear and thoughtfully licking the lead point.

'Nguyen. N-G-U-Y-E-N.'

'Eh, why dae ye need tae know this, Frankie, if ye don't mind me askin'?'

'Just a wee bit of insurance, that's all.'

'Nae bother, son. I'll get right on tae it.'

'Thanks Sammy, you're a pal. I'll be in touch.'

'Eh Frankie, before ye go.'

'Aye?'

'Nae kiddin', I've just got hold ae some smashin' black puddin', you've never seen anythin' like it. I'm tellin' ye, if Jesus wis alive, he'd be wantin' some for him and the Apostles. His maw as well. If yer wantin' some ye'd better get in now, son, because I can't guarantee how long it'll last.'

Frankie sighs. 'Put me down for half a dozen.'

'You're a wise man, Frankie. I've always said that, so I have. You've got a good heid on yer shoulders. Aye. A good heid.'

Sammy strolls briskly back into the kitchen and dumps himself on a chair to resume his meal. He opens a bottle of beer and shakes a storm of salt and pepper over his chops and potatoes and the room warms to the sound of a contented sigh as he reaches for the tomato sauce.

A ndrew and Fergus McCludgie were always big for their age. While most other Glasgow boys of their generation spent much of their early years pale and sickly and racked by coughs and mysterious infections, spontaneous eruptions of spots and boils and the occasional life-threatening fever, they were always immune from maladies of any kind. Where other children went off their food, or would only drink boiled water with sugar from a particular plastic cup bearing a picture of a fluffy yellow duck, the McCludgie twins were strangers to problems of the digestive tract. Everything went in and out according to God's plan or, indeed, at a greater rate and volume than He had ever anticipated. Anything that was edible was eaten, anything that was drinkable was duly drunk. At the breast, their infant toothless mouths created a vacuum strong enough to clean a shag pile carpet. So ferocious was their appetite that the district nurse insisted their mother, Mrs Agnes McCludgie, five foot two and six stone eleven, should immediately desist from continuing to feed them for fear that she would be sucked inside out, and her body left withered and free of anything resembling moisture within it.

While the other children in their street were afflicted by perpetually running noses, rickety legs and bony concave chests framed by shoulders that slumped like deflated tyres, the McCludgie boys had bones like rock and skeletons that were straight and true. Their chests were barrels of oak and their nasal passages remained dry and clear even when confronted with the dankest, most miserable, most snot-inducing Glasgow weather.

They were a majestic pair of galloping Clydesdales in a field of consumptive Shetland ponies. Not for them a prancing sky-blue perambulator with decorative lace around the hood. They were paraded around the scheme in something resembling a Wells & Fargo stagecoach that had been designed and welded together with industrial strength components by their neighbour and honorary uncle, Frankie Canyon, who at that stage was still working the night shift at the shipyards.

The veins of too many other boys in the street were filled with the lank blood of scrawny Irish Catholic immigrants who, when they stepped gingerly off the boat many decades before, were strangers to any meal other than the potato, boiled, mashed or souped. But the McCludgie boys had inherited a thick porridge of virile corpuscles from their paternal grandfather, a six foot seven highlander who regularly feasted on Aberdeen Angus and tossed cabers for sport when not dragging a plough across the field.

Now, at the age of nineteen, the twins had developed into perfect physical specimens of rampant masculinity. As tall as trees, as muscular as Mr Atlas, as handsome as only young men in their radiant prime can be, they also were possessed of a fierce loyalty to their family, friends and neighbours, a blind fidelity that was not compromised by finely tuned intellects or a highly developed sense of right and wrong.

In short, the Magnificent McCludgies would never come top of the class, or even linger near the middle, but their capacity for excessive physical violence knew no bounds when it came to defending the interests of their loved ones. Which is why their Uncle Frankie has asked Andrew and Fergus to post themselves outside the main entrance to the London School of Economics and keep a keen eye out for two Vietnamese undergraduates, who at twelve-thirty on a Thursday afternoon, might be venturing out for a bite to eat.

Unfortunately, the McCludgie boys feel they have underestimated the cosmopolitan composition of the student body, not expecting to be confronted with such a dim sum of students from all over Asia. The study of the particular distinguishing racial characteristics of Vietnamese, Chinese, Taiwanese, Burmese or any other 'ese' was not something to which they had devoted many of their leisure hours. But, armed with photographs of the two lads, supplied by Sammy's nephew Nathan, they are optimistic that they will be able to recognise young Pham and Vong and, with the right mixture of charm and intimidation, be able to convince them to get together for a quiet drink and a bit of a chat.

Fergus pulls out a pack of cigarettes from his jacket pocket and offers one to his brother. Having both smoked anything they could get into their mouths and puff on since they were eleven years old, they were always well prepared for a quick fag, with several packs of cigarettes and boxes of matches generally found on their person at any time of the day or night. The twins bend slightly to light up, cupping their cigarettes from the breeze, and inhale deeply with a noisy blend of relief, satisfaction and pre-cancerous cells.

'Thanks pal,' Andrew says.

'Nae bother,' Fergus replies.

'Wait a minute, is that them?' Andrew says suddenly, nudging his brother in the ribs and pointing to two young Asian men heading towards them. 'Where are those photies?'

'I thought you had them.'

'Away ye go, ya bampot, I gave them tae you.'

Fergus furiously searches through his clothes until finally he finds the crumpled passport-sized photographs in a small pocket hidden on the inside of his trousers. 'They were in my secret pocket,' he says, relieved.

'Aye, that secret pocket's so fuckin' secret you can never remember where it is. Geez them here.'

The twins squint at the pictures and then at the two young men almost upon them before looking again at the images like two fans transfixed at a tennis match.

'Aye it's definitely them,' Fergus says. 'They look like twins. Ye widnae credit it, eh? I mean what's the probability of two twins from Glasgow meeting two twins from Vietnam on a busy street in London?'

'Fuck all probability if you ask me.'

'Ye just widnae credit it,' Andrew says again, forever amazed at the infinite wonders of the universe.

'Right, let me dae the talkin',' Fergus says as they stride towards their assignment.

Fergus bails them up with a quick nod and a shuffle of shoulders, his hands thrust deep into his pockets. 'Eh, excuse me, is your faither called Cam, an' that?'

The two young men look at their interrogator as if he were from another planet, which indeed some of his fellow students at the LSE believed Scotland to be. They look at each other uncomprehendingly, not being acquainted with this particular variation of what they presume to be the English language.

'Youse two are fae Vietnam, right? So is your da called Cam?' Fergus asks again, slightly frustrated.

Again there is no response other than looks of pure bewilderment. Andrew decides to try his luck, speaking slowly and in the sort of English he has heard on the BBC. 'Hello. My . . . name . . . is . . . Andrew,' he smiles. 'And this is my brother Fergus.'

'Ah, nice to meet you. My name is Pham.' 'And my name is Vong.'

'Is that right?' the McCludgie boys reply, not a nanosecond apart. 'Very nice to meet you too.'

They shake hands vigorously, the smaller, more delicate pair wincing at the bone-crushing grip of the two lumbering giants before them.

'How can we help you?' Pham asks, wondering what these two babbling men could possibly want with them.

'Do . . . you . . . have . . . a . . . father?' Andrew inquires, each syllable a study in perfect mother-speaking-to-the-posh-relatives English.

'Yes, we have a father,' Pham says. 'And a mother.'

'Is . . . your . . . father . . . called . . . Cam?'

'Yes,' Pham and Vong say hesitantly.

'That's the game then,' Fergus says, excitedly. 'Cause we've goat a wee message fer you fae yer faither. Fancy a bevy?'

After Andrew translates his brother's mysterious invitation, the young Vietnamese students need little encouragement to join the McCludgies for a drink. Having been in London for only a few weeks, they have yet to make any new friends and are keen for some company, however tall, Celtic and lacking in O-levels it may be.

It's a rare and fine day so they decide to walk because, as Pham points out, there is much to see in this most historic of cities and taxi fares have gone up something shocking. Along the Strand they go, through Covent Garden, and across Charing Cross Road, stopping along the way for the inevitable pint or ten, a nervous dalliance with some snake wine down a back alley, several bowls of won ton soup and chilli pork at Poon's and a few mountainous helpings of pie, mash and beans at the Frog and Firkin. Seven hours after they first set out on their twenty-minute stroll they are standing unsteadily outside what appears to be a bar but which has no sign above the door or on the small circular window.

'Is this the place?' Fergus asks his brother.

'I don't know, there's nae sign or anythin',' he replies, pulling a crumpled scrap of paper from his trouser pocket. 'This is definitely the address, but.'

'Perhaps, my friends, perhaps we should just go inside and as you say in the Bonnie Scotland, have a fucking look,' Pham says, giggling at his brother.

The four tumble their way inside and meander to the bar where a perfectly coiffured barman is inspecting his teeth in the mirror, his mouth a pearly heaven, a dentist's holiday in the sun.

'S'cuse me pal. Is this BLAB!?' Andrew inquires.

'Certainly is, my son. What can I do for you?'

'Two pints o' heavy and two large glasses o' snake wine, thanks Jimmy.'

The barman is surprised. 'Funny that. I had a couple of Jocks in here a few days ago asking for pints of 'eavy and I'll tell you the same thing as what I told them.'

'And what's that?' Andrew asks.

'We ain't got none.'

'Nae snake wine either, I suppose.'

'No snakes. No snake wine. How about some Corona beer? It's imbued with the spirit of old Meh-hee-coh.'

'Is that right? Aye, well, fuck that. I don't want any poncy Mexican beer wi' dods ae fruit in it. Geez four McEwan's Exports.'

Vong nudges his brother in the ribs, pointing to the huge bowls of fruit hanging from the ceiling. 'This place is wicked,' he says.

Suddenly a voice screeches out from the lounge area beyond the bar where two women are sitting drinking Barbara Windsors at a small lamp-lit table. 'Christsake, where have yeez been? We've been worried sick. You were supposed to have been here hours ago. What time dae yeez call this?'

'Oh hello, Auntie Stella. Hello, Auntie Eileen. Yeez all right?' Andrew says, beer in hand.

'Naw, we're no bloody all right. You two need a right good skelp. We thought you'd been run over by a bus or abducted or something.'

'Easy, Stella, and don't mention the word abduction in present company, if you know what I mean,' Eileen says, placing a restraining hand on Stella's elbow. 'Everything's fine and they're here safe and sound and they've brought these nice boys along with them like we asked them to, so things couldn't be better. Hello boys.'

'Hello, beautiful ladies,' Pham and Vong say in chorus, attempting to kiss the women's hands. Finding the downward motion disorienting, they abandon any attempt at gentlemanly introductions and return to being amusingly drunk.

'Well, aren't you a couple of charming boys,' Eileen laughs. 'Are you having a nice time with Andrew and Fergus? They'll look after you, don't you worry about that.' She turns to the McCludgies, whose eyes are firmly locked on the perky bobtailed bottom of a cigarette girl who is languidly smoothing out a wrinkle in her stocking, oblivious to the acute groinal discomfort she is causing her male clientele. 'Boys! Boys!' Eileen says in a vain attempt to grab their attention. 'You two know what to do, right? 'We'll be in touch. Stella, we'd better be off or we'll miss the plane.'

'You don't want another Barbara Windsor for the road?' Stella asks, hopefully.

'I think one Barbara Windsor is more than enough,' Eileen replies, gathering up her bags.

Andrew and Fergus and Pham and Vong stand arm-in-arm by the open door and wave energetically as Eileen and Stella jump into a taxi, Heathrow and Saigon bound.

'**D**aniel! You bastard! How the bloody hell are ya?' Saturday night at the Blue Moon and the place is jumping with blokes playing pool, swilling draft Tiger Beer and instructing some of the visiting girls on the finer points of throwing a dart. But all heads turn as two elderly men burst through the front doors of the bar, their arms spread wide and their eyes alive with excitement at the recognition of a long-lost friend.

Danny stops midway through pouring a beer for his brother, who is perched on a stool in front of him, but he is unable to immediately grasp the situation. The voice is familiar but out of context, the faces are ones he has known, but they were younger then. But the eyes, he knows those eyes and the warmth that beams from them, and the memories come flooding back.

'Young Bob! Happy Jack! Jesus Christ. What are you doing here? Bloody hell, I can't believe it. How are you?'

'All the better for seeing you, me boy,' Young Bob says, extending his hand to the man he once thought of as a son.

'I can't believe it. I just can't believe it.'

'Well, you'd better believe it because here we are in the flesh. Isn't that right, Jack?'

'That's right mate, in the bloody flesh. Here, we brought you something from the old place,' Jack says, handing over an elegant brown paper carry bag with the words 'William Mortimer & Sons, Boucherie and Charcuterie' printed on it.

Danny peers into the bag and withdraws several tightly wrapped bundles which he opens immediately, peeling away layers of plastic wrap, newspaper and bits of string to reveal a leg of spring lamb, two dozen Mortimer's old-fashioned pork sausages, a special gift box of Chicken Luncheon Delight, four black puddings and six tins of pâté.

'Pâté?' Danny says, scrutinising the tasteful black label with gold lettering.

'Yeh, mate,' Young Bob says. 'They've opened a fancy new delicatessen for all the yuppies that have moved into the area, it being close to the city an' that, and they even make their own pâté. You can still get snags there, of course, but they're posh snags with herbs and grog in them. You know, like veal and pork sausages with red wine and sage. You'd be scared shitless to throw them on the barbie unless you'd given it a bloody good scrub first and had it blessed by the Pope, eh?'

'Looks just like the old Mortimer's Meat Paste to me,' Danny says, pulling back the ring tab on the can of pâté and giving the contents a good sniff.

'Probably is, mate. They just stick it in a fancy can and double the price. Gets them in every time.'

Danny surveys the open bundles in front of him, obviously pleased. 'Thanks fellas, this must have cost you a fortune.'

'I wouldn't go that far, Daniel. We've still got a few contacts in the old place. Isn't that right, Jack?'

Happy Jack taps the side of his nose with his forefinger and gives a knowing wink. 'That's right mate, a few contacts.'

The three former meatworkers laugh loudly, recollecting happy memories of the old days when more food walked out the front gate than was driven out in the official Mortimer & Sons delivery vans.

Danny introduces his friends to Frankie and Jimmy and a few valued customers in the bar. He places fresh beers in front of them and makes a celebratory toast to old friendships, old times and herb-free meat products. Frankie quietly points out that a sprig of rosemary goes quite well with roast lamb.

'What brings you here?' Danny inquires.

'Aw, you know, it gets you out of the house, mate, and I couldn't stand the thought of another caravan holiday,' Young Bob replies.

'No, seriously. Vietnam is not exactly on the tourist map for blokes like you.'

'Well, the wives 'ave been on at us for a holiday, and then I ran into one of Mai's Vietnamese mates from the works and she told me you were having a few problems, so we thought we'd come over and lend a hand. Safety in numbers and all that. And get a few brownie points with the wives, eh Jack?'

'Thanks pal, I appreciate it,' Danny says, touched at the loyalty of his friends and still shocked to see so many familiar faces in his bar.

'No worries, son. Where is Mai anyway?'

'She's upstairs with the baby.'

'Baby? Bloody hell son, well done,' Young Bob says, surprised. 'What is it, a boy or a girl?'

'A boy.'

'Lovely, mate, lovely. What's his name?'

'Robert, his name's Robert.'

Young Bob rests his beer on the bar and stares at it quietly, watches the amber bubbles rise slowly to the surface. 'Daniel, son, you break my heart.'

'I thought he was named after Robert the Bruce, Danny,' Frankie says.

'No, Robert the Fitter and Turner,' Danny replies, smiling at Young Bob.

They sit at the bar, happily ensconced on their stools or standing up smoking cigarettes, swapping stories about Danny's misadventures as a boy, a young man and a father, all of which seem to feature greyhounds, horses, chickens and the occasional pair of geckoes crawling up a wall. Young Bob talks of life as a retired tradesman and about his periodic visits to the slaughterhouse to re-calibrate the sensitive blades of The Big Chopper, a skill no other fitter has mastered as well as the great machine's original guardian. A blade out of alignment, he reminds them, is an accident waiting to happen. But he's given up breeding the dachshunds because the little buggers kept getting under his feet and he's not as nimble on his pins as he used to be. Sure, he misses the works and his mates there, but he says a bloke can't work forever can he? He's got his health, which is a bloody good thing, because he's seen blokes retire and three months later they're six feet under. What's the point of that? No wreath from the old bosses either.

Happy Jack's still generally pleased with the world, except for a bit of arthritis and some deafness in his right ear from all those years as a young bloke working at the mines in Queensland, blowing the shit out of mountains. Gelignite Jack he was known as then. He spends a lot of time helping his four sons pull out, and put back in, engines and gearboxes from their respective cars, which spend more time off the road than on it.

'Where are your better halves, anyway?' Danny asks.

'In the end, Lorna didn't come because she didn't fancy the heat or the food, so she's gone on a cruise to Fiji with Jack's wife Nancy. But she sends her love.'

'Well, I'm amazed you two found the place,' Danny says, pouring another beer for his Australian visitors whose thirst for liquid refreshment, he notices, has not diminished over the years.

'We did get lost and we ended up in something called a beer *om.*'

'*Om* means cuddle, mate,' Danny points out.

'Yeh, well we know that now, don't we. I thought it was some kind of Buddhist drinking establishment. Anyway, so we go in there and no sooner have we sat down than these two sheilas have the saveloys right out of our pants. You've never seen anything like it. If we hadn't put a stop to it we would have got the full treatment, I tell ya. Jack here nearly had a heart attack, isn't that right, mate.'

Happy Jack nods, smiling. 'The full treatment,' he says.

'Funny old country this,' Young Bob says, shaking his head.

'Not all the time,' Danny replies, taking another sip of his beer.

'Yeh, so I hear. So what can we do to help, mate? Gelignite Jack here could always blow the bastards up, eh?'

Jack mimics perfectly an explosion of rocks, gravel and body parts. 'Bo . . . oo . . . mm!'

A senior policeman walking into a crowded bar generally does not foster an atmosphere of convivial abandon. And indeed this is the case when Inspector Hoanh strolls into the Blue Moon, taking in the studious pool players, cigarettes dangling from their lips, the Saturday night revellers determined to drink themselves onto another planet, the solitary tourists in search of some friendly company, the surprised working girls tugging at their handkerchief-sized skirts in a vain attempt to stretch them to somewhere near the vicinity of their thighs. The place slows to a halt like an old wind-up gramophone that has run out of revolutions, and the general rumble and hubbub becomes an uncomfortable undercurrent of nervous coughs and whispers. Even Aretha Franklin on the stereo seems to reduce her rollicking up tempo number to a soulful lament.

Inspector Hoanh takes one more semi-circular sweep of the subdued bar, like a captain of a submarine scanning the dangerous ocean above for enemy craft, before recognising Frankie in the corner. 'Mr Frankie! I was hoping you'd be here,' he smiles. 'I am very happy to see you.'

Frankie raises an acknowledging thumb and at once the music becomes louder, the talk more animated, the girls more amorous, the evening full of endless possibilities. A further round of introductions is made with Frankie doing the honours. Inspector Hoanh at first declines the offer of a drink, but when pushed accepts two fingers of Black Label with three cubes of ice.

Frankie leans across and whispers in Young Bob's ear. 'I think he's after you blokes and those contraband sausages you sneaked into the country. Aye, I think Interpol has been on the blower. Be careful what you say.'

'Jesus mate, and after we slipped those airport customs blokes six snags and a tin of pâté each to look the other way,' Young Bob replies, not missing a beat. 'I told Jack we should have given them a black pudding as well.'

'Aye, a bit of offal will always see you right.'

Through his sources on the street, Hoanh had heard that Mr Five Oranges' men would be paying a visit to the Blue Moon tonight and thought it would be a good opportunity to renew his acquaintance with some of the city's more notorious criminal identities.

'I don't understand, Inspector Hoanh. Why is Nam Cam so determined to get money out of me?' Danny says. 'I mean, I'm just small beer, compared with all the other stuff he's into.'

'That is true. But it is a matter of principle to him. It would be a sign of weakness if he let you off the hook. Then maybe some other of his clients would take advantage. *Anh hieu*?'

'Yes I understand that, I suppose. But don't you think he's going a bit far, getting his thugs to rough me up and threaten me with knives and a one-way trip to the bottom of the Saigon River?'

'Maybe, maybe not. After all, you owe him twenty thousand dollars, is that correct? That is a lot of money in Vietnam, you know that. Besides, Cam, he is also a little bit crazy.'

'More than a little bit, I'd say,' Frankie says, joining in the conversation. 'You know the other night when we met up with him, he was telling me his favourite nature documentary is the one about the giant sea turtles that crawl out of the sea and onto the sand of some island somewhere and then dig a hole and lay hundreds of eggs and then head off back to the sea again.'

'What's so bad about that?' Danny asks.

'Well, he says the best bit is when all the wee baby turtles hatch and start scrambling across the sand to the safety of the water, but they don't make it because they all get eaten up by seagulls. That's the bit he says he likes the most. Some guy, eh?'

'Aye, a real nature lover,' Danny says.

Mai appears at the bar with Robert clinging to her hip. She says he can't sleep so she might as well be here rather than upstairs on her own. She warmly embraces Happy Jack then Young Bob, who immediately takes his young namesake into his arms. The Youngest Bob, he thinks to himself. Danny introduces Mai to Inspector Hoanh and before long they have established that they are indeed related through a maternal great-grandmother.

'Welcome to the family,' she says, kissing him on both cheeks.

'Thank you,' he replies, blushing.

'But you know, being a member of a family brings with it certain responsibilities.'

'*Da phai*,' Hoanh replies gravely. 'I am well aware of that. How do you call it, Mr Francis? Blood is thicker than . . . ?'

'Than water, Inspector Hoanh. It's all about blood, eh. That's what it seems to me anyhow.'

'Aye, and it's a bloody sight thicker than Mexican beer and yon rice wine ae yours an' a',' Jimmy laughs, winking and raising his bottle in the inspector's direction.

What with all the toasting to old friends and new family members, and a few more beers and a few more chasers, Jimmy is feeling like a new balloon before a party. He thinks he might give them a song in a minute. Something by Elvis. He's in an Elvis kind of mood. 'Teddy Bear', maybe. Or 'Heartbreak Hotel'. Aye, that's the one. He curls his upper lip, like a snake about to strike, twists himself an imaginary quiff and begins to sing . . .

'Hello again.'

Jimmy's inspired Elvis impersonation is interrupted by the delicate scratch of a long fingernail across the back of his neck and the familiar husky tones of a young woman telling him how much she has missed him. 'So much,' she says, rubbing her thigh against his and digging her nails into his chest. 'So . . . o . . . oh much. Ooh you get big handsome when you wear that shirt.'

'Aw, hello Jade, darlin'. Didn't I see you yesterday?' Jimmy says, puzzled, his trousers nonetheless suddenly feeling tighter than they were a minute before.

'Yes, but it seems long time to me,' she says trailing a featherlike kiss across his forehead.

Jimmy's head swims momentarily in a sea of pleasure, across a coral reef of new and dazzling sensations, before catching a wave of rippling delight onto a white sand beach of warm, sticky joy.

'Aw, wait a minute here,' he says, suddenly shipwrecked. 'You're no a *she*, you're a *he*. That's right, Danny was talking about you in the car the other night. Aye, and they had a good laugh, an' a'.'

The woman, for a more feminine creation you would be hard pressed to find anywhere, uncoils herself from Jimmy's lap, smooths down her dress and dabs at what looks like the beginning of a tear in the corner of her eye. 'But I am almost a *she*. I have just one more operation to go,' she says plaintively.

'You mean cosmetic surgery?' Jimmy says, his interest perking up.

'Shooah.'

'You mean, like penis enlargement?'

She shakes her head vigorously. 'No, no! Not make bigger. Make go away!'

'Is that right?' Danny says, the penny finally dropping. 'Ye know, I've got a magazine that goes right intae all that stuff, wi' pictures and everythin'. Fascinating, so it is. Wid ye like tae see it?'

'Yes,' she nods, her face brightening, like the sun peeking out from a cloud after a brief burst of spring rain.

'Right, I'll away upstairs and get it. Are ye interested in interior decoration at all?'

But before he can move, before he can shift her hand from his knee, before he can even begin to remember whether the magazine is still in his bag or whether he has unpacked it, the sound of fury crashes through the bar, reverberating across the tables and chairs and up the walls and under the floor, once again rendering the place silent as a church before morning mass.

'James William Stewart, take your hands off that girl this minute or I'll bloody well kill ye, so I will!'

Jimmy looks sheepishly towards the door. There is only one person in the world who ever calls him James William as if she was cleaning up dog shite from the new carpet.

'Aw, hello Stella. Nice tae see ye.'

'Nice tae see me my arse. I cannae leave you for a minute,' she says, charging through the stunned clientele to Jimmy's table.

'Fourteen hours on bloody planes and what do I see when I get here? You and this . . . this . . . woman, doing God knows what.'

'She's no a woman,' Jimmy whispers, optimistically.

'Jimmy, when are you gonnae grow up, eh? First that slag of a conductress and now this. I'm telling ye, Jimmy, I've had enough, so I have. Ye're just lucky I don't have that poker wi' me, so ye are.'

'She's no a woman,' Jimmy says again, louder this time. 'She's a man.'

Stella stares at him, cynical disbelief tattooed all over her face. She suspends her furious tirade and, hands on hips, runs her sceptical eyes over this so-called bloke's shoulder-length hair, the full mouth, luscious with lipstick, the fine neck as slender as a sapling, the rippling coffee-coloured breasts pushing against the thin fabric of the dress that barely contains them, the welcoming half-moon hips, the silky smooth thighs that would make a lover weep with unbearable longing.

Unconvinced, Stella moves closer, like a crouching lioness towards an unsuspecting antelope, and quickly shoves her hand into her victim's soft black underwear to find a small limp penis hiding within the folds of her buttocks, like a slug between two rocks in the garden.

'Jesus, Jimmy. Yer no gay are ye?' she asks, alarmed, Jade's little buried treasure still pinched firmly between her thumb and forefinger, a louse caught in a pair of tweezers.

'Ye know very well I'm nae such thing. And you can let go now, the boy's gaun blue there.'

'Oh aye, sorry son. Away ye go now, there's a real woman on the premises. And you, Jimmy, can get me a vodka and orange. I've got a right thirst on me. This country's like a fan-forced oven, so it is.'

Frankie and Eileen embrace by the bar, her head on his shoulder, his hand on the small of her back. He kisses her gently on the ear and she strokes his hair. He caresses her cheek. She grinds her groin into his.

'I've missed you,' she says softly.

'Aye, me too. Everything all right? The cat still alive?'

'Aye,' she laughs, tickling his ribs. 'I did put some whisky in his milk though. He stoatered about for two days, dead drunk. Nobody eats my fish and gets away wi' it.'

'That would have showed him. I hope you didn't use the single malt.'

'No, the blended.'

'Good. How'd things go with the McCludgie boys? Did they get what they were after?'

'Aye. The four of them were in that funny bar the last time I saw them and they were going to head back to the hotel. God only knows what they'll be up to.'

'Well done. Here, you've got some people to meet,' Frankie, says, taking her by the arm.

Apart from the universal mode of communication known as profanity, music is the international language. Everybody says that, especially people in the music industry. When there's a famine in Africa, a bunch of ageing popstars get together, belt out a few tunes for charity and raise twice the gross national product of Equatorial Guinea. When there's a war on somewhere on Christmas Eve, there's a fair chance everybody will drop their weapons for a while and have a right good go at "Silent Night". When folk are standing miserable at the bus stop on a freezing winter's morning, a few verses of "Marie's Wedding" will warm their hearts, if not their feet. And so it is with Fergus and Andrew, Pham and Vong, who, after several more pints of McEwan's Export at BLAB!, and a few bottles of Newcastle Brown just for the hell of it, are warm and snug and pissed as newts in the McCludgies' hotel room which, much to their great joy, is equipped with the latest in karaoke technology.

Fergus, the more sentimental of the twins, is moaning his way through 'Nobody's Child', a song often sung by his mother throughout a lifetime of family get-togethers and New Year's Eve parties. It is a tune her son has taken to his heart like a thirsty fish to water.

'Fucksake Fergus, enough of that shite, geez some Kylie Minogue or somethin', the wan where she wiggles her arse aboot. Or whitsisname, Robbie Williams, the wan where he wiggles his arse aboot an' a',' Andrew whines, his face an art student's exercise in eye-scrunching, tongue-shrivelling distaste.

'No, I like this song. It's very sad,' Pham says, looking tearful. 'In Vietnam we like the sad songs. Have you ever heard "Moonlight Over Lake Ping"?'

'Can't say I have, naw,' Fergus says.

'Very beautiful song. Very sad. Break the fucking heart, cock. I will sing it for you. *Khong sao*. No problem,' Pham says, hoisting himself up from the settee.

Andrew tugs him back down. 'Wait a minute. So you know what you have to do when we get the phone call, eh?'

'Yes, we know what to do. Do not worry.'

'It wullnae be me that'll be worried if you fuck it up, I can tell you that right now.'

'No problem. We are happy to do it. My father is, how do you say, a prick. He bullies us like he bullies everybody. *Anh noi that*. It's true. Yes, I am not joking you, my friend. He sent us here to learn about big business and how to make investments. We are his investment in the future. Is this not correct, Vong?'

Vong takes a swig from a half-bottle of the famous Grouse and waves merrily at his brother.

Pham gestures to Andrew to come closer, like an excited child with a secret to reveal. He whispers in Andrew's ear. 'You know, my father, one time he kill a policeman. That man's son is a policeman too, an important police inspector. In Saigon. But my father, he never get caught. His friend, he tell me this.' He squeezes Andrew's forearm. 'But please, don't you tell anybody. Big problem for me, OK?'

Pham leaps up from the settee, his drinks spilling on the carpet, occasional patches of which can be glimpsed through the sea of stains. 'Now I want to sing. Sing like a bird!'

'Naw, just hold on a minute. It's my turn,' Andrew says, already up on his size sixteen feet. 'Hey Fergus, geez that fuckin' microphone. I'm gonnae sing a real song.'

'Aw aye. And what's that shitheid?'

'"Viva Las Vegas", son. "Viva Las Vegas."'

When Nguyen Nam Cam pushes open the swinging doors of the Blue Moon with what observers would later describe as an arrogant and supremely confident thrust of his upturned palms, he isn't prepared for the scene before him. Danny and Mai, Frankie and Eileen, Jimmy and Stella, Young Bob and Happy Jack, Inspector Hoanh, Benny and Jade the ladyboy, are seated around a long wooden table like the twelve apostles at the Last Supper with one gone out to get the takeaway. He is surprised because he thought he had demonstrated that he is not a man to be messed with, and that while he is indeed generous and patient, some would say too much so, he has his limits and those limits, believe you me, have been reached. He is not to be taken lightly. He has come here, in good faith, expecting what is due to him, and what does he find? A party. People drinking and singing and laughing like they had not a care in the world. Perhaps he had shown them too much hospitality when they came to his house. Perhaps he should have broken a few of their fingers or dumped them in the canal and let them swim home through the reeking debris and pungent sewage. This is what happens when you try to be civilised. People start to relax. He should have known better. Yes, he will know better next time. They seem surprised to see him, these Scotsmen and their women. But it is good to surprise people. It keeps them on their toes, does it not?

Sometimes they have to be reminded who they are dealing with. Cam laughs to himself. They are dealing with me, that's who! He smiles at Inspector Hoanh. What is he doing here? Like father, like son, isn't that what they say? He may have to deal with the son as he did with the father.

Once again, the bar grinds slowly to a halt as Cam, flanked by two of his smoother associates, like two razor-sharp creases on a pair of trousers, fixes a gaze thick with malevolent intent on Frankie and Danny Canyon, who are just this minute into the first verse of "You've Lost That Lovin' Feelin", with Danny doing the high notes, his eyes closed, his mind full of wild imaginings that he is indeed a Righteous Brother. When the only voice he can hear is his own, he finally realises that all is not as it should be at the Blue Moon on a Saturday night. If someone had suddenly pulled out a trumpet and played "The Last Post", it would not have sounded out of place.

'Jesus Christ, the cat died or something?' Danny says, looking around.

'I bloody well hope not,' Frankie replies, well aware of the presence of the new arrivals but choosing to ignore it nonetheless. 'Eileen, what did I say about the cat? You were not to go anywhere near it with a frying pan or any other kitchen utensil.'

'I didn't touch the stupid cat,' Eileen says, miffed at the very suggestion.

'What cat? Where is this cat? I don't see any cat,' Jade says, puzzled, surveying the room for something furry with a tail.

'Eh, I'll have one more beer and a vodka and orange for the wife here,' Jimmy says, his glass empty.

Danny turns in his chair, sensing some new customers have just arrived. Among them is a face he doesn't particularly want to see, indeed had not expected to see. There is something about those eyes. No matter how much the man laughs or jokes, Danny suspects he would never be able to make his eyes laugh along with him. Any light within them had long ago been extinguished.

Their eyes meet like a fatal two-car collision at a busy intersection.

'Ah, you are having a party, Mr Danny. Some karaoke, I love the karaoke!'

'Aye,' Danny says nervously, uncertain whether to offer Cam a drink, hit him with a pool cue or make a dash for the door.

'Actually, we're just having a bit of a sing-song to raise money for what Danny owes you,' Frankie interjects. 'But we don't seem to be doing so well. How much have you got, Jack?'

Happy Jack, nominated as treasurer for the night, and, as such, responsible for soliciting donations from customers impressed by their renditions of songs under the category of Sibling Groups from the Sixties and Seventies (genuine or expedient), counts their takings with a disappointed shake of his head. 'Thirty-eight dollars and a few thousand dong. Oh, and a packet of chewing gum. Spearmint.'

Cam's complexion, generally fair for a man of his background, quickly takes on the burnished hue of a ripe chilli pepper. His companions, familiar with their employer's sudden changes of mood, assume a more military-like bearing, casting nervous glances around the room, which is now silent but for the ever-present hum of the refrigerator struggling up the steep incline that is a steamy tropical climate.

'Please, Mr Daniel, I'm in no mood for this joking and I do not have any time for it. I am a businessman and I have come to complete my business with you,' Cam says, with exaggerated civility.

What remains of Danny's confidence evaporates like overnight dreams when the morning sun streams through the curtains. Perhaps he should've stayed in Melbourne with his mates at the meatworks. The smell was bad, but the money was good. Taking risks is not all it's cracked up to be—there is always something to lose. Sometimes there's something to be said for playing it safe.

'Mr Cam,' Frankie says, rising and indicating the vacant chairs beside him, 'please, take a seat and we can have a wee drink and get this business over with, eh. Really, my brother was just having his little joke. He's had a hard week and might have had a couple of drinks too many.'

Cam stands perfectly still, a lamppost in a windy street, considering this offer. 'The man who owns the bar should never drink his profits,' he says, deciding to take it up and indicating that his companions follow him.

Frankie nods to the barman who brings three glasses of what looks like milk poured over ice and places them ceremoniously in front of the three men.

'What is this?' Cam asks, unimpressed.

'Saigon Tea,' Frankie replies, his face a veil of enthusiasm.

'But this is the drink of bar girls.'

'Not this, Mr Cam. This is my brother's special Saigon Tea. He only serves it to honoured guests. It's the Glasgow version with the finest Scotch single malt whisky in it. The Laphroaig. I'm sure a man of your experience would know of it.'

'Ah yes, I have heard of it. It is very famous.'

'Aye, it is,' Danny joins in. 'It's from the Isle of Islay on the west coast of Scotland. Laphroaig is a Gaelic word that means "the beautiful hollow by the broad bay".'

'Ah yes,' Cam says, lifting his drink to his nostrils and savouring the peaty aroma. 'The beautiful hollow by the broad bay. It sounds like a Vietnamese song, yes?'

'Aye, it does that.'

'Do you know "Moonlight Over Lake Ping?" My son, he sings it very well.'

'Is that right?' Frankie says, raising his glass. 'Anyway, cheers, eh. All the best.'

'May yer lum ay reek,' Jimmy says, to the uncomprehending looks of those around him.

'Here's to you,' Danny says, giving his brother a sly wink.

'Down the hatch,' Young Bob exclaims with a grin as broad as a side of lamb.

'*Chuc suc khoe*,' Cam says, as the pale nectar slips down his throat like a slow sinuous ride through the tunnel of love.

Cam floats in the small lake near his village in the hollowed-out log his brother and he call their boat. He trails his fingers in the warm brackish water and their fishing poles dangle across the side, like palm trees heavy with fruit, waiting for a fish to bite. The dappled sunlight dances across his face, a flickering beam on his shaded eyes. He can see his mother on the bank, waving to them to hurry up and catch something. The rice is already in the pot. See the smoke rising from the house! See how it is embraced by the evening sky! His father will soon return from the fields, weary and burnt by the sun, and they will eat. Look at this glorious day, the clouds must be hiding behind the moon, because there are none to be seen. It is a day to dream of greater things . .

'OK, wake up dickhead. Wakey, wakey!'

Cam is roused from his dream by something sharp intermittently pressing against his chest. In his murky semiconsciousness he tries to brush it away, but finds he cannot move his arms. He knows they are there, he can feel them, but something or someone is holding them back. He struggles and tries to push himself up, but his legs do not respond.

'C'mon, mate. Up you get. You can't seem to hold your drink, son. Weak as piss, you are,' Young Bob says, poking his slumbering captive with a pool cue. 'Hey Danny, this cue needs a new tip. Look, the rubber's all worn away.'

'Aye, I'll get right on to it in a minute,' Danny replies, testing the sharpness of a meatworker's boning knife on his thumb. Drawing blood, he decides it will do.

Slowly, Cam awakens in a thick fog of uncertainty and rouses himself into a hesitant awareness. Suddenly, he can feel the ropes around his feet, the thick black tape that binds his arms to the chair. Through blurred vision he can just make out the shapes of his two companions similarly bound on either side of him, two thieves on the mount.

As his eyes begin to focus clearly, he can see several faces before him, staring intently at every flicker of his eyelids, every moan of pain, every vain attempt to break free of his predicament. Has he died and gone to another place? Is this the other life all Buddhists dream of? But then, it all becomes clear, like the sky after the wet season rain. The bar, the singing, the promises. The beautiful hollow by the broad bay. The fucking Saigon Tea.

He tries to talk, to shout, to tell them what a mistake they are making and that all that awaits them is an agonising end and an eternity spent on the filthy bottom of the Saigon River, but the scrap of towelling jammed into his mouth makes him gag.

'Look, he try to talk,' Jade says, parading in front of him like a model on the catwalk, all hips and legs and shimmering breasts.

'I wish I had a body like that,' Stella whispers to Eileen as she hands her a video to slip into the machine. 'Minus that one wee bit, ye know.'

'Och, it needs rewinding. Why do people never rewind the videos?' Eileen says, crossly. 'I hate that.'

'OK, that's enough,' Frankie says, the tone of his voice alerting the others that he is not to be argued with. 'Jade, Stella, away ye go outside. You too, Eileen. We'll see you in a wee while.'

Jade begins to protest, but before she can say anything Eileen takes her by the arm and leads her out the door end of the bar, followed by Stella who appears relieved to be leaving. Frankie gestures for everyone to be quiet and he undoes the gag around Cam's mouth. He raises one finger to his lips, warning his prisoner not to speak. He nods to Young Bob, who presses the play button on the video recorder.

From somewhere in the corner—he just can't manage to twist his head far enough to see from where exactly—Cam hears the sounds of fear creep out into the half-lit room. The sharp crack of a bullet, the raspy breath of skin-licking flames, the fruitless moans of despair that no one will answer.

We must kill them. We must incinerate them. Pig after pig. Cow after cow. Village after village. Army after army.

Frankie pulls up a chair and places it next to a defiant Cam who begins to threaten his captors before Frankie rams his hand across his mouth and again raises a finger to his lips. 'Mr Cam. My friend, my pal. Please don't speak. I've asked you nicely. A nicer request you couldn't get. Isn't that right, Jimmy?'

'Aye, that's right enough, Frankie. A very nice request. Polite as anythin'.'

Frankie taps his fingers on the back of Cam's chair, searching for the right beat, the right note to hit. 'So here we are. Can I get you something, a cup of tea maybe? No? Nothing? Maybe later, eh, when we're all friends again. That's the game. So, what are we going to do? I mean, this is not a situation we wish to prolong. You know what I mean? I have to get back home to my work. I've got responsibilities and I'm sure you have too. So why don't we just forget all this business about the twenty thousand dollars and we can all get on with our lives. It's not as if it's all genuine debt, is it? And my brother shouldn't have to pay you so that he can run his bar without getting his head kicked in. And the money he lost on cock-fighting, it's mostly interest isn't it? Now, you and I know that's not fair. Danny is just an honest man trying to make a living. He's a got a family to support, a lovely wee wean. You, Mr Cam, are taking food out of that baby's mouth. Do you realise that? How could you?'

This is the way the fucking world ends. Look at this fucking shit we're in man. Not with a bang, but with a whimper. And with a whimper. I'm fucking splitting, Jack.

'As my friend Dennis Hopper says, sometimes people go too far. We all have the potential to go too far, Cam, old pal. We have to know when to stop, and this, my friend, has gone on long enough. So what do you say, let's all shake hands and let bygones be bygones? You can't get fairer than that, can you Jimmy?'

'No, ye certainly cannot, Francis. That's a deal and a half, that yin.'

'A deal and a half. So what do you say, Mr Cam? Yay or nay?'

Cam looks around the room at the expectant faces assembled before him but can barely contain his laughter. He heaves and scoffs and chortles till his eyes are wet with tears. 'You make a big joke, yes? You know, Mr Frank, you should never underestimate anybody. Do you think I am stupid? My men know where I am and if I do not return to my house they will come to this bar. I have many men, Mr Frankie, and by my calculation they will be here very soon. Then we will see who is Mr Clever Dickie.'

'Clever Dick, Mr Cam, Clever Dick. I'm sorry to disappoint you, but I might have some bad news on that front. You see, my pal here, Inspector Hoanh, has already sent a fair few of his men to your house to pay a wee visit and, if my calculations are correct, your boys should all be locked up about now, isn't that right Inspector?'

The Inspector smiles and nods at Cam in friendly acknowledgement. 'Yes, that's right. Twenty of my best men are at your house this very minute. Times are changing, Mr Cam. Some of us have had enough of the way things have been. My father felt the same way, Mr Cam. Do you remember my father?'

'Your father was a fool.' Cam spat out the words like they were a distasteful memory.

Hoanh explodes and smashes his fist into the side of Cam's face. After the initial shock, Cam just smiles to himself like a man enjoying the private remembrance of an old joke. 'Ah, Mr Hoanh, you are so stupid. You surprise me. How long do you think it will last? When I pay off your superiors everything will return to the way it was and you, Inspector, will be a dead man. You can join your father in the next life. And as for you,

Mr Frankie Canyon, when you go home you had better say a long goodbye to your brother because maybe you will not see him again.'

'Is that right?' Frankie says, feeling his face redden with a sudden surge of anger.

'Yes, I am afraid so. And, I am sorry to say, I have two sons in London and they might have to pay your family a little visit in the Bonnie Scotland.'

Frankie casts an anticipatory glance at Jimmy who consults his watch and picks up the telephone. He dials a long number and, after a few nervous seconds, he hands over the phone. Frankie holds it against the ear of his smugly confident captive, who appears not the least bit surprised to be taking a telephone call while bound and taped to a wooden chair in a room full of hostile adversaries. He acts as if he were untouchable, as if he believed that any dire situation he encountered would be resolved in his favour. Setbacks are temporary, triumph is inevitable for people like him, people with real power.

Eternally fascinated by the workings of the human body, Frankie watches the colour drain from Cam's face, like water down a plug hole. Then, through some magical reverse of gravitational force, he sees Cam's complexion become a palette for all the colours of the rainbow, including some devilish new pigments of sinewy, blood-pumping, purplish rage.

Frankie takes the phone away from Cam, who is trembling like the doom-laden moments before the earthquake finally rips the firmament apart. He holds it to his ear. At the other end of the line, in a Soho hotel, Pham and Vong are wailing and moaning as if engulfed by flames and their burning flesh were being rendered down to tallow and glue. If he is not mistaken, it sounds like something from *Led Zeppelin Two*. The frightening din subsides and Fergus McCludgie comes to the phone.

'Hello. Is that you, Uncle Frankie?'

'Aye, it's me, son.'

'Is that what ye wanted?'

'Aye, that was perfect. It sounded like they had died and gone to hell.'

'Well, we told them they'd be deid if they didnae do what we told them. But they've had so much tae drink, and what wi'

Andrew threatening tae drag them back tae Glasgow and beat the shite out of them, they seemed quite happy tae go along wi' it, ye know. They're no bad boys really. They don't like their auld man much, I can tell ye that.'

'We feel the same way over here, son. Anyhow, well done. Give my best to your mother when you get back.'

Cam pushes and pulls and struggles against his confinement. A man is only a prisoner inside his head, he tells himself repeatedly. Be strong. Be positive. In control. But his gaolers just laugh and mock as his efforts prove fruitless and his frustration erupts like a boil that has just been lanced.

'You will regret this! You will regret this! When you hurt my sons you go too far. Too far, do you hear me?'

'Aye we hear you,' Jimmy says, wandering over to the three men, straightening their ties, patting down their hair, adjusting their crumpled jackets, mopping their sweaty anxious brows. 'Yer lookin' a wee bit worse for wear, boys. Would yeez like a wee break, eh? A nice cold drink and long soothing hot shower. A bit of a lie down. A bite tae eat? How would that be? Would yeez like that?'

The two other men, shattered, exhausted and almost broken, nod with relief, one of them whimpering quietly into this chest. Cam says nothing, looks at no one.

Jimmy stares at them, and then at his friends, as if seeking their counsel about what to do next. He takes Frankie aside, nervously rubbing the greying bristle on his chin. 'Here Frankie, dae ye know what yer doing here, son? These are serious people we're dealing with now. They're no John Cameron and yer no down by the canal now. Yer in Saigon and it's their territory, no yours. And what about Danny and Mai and wee Robert? This could a' come back tae haunt them, know whit I mean? We'll be back in Scotland and they'll still be here waiting for the next brick through the windae.'

Frankie sighs deeply. 'I know, Jimmy, I know. To be honest, I don't know if what we're doing is the right thing or no. But it seems to me we haven't got any other choice now. I've tried negotiating wi' Cam, but he's no interested. I'm telling you, I wish my faither was alive. I could do wi' his advice. He was always good wi' the advice.'

Frankie nods at Happy Jack and makes his way to a small storage room at the back. Jack walks determinedly to a fridge in the corner and withdraws three packages of what looks like dynamite, long fuses sticking up like antennae from the head of an alien. With black plastic tape he straps one package to the leg of each chair, moves a step back to survey his work and takes out a box of matches from the side pocket of his trousers.

'This is our friend, Gelignite Jack,' Danny says, placing a respectful arm around his shoulder and giving it a friendly squeeze. 'He is very good at his job. He used to blow up mountains. Isn't that right, Jack?'

'Yeh, bloody big mountains, mate.'

All heads turn as Frankie appears wheeling a large metal cylinder of acetylene gas, to the nozzle of which is attached a rubber hose and a welding torch. He's wearing a protective mask that envelops his head like the primitive brass helmet of an early deep-sea diver. Through the mask's small and slightly misted rectangular window can be seen the weary eyes of a man who has clearly run out of patience. Time to peel himself an orange. He turns to Jack and quietly and calmly asks him for a light.

Danny moves towards what were once three full-grown adults, two of whom have regressed to blubbering children at the sight before them. Did it all have to come to this? With his glistening boning knife dangling with intent from his right hand, Danny confronts Cam's steadfastly impassive gaze before moving directly behind him, a shadow over a grave, and with his newly sharpened blade, pierces his skin just below the jaw line. As one lonely trickle of blood meanders down to his shirt collar, leaving a permanent crimson stain on the expensive cloth, Cam's eyes glaze over and once again his beloved mother beckons him from the riverbank to the breast-milk warmth and safety of a delicious and trouble-free unconsciousness.

Frankie wearily removes his mask and looks to his brother, who is wiping his knife on the back of Cam's shirt. 'What do you think then, Danny? It's no like the pictures, is it, this stuff? You can be Humphrey fuckin' Bogart in your mind, but when it comes to the real thing . . .'

'I know, Francis, I know,' Danny sighs, the exhaustion, fear and anxiety of the last few months finally catching up with him. 'Anyway, I don't think he'll bother us again.'

But the silent relief of their victory is suddenly and unexpectedly shattered by three loud and resonant raps on the door. Frankie and Danny immediately head towards it but Inspector Hoanh motions them aside and raises his fingers to his lips, indicating that they keep still and quiet. He is afraid something has gone wrong and Cam's men have managed to get here after all. Hoanh draws his pistol from its holster and positions himself to the right side of the door. With his left hand he quickly pulls on the handle and he jumps into the doorway, legs spread and his gun aimed menacingly at whoever stands before him.

The young man in front of him rattles with fear and the bundle of boxes he is carrying tumbles to the floor like a stack of cards. 'Pizza?' he says, his voice thin and quivering. 'Pizza for Mr Jimmy?'

Frankie Canyon sits on the step at the entrance to the Blue Moon sipping slowly from a cup of thick dark coffee and letting the morning sun wash over his face. He thought he would get up early and take a last solitary look at this crazy lovable city, perhaps take a final walk down to the Saigon River to watch the boats heading out to sea and the ferries casting off for Vung Tau where the passengers will gaily disembark to wade in the warm blue water and eat fresh boiled crab on deckchairs in the sand. He had contemplated a casual stroll down Le Duan Street, then down past Mai's old family home in Alexandre du Rhodes and then maybe on to the presidential palace for a wander around the old gardens. Perhaps a bit of last minute shopping at the Ben Thanh Market. Benny suggested he have a massage at the Palace Hotel. Very OK massage there, he had said, thumbs up. But as the morning wore on, and he refilled his coffee cup and ate freshly-baked croissants with strawberries from Dalat, time drifted dreamily away and he was content to simply observe the exotic parade that passed in front of him. If his last few hours in Saigon were to be spent sitting barefoot on a step at the door of his brother's bar and he would be quite happy with that. After all, he's had enough activity in the last few days to last him a lifetime. Still, he can understand why Danny loves it here, despite the troubles he's had. And with a bit of luck he should be all right now, what with Cam and his pals all set for a lengthy spell in gaol and Inspector Hoanh having taken care of the bent coppers who were bleeding Danny dry. Being part of the family, the inspector might work extra hard to keep the hounds at bay for a while. But Saigon being Saigon there'll always be another Cam, another Mr Five Bloody Oranges around the next corner just waiting for a chance to move in for his share of the action. One man's misfortune is another man's opportunity and all that. Danny's promised Mai that he's finished with placing bets on angry young chickens, although she says she'll believe it when she sees it. He even said that they might come to Glasgow to see the family and to have a holiday, maybe take Mai and Robert up to Ullapool for a few days. Benny wants to come as well to buy a kilt, but Danny said although he would undoubtedly look splendid in a length of the finest Royal Stewart, he has to stay behind and look after the bar and keep Jade the lady-boy and her lithe-somely provocative pals from running rampant while Danny's away. They'd have their gloriously manicured hands down every foreign crotch in the place if someone wasn't there to impose some sense of decorum. Danny told Benny he could go next time and apparently he's already started saving up his wages for the ticket. Christ, Frankie reflects, Benny Le in Glasgow. What a thought. It would be a shock for both cultures, right enough. Young Bob and Happy Jack said they might take a bit of a caravan holiday around the Highlands with the balls and chains and they'd be in touch. They promised to bring along some Chicken Luncheon Delight for Stella, who's taken quite a fancy to it.

Frankie begins slicing a ripe mango that he bought from a passing vendor. She told him she'd walked an hour and a half from her village in Tu Duc to sell her fruit in the city, so he bought ten mangoes and a mountain of bananas. He'd never eaten a mango before in his life but quickly came to the conclusion that it was the fruit of the gods.

'All right, Francis?' Danny says, emerging from the cool darkness of the bar and sitting beside his brother in the bright morning sunshine.

'Aye. Couldn't be better. Mango?'

'No thanks. Stuffed myself stupid with them when I first came here and I can't quite come at them any more. I'll have a banana though.'

'Help yerself.'

Danny breaks a banana from the bunch, peels it and bites into the pale creamy flesh. 'Are you all packed then?'

'Aye, although we seem to be leaving with more stuff than we came with. Eileen and Stella have taken a right shine to the local shops. Bloody Jade's been taking them all over the place. I don't know what we're going to do with all those conical hats.'

'They make nice lampshades, Francis.'

'Is that right? I suppose Eileen will think of something to do with them. She likes hats.'

Frankie takes another sip of his coffee and gazes at the circus of life on the street. A fat tourist struggles out of the doorway of the hotel opposite, juggling two cameras, a small green backpack and a large map that he is trying to fold into a manageable shape. Two young men on a motorbike quickly mount the kerb. One deftly jerks the cameras from around the man's neck and they accelerate nonchalantly off towards the river. The stunned man stands motionless for a moment, as if waiting for someone to explain to him what has just happened and what he should do now, before hurling his map on to the ground and furiously kicking it into the gutter. A local beggar with no legs pushing himself along on a flat board with wheels, his hands wrapped in tattered cloth to protect them from the abrasive bitumen road, politely appeals to the now livid foreigner for some small change. The visitor curses him loudly, picks up his map and his bag and stomps back into his hotel. The legless man continues his slow knuckle-grazing journey along the street, all the while smiling broadly at passers-by and holding up one ragged upturned palm for a donation.

'It must be difficult having no legs,' Frankie says.

'Aye, it would tend to cramp your style,' Danny replies, peeling another banana.

'I suppose you'd save a lot of money on shoes though,' Frankie shrugs, almost apologetically.

'I see the standard of your jokes hasn't improved.'

Frankie laughs in acknowledgement. 'How would that bloke have lost his legs anyway?'

'Och, he's probably stepped on a landmine in a field somewhere in the countryside. By the look of him, he was probably just a kid when it happened.'

Frankie sighs. 'Christ, what a thing to happen to a wee boy. At least in Glasgow all you have to worry about stepping on are chewing gum and dog shite.'

'People still get blown up here, you know. There's still unexploded landmines and bombs all over the bloody place.'

Frankie can't believe it. 'What, from the war?'

'Aye.'

'My God. You don't know how lucky you are sometimes, eh? I might live in that stinking scheme, but at least I can walk to the pub of a night time and be fairly confident of getting there with my arms and legs still attached to my body.'

'Aw aye, but from what Jimmy tells me you could quite possibly lose them there while you're having a pint. That pub of yours sounds like a right madhouse.'

'Aye, it has its moments. At least it doesn't have a smorgasbord though. That's one thing in its favour.'

Danny looks at his watch and then at his brother. 'We'd better be off to the airport, Francis, or you'll miss the plane.'

'Christ, is that the time? Aye, we'd better be off right enough,' Frankie says, pulling himself up from the step. 'We're a' ready anyhow.'

Danny stands up and holds the door open for Frankie to enter the bar. He catches his brother's eye and holds it. 'Thanks, Francis. Thanks for coming.'

Frankie grins and pushes him first through the doors. 'Aye, well, just stay away from the fuckin' chickens next time.'

'Aye. Tell Annie and Fiona I was askin' for them. And the weans.'

Inside the Blue Moon, Eileen, Stella, Jimmy and Jade are playing a final game of pool. Jimmy is on his fourth Corona and the two women are sipping iced tea. Jade is sprawled over the table, cue in hand, her skirt hitched up to the curve of her buttocks, her breasts pressed against the side cushion as she stretches to reach the white ball.

'Very nice lingerie you're wearing, Jade love. I'd quite fancy a few pairs ae those masel', Stella says to her new pal, with whom she's spent the previous couple of days swapping beauty tips and trying on each other's clothes. 'What do you think, Jimmy?'

Jimmy's gaze inches its way up the back of Jade's taut tan legs from the delicate silver bracelet circling her ankle to the fine lace edging the bottom of her black silk knickers. He swallows hard and shakes his head in disbelief at how such a glorious specimen of womanhood could in fact have been born naturally equipped with a small brown willie. Sometimes, the vagaries of life were just beyond him. 'Aye, well, whatever you think Stella. I might just get myself another beer.'

As Jimmy moves towards the bar, one eye still on Jade's perky left nipple, which has somehow managed to escape from its silken upholstery, Mai runs from the back room weeping.

'Hamish! Hamish! They've kidnapped Hamish.'

'Fucksake, not again,' Frankie says.

'Who's Hamish?' Eileen asks, concerned but uncertain about what's going on.

'My little dog. My pretty little dog,' Mai cries. 'It's always getting itself kidnapped.'

'Aw no. I had a wee bird called Hamish,' Eileen says, becoming tearful at the memory of her dear departed deep-fried friend. 'He was some budgie that yin, I kid you not,' she moans.

Danny takes both of his wife's hands in his, squeezes them tight. 'How do you know Hamish has been kidnapped again, love? Maybe he's just got out of the house and wandered off. Gone for a pee, maybe.'

'No. No. They telephoned. They want two hundred and fifty thousand dong and they'll give him back.'

'Christ, this dog's costing us a fortune, so it is,' Danny moans.

'Aye, tell me aboot it,' Jimmy interjects. 'See ma dug Blackie. Three pun a mince a day, and half a dozen cans of chicken noodle soup. Is that no right, Stella?'

'Aye, that dug's a gannet, so it is.'

'Maybe we should send Happy Jack to see the doggy nappers,' Mai says. 'He could blow them up.'

'Maybe that's taking things a bit far, Mai,' Danny replies.

It's decided that Danny has no choice but to go and see if he can locate Hamish and negotiate with the dognappers, so Benny will have to drive everybody to the airport. Benny and Frankie haul the luggage, the misshapen bags of straw hats, three bottles of rice wine, two hand-embroidered tablecloths each featuring a spray of purple irises, a large lacquerware painting of Ho Chi Minh and a dozen bottles of Corona beer into the boot of the car. Frankie jumps into the front seat next to Benny and the others squeeze in the back.

'Christ, it's like an oven in here, so it is,' Stella says, peeling her skirt from the scalding seat and cooling herself with a handpainted wicker fan she bought from the market. She and Eileen wave farewell to Mai and young Robert, who's shielding his face from the sun's glare by burying his head in his mother's shoulder. Jade is weeping and blowing a rapid succession of kisses. Jimmy can't help but notice there's a certain attractive vulnerability about her when she's crying. 'Here hen,' he says, handing her his favourite magazine with the special cosmetic surgery sealed section. 'Take this. You need it more than me, eh.'

Danny motions to Frankie to wind down his window and he extends his hand. 'Thanks again, Francis. Have a safe journey home, eh? I'd better go and find this fuckin' dog. I'm telling you, if it's no one thing here it's another. Next thing they'll be kidnapping the wean.'

'Aye, away you go then. I'll see you when I see you. A' the best.'

Benny pulls out from the kerb in a staccato dance that leaves a cyclo driver with a broken wheel and Eileen with a minor nervous breakdown as he narrowly misses an elderly woman pushing a cart full of watermelons. 'OK, we go, no worries,' Benny says, turning and beaming to the disconcerted women in the back.

Jimmy raises a bottle of beer in his Vietnamese pal's direction. 'Right ye are, son. On ye go.'

Benny accelerates rapidly and in no time they are speeding down Pasteur Street. To smooth their progress he decides to ignore any attempts at traffic regulation by red lights and frantically gesticulating policemen and to exercise the God-given right of all Vietnamese commuters to travel the wrong way down the street whenever they feel like it. At the top of the street Benny misreads the corner and almost collects four young men innocently enjoying a late-morning bowl of beef noodle soup at a pavement café. 'Luh-kee!' he laughs, acknowledging how close he came to skittling their roadside table. He nods to Frankie. 'Very delicious soup there, mate. I not joking you. Next time you come Vietnam we go. No worries.'

'Aye, thanks Benny. If I ever get out of this country alive, I'll look forward to it.' Frankie recognises Nam Ky Khoi Nghia Street from the journey into town when he first arrived and figures they should be at the airport in about fifteen minutes. He leans back and tells the others it shouldn't be long now. Jimmy is asleep and singing what sounds like "Dock of the Bay" by Otis Redding. Frankie smiles in appreciation and winks at Eileen who reaches over and smooths his hair. Stella points excitedly to a long wooden cart full of sugar cane being pulled by two huge buffalo that are ambling along at a leisurely rural pace amid the urban traffic madness. 'There's something ye'd never see in Glasgow, eh Frankie.'

'Aye, there's definitely no many buffalo wagons travelling down Argyle Street these days, Stella. Did you know that of all the feared animals in the African plains, the buffalo is the most feared? Left to themselves, buffalo are gentle creatures but when threatened a different animal emerges. You know, they have fearsome strength and in some parts of the country are the main killers of lions.'

'Is that right?'

'Aye, it is. And they have to live near water, your buffalo. A large bull can drink a hundred pints a day.'

'Sounds like Jimmy and yon Mexican beer,' Stella says, resigned to the fact that her husband has again struck up a close and meaningful friendship with a new brand of liquid refreshment.

Suddenly Benny wrenches the steering wheel sharply to the left to avoid colliding with a late model BMW that screeches unexpectedly from a side street and glues itself to their rear bumper bar. The car sticks to Benny's tail as he weaves his way recklessly through the busy traffic.

'Jesus, Mary and Joseph,' Stella shrieks. 'What are they playin' at?'

Frankie pokes his head out the window and peers at the car glued to their rear. 'Can you see who's in the car?' Frankie says.

'Naw, the windows are a' tinted,' Eileen says.

Benny picks up speed as he heads down Nguyen Van Troi Street. But he is unable to shake off his pursuers despite employing some deft driving moves he's picked up from reruns of old episodes of *Hawaii Five-O*. He plants his foot to the floor and speeds past the Tan Son Nhut cinema like a bullet out of a gun. Jimmy momentarily emerges from his

Corona-fuelled torpor and glances out the window at the hoarding advertising *The Fugitive*. 'Aw, we gone tae the pictures then? Very nice. Look, Harrison Ford's in it. Good auld Indiana Jones, he's the man, eh?' he slurs, before slumping against the side door and falling asleep once again.

Eileen turns and grips the parcel shelf, glancing fearfully back at Frankie as the car continues to stick to their tail like fly shit to the ceiling, mirroring every hairpin turn, sideways slide and frantic dash Benny makes.

'Who are these people, Francis?' Eileen says, her anxiety increasing with the speed of Benny's driving.

'Maybe they the friends of Mr Five Oranges,' Benny says, looking at Eileen in the rear-view mirror and clipping the wheel of a fruit stall and sending a mountain of jackfruit tumbling down the street.

'Great, that's all we need,' Frankie replies. But it couldn't be, could it? The last he'd heard, Cam and his boys were safely behind bars with a promise from Inspector Hoanh that he'd throw away the key. Maybe Cam had more friends than we knew about. Christ, just when you thought things had been wrapped up, brought to closure, as they say on the Oprah Winfrey show. Nothing's certain in this life. Why can't you ever take anything, just one fucking thing, for granted? It's his own fault, Frankie thinks. He's been complacent, gallivanting around Saigon for the last few days, seeing the sights when he should have been mopping up, making sure that there would be no comebacks from Danny's tormentors.

'Go faster, Benny, go faster,' Stella yells, her voice a guttural tremor of trepidation.

Jimmy wakes, disturbed by the commotion. 'What, is that us there then? That was quick.'

Stella loses patience with her husband and belts him over the head with a hand-embroidered door stop she'd bought to keep out the draught from the living room back home. The snake explodes in a storm of wood shavings.

'Once we get into the airport we'll be all right,' Frankie says, brushing some pine dust from his shirt. 'They won't have plane tickets and the polis will stop them at the terminal. Isn't that right, Benny?'

'That's right, mate. No worries, for sure,' Benny replies unconvincingly, while hauling the steering wheel around three hundred and sixty degrees and shooting past the security guards at the airport gate. He glances in the rear-view mirror and sees the BMW still right there behind him, like a dog chasing a cat up an alley. 'Bloody hell, mate. Big trouble. Big trouble.'

Frankie fingers the antique brass letter opener in his trouser pocket that he'd no doubt paid too much for in Dong Khoi Street. He curses to himself. Just when a man needs a weapon, all he has is a blunt dragon's head knife that's only good to open yet another gas bill. He braces himself against the dashboard as Benny slams on the brakes and the Citroen squeals to a smoky tyre-screeching halt outside the international departures terminal. He pushes against the door and leaps out of the car as the BMW roars to a stop behind them. He pulls the brass knife from his pocket and grips it with intent. Jimmy finally comes to his senses and smashes his beer bottle against the kerb and brandishes the jagged weapon that remains. Benny adopts a threatening karate pose. Stella is impressed. 'Hey Eileen, look at that. Wee Benny knows karate, just like yon Bruce Lee. I like a man who can defend himself, don't you?'

Frankie yells at the women to stay in the car. Slowly the two rear doors of the BMW creep open like wings on a bird and two large square heads with number two crewcuts emerge grinning from ear to ear.

'Hello Uncle Frankie, ye all right?' Fergus and Andrew McCludgie say in unison. 'Hello Uncle Jimmy. Dae ye fancy a pint?'

Frankie decides the letter opener might do the trick after all and moves angrily towards them. 'What the fuck are you doing here? You scared the shite out of us. Wait till I get a hold of you.'

The two boys step back as Pham and Vong Nam Cam jump out of the front of the car smiling broadly. 'We bring them to Vietnam for holiday,' Pham exclaims joyfully. 'Tonight we go karaoke!'

'Aye,' Fergus adds. 'We just wanted tae say cheerio before ye left, but we just missed ye at the Blue Moon.'

'That's a fuckin' hell of a way tae say cheerio,' Stella screams, clambering out the back of the Citroen, waving the remnants of her door snake. 'I'll gie ye cheerio, ye wee buggers ye. It's a good skelp on yer arses ye need. Just wait till I see your mammy.'

'Some country that Vietnam, eh,' Frankie says, slumping back in his seat and wiping his brow with a warm towel.

'Aye, I wouldn't mind going back one day,' Eileen replies.

'Well, we should, once we recover from this trip. The McCludgie boys nearly gave me a fuckin' heart attack, so they did,' Frankie says, staring at the small movie screen on the wall at the front of the economy class section. A matriarchal elephant is rubbing her tusks and trunk against the sun-bleached skeleton of a long-deceased family member.

'Did you know that elephants are the only animals in the world that revere their ancestors and make special journeys to visit their remains?' Eileen asks, snuggling up to her husband.

'Of course, doesn't everybody?'

'So, Francis, it's back to Glasgow and back to the grind, eh?' Eileen says, taking a sip of champagne and a bite of her salmon sandwich, which she happily notes has been cut into neat little triangles.

'I suppose it is. Still, it's been an adventure, one of yon life experiences.'

'Aye, it'll take us the rest of our life to pay off the cost of the plane tickets.'

'Och away, I'll do a bit of overtime, we'll be fine. It's been worth it, whatever the cost. We did the right thing and that's a good feeling,' Frankie says, affectionately squeezing Eileen's arm. 'Besides, it'll be something we'll remember when we're auld and decrepit and all we can manage to do is to sit in front of the telly and dribble and watch *Neighbours*.'

'My God, Francis, that's a fate worse than death. I hope we can have some more adventures before we get to that point, at least while we've still got our own teeth anyhow.'

'Aye, well we've got the taste for it now, eh. Who knows what might lie ahead. We just have to make it happen, Eileen, that's the thing. Our lives are in our own hands.'

'Aye, I know that now, Francis,' Eileen says, slipping her hand inside his shirt.

Frankie smiles at her and takes a nip of his whisky. 'Eh, where are those two?' he asks, noticing the vacant seats across the aisle.

Eileen's face crinkles with mischief. 'Stella's drafting Jimmy into the Mile High Club.'

'Jesus, Mary and Joseph. Wonders will never cease. I suppose you put her up to it.'

'I might have,' she says sheepishly.

'You're a wicked woman, Eileen McVeigh.'

'Wait till I get you home, then I'll show you how wicked I really am.'

'Is that right? Well, remind me to strap on my seat belt.'

'Aye, get ready for a mid-air explosion, sweetheart. By the way, that reminds me, was that real gelignite Happy Jack threatened to blow up Cam and his pals wi'?'

Frankie laughs. 'No. Looked like the real thing, though, didn't it? It was eighteen of those frozen jumbo pork links he and Young Bob brought from Australia.'

'My God. The crafty buggers. What was it that Young Bob was always saying?'

'A sausage never sleeps?' Frankie says.

'Aye, that's it. A sausage never sleeps,' she replies, slipping a warm and hopeful hand between his legs.

Nguyen Nam Cam sits quietly on a straight-backed bamboo chair, his hands folded in his lap, his right leg crossed over his left knee. He closes his eyes and tilts his head back as the sun's rays splinter through the bars on the small cell window. They flicker and dance across his face in time with the gently swaying acacia trees in the prison yard outside. There is a light breeze, a warm breath of country air that reminds him of his childhood. It brings with it the smell of frying fish and chicken sizzling on the grill, the sound of buffalo bellowing in the fields and his sisters yelping with delight as they plunge into the cool river. It's as if he can reach out and touch them, feel the wetness of their skin. Memories wash over him, bathe him in pleasure. It is not so bad here. The fresh air does him good, the small amount of manual labour that he hasn't managed to buy his way out of keeps him fit. His Armani suits will fit better now, will sit well on his newly muscular shoulders.

Cam hums contentedly to himself, a few bars of "Moonlight Over Lake Ping". What a song! He wonders how his sons are now that they are on temporary reassignment from the London School of Economics to his brother's farm in the Mekong Delta. Children can be such a disappointment. You do everything for them, give them opportunities that he certainly never had, and what do they do? They spit in your face.

That's gratitude for you. But he blames himself. He indulged them. But no more. No more fancy cars, no more allowances, no more parties, no more university. From now on it's boiled rice and chicken feet. It will do them good, toughen them up, make them hardy like he is now. Yes, like him. They told him that they didn't approve of his lifestyle. Well, let's see what they think when they are up to their arses in pig shit and paddy water.

Yes, it's not too bad here, not too bad at all. It never fails to amaze him, the power that money wields. A bit of cash in hand curries many favours. A few dollars here, a few dollars there, can iron out the annoying little wrinkles of prison life. The satellite television in his cell has certainly made his confinement more enjoyable. Twenty-four channels including Discovery. Tonight it's *Wonders of the World: Australia's Great Barrier Reef.* It's one of his favourites. Perhaps he will tape it and send a copy to that Mr Frankie Canyon. The programme has many sharks in it and they both love to watch sharks on the hunt. Predators of the deep. Aren't we all?

Cam casts an appreciative gaze around his home for the next little while, little being the operative word. Once the money reaches Inspector Hoanh's Saigon superiors and his contacts in the Ministry in Hanoi, his time here may be even less than little. It will be so brief as to be almost an illusion, a minor hiccup in his inexorable rise to power and fortune.

The late afternoon sun blushes through the window, giving the walls of his cell a warm dusky glow. He certainly chose the right colour of paint, Tropical Blue, and the guards did a lovely job of it. The Persian rugs give the rough stone floor a certain rustic charm. Very Normandy farmhouse indeed. His own paintings hang around the room. They are not bad, if he says so himself. There is nothing like a few women wearing conical hats and harvesting rice in the field to imbue the space with peace and tranquillity. You know, if it wasn't for those foolhardy Scottish men, he would never have discovered this artistic side of himself. They have certainly contributed to his personal development, there's no doubt about that. And he is grateful. But there are other matters to be taken into consideration concerning his feelings towards the brothers Canyon.

Cam reaches for the remote control on the coffee table and in an instant the sounds of Stan Getz and Astrud Gilberto dance slow and close around the room. "The Girl from Ipanema". Seriously sublime. He glances at his watch. One hour until dinner. Fried crab in tamarind sauce. To drink? A bottle of 1999 Cabernet Franc from Francis Ford Coppola's own Californian vineyard. That Francis Ford, he's the man. Once it was the smell of napalm in the morning, now it's enticing red fruit aromas at night. He shakes his head and laughs. Isn't life strange? But enough of this whimsy. He must finish this letter so he can catch the post in the morning. Where was he? Ah yes. 'Prison is good, but could be better. Wish you were here. *Hen gap lai.*'

Yes, Mr Frankie, see you again, he smiles to himself, slipping the crisp white notepaper into an envelope and sealing it shut. See you again.